FOCUSED

KARLA SORENSEN

This is dedicated to the ones who've ever felt like they needed to prove their worth.

I promise, the right people will always know exactly how valuable you are.

CHAPTER ONE

MOLLY

IF I'D KNOWN that my new boss was Cruella de Vil, I would've color coordinated my outfit for work that day. She matched the colors of the Washington Wolves perfectly. She was all sleekness and shine with her black dress, white jacket, red shoes, red lips, and a silvery white bob that fell just below her glass-sharp chin.

"Molly Ward, is it?" she asked quietly. Like the kind of quiet where I felt like if I answered wrong, she'd press a button, and I'd fall through a secret trap door.

I nodded. "Welcome to Washington, Miss Kelly. I've been looking forward to meeting you."

One perfectly manicured eyebrow lifted like it was being pulled oh, so slowly by someone tugging a string. Briefly, she glanced down at something on her desk, my employment file, presumably. "You've been here a long time."

I smiled. "My whole life, practically. But as a paid employee, for four years now."

I waited for Beatrice Kelly, the brand-new chief marketing officer of the Washington Wolves, to smile back, but she didn't.

As I stood in front of her desk, my nervous fingers twitching together behind my back, she appraised me openly, her gray eyes (because even her eyes matched) traveling from the top of my head to the soles of my feet, clad in sensible brown leather flats.

Personally, I found sensible footwear incredibly sexy because I enjoyed the ability to walk without pain at the end of the day when my shoes came off.

For some reason, those shoes offended her. I saw it the moment her gaze touched the rounded toe and tiny leather bow in the middle.

I glanced down, like the shoes would explain to me what they'd done wrong and why we were now in trouble with my brand-new boss.

I miss Ava, I thought for the thousandth time, my heart squeezing over the loss of my old boss, Ava Hawkins. Why they had to up and move across the country to be closer to her husband's family was beyond me.

"Have a seat," Beatrice said, still not taking her eyes off my shoes. I slid into one high-back black chair and folded my hands in my lap, wishing desperately to have something to keep them occupied. My whole life, I was the worst fidgeter in the universe when I was nervous. And this moment right here was sliding right into the top ten moments of all time. "Tell me what you love about your job, Molly Ward."

My brain raced at the unexpected question because I felt very much like I was being tested on some unseen scale. Quite irrationally, I wanted to glare at my shoes as if they'd gotten me into this mess.

"I love so much about my job, Miss Kelly," I said honestly. "I could probably talk your ear off for hours telling you all the reasons."

She hummed. "Marketing liaison suits you then?"

"It does." I took a deep breath because I knew this was one of those moments when false modesty would get me nowhere with

2

my kinda scary, really matchy-matchy boss. "I'm good with people. I make them comfortable and anticipate their needs well. So when I finished my internship, Ava knew that I'd do well dealing with our advertisers, and I believe that I have. For the past four years, I've built strong relationships with our advertisers and we haven't lost a single major sponsor since I took over that role. They trust me, and I've earned that trust."

For a split second, I held my breath, worried I'd gone too far, based on the speculative gleam in her eyes. My restless hands itched to reach up into my hair and redo my bun for the thousandth time. It was a bit of a running joke among my coworkers that you could tell I was stressed when my hair moved positions more than two times throughout the day. This morning, knowing I'd be meeting my new boss, I'd anchored every strand of my dark hair so firmly into place that only a crane operator would be able to get it to budge.

"May I be honest, Molly Ward?"

"Of course." And also, why did she keep saying my full name?

Beatrice settled back in her large leather chair and studied me again. "I wasn't looking forward to meeting you."

Ever heard the air being let out of a balloon? That slow, sad hiss of air until the only thing left was a droopy piece of crumpled plastic? Yeah, now imagine it happening to an unsuspecting twenty-five-year-old, eager to get to know her new boss.

"Oh," I exhaled. "Okay?" As soon as the words slipped out, I wanted to take them back.

This wasn't okay. Not okay at all. I'd known these halls and practice fields and offices since I was fourteen years old. Everyone here loved me! I was Molly freaking Ward. I was good at my job. No, I kicked ass at my job. "Actually," I said slowly, gathering my nerve and lifting my chin, "I'm sorry to hear that because I was looking forward to meeting you. I love this organization, I love my job, and I'm very good at it. If it's something I've

3

done in the past that I can improve on, please tell me, so I can fix it."

Boom. I saw the spark of grudging admiration in her eyes, there and gone like a flash of lightning.

"Aren't you curious as to why I wasn't?" she asked, resting her jewelry-free hands lightly on the desk in front of her.

Not particularly.

Okay, fine. That was a lie. If I knew, I could do every damn thing in my power to change it. Change her perception of me. In college, I was a 4.0 student. Any unfocused energy that I'd wasted in high school turned into a bright, shiny red laser trained straight at hitting the dean's list every semester. It took me no time at all to realize that even if I wasn't the smartest person in the room, I could damn well be the hardest worker, and that had my name on the list every single time.

I took a deep breath and nodded. "A little."

Her scarlet red lips curled up in the slightest of smiles, something I'd come to know as the ultimate sign of amusement for Beatrice. "You probably don't struggle with people liking you, do you, Molly? I imagine it comes very easily to you."

Did it?

I suppose it was naïve of me to think she hadn't already answered that question in her head.

"It doesn't *always* come easily," I heard myself saying.

Now the edges of her smile stopped, frozen on a face that showed nary a wrinkle, despite the color of her hair. "I'm sure it's difficult to make friends. You're beautiful. Charming. Privileged. Your brother is a football legend and now a celebrated coach within these very halls. Your sister-in-law, Paige, is a former supermodel who could walk in New York Fashion Week tomorrow if she wanted to. You scored a job fresh out of college that ten-year industry veterans would kill for. Obviously, you're doing something right, Miss Ward."

The emphasis on my last name had me sitting up straight in the chair.

Like she was sitting on my shoulder, I could hear my sister-in-law's voice, the veritable devil with flaming red hair, the one who always battled for my sisters and me when someone came against us.

This bitch can go screw herself. She doesn't know you, and she sure as shit doesn't know our family, Paige whispered. My inner Paige wasn't wrong.

But on the other shoulder was my brother, Logan, the man who'd all but raised my three younger sisters and me after our mom bailed. And I knew what he'd tell me to do. Show respect. Do my job. Prove her wrong in the right way.

Inner Logan wasn't wrong either.

"I know what I must look like to you," I told Beatrice. "How my life must look. But you've only just met me, Miss Kelly. I'm a hard worker; otherwise, I wouldn't have this job, no matter what my last name is."

"We'll see," she mused.

Her attention flicked back to something on her desk, and my molars ground together at her flippant tone. She held up a file and handed it to me over the immaculate expanse of her desk. The black and red Wolves logo was stamped on the front, and I opened it up once I had it firmly in my hand. My eyes skimmed quickly over the cover page, eyebrows popping in surprise.

"Amazon?" I asked. "That's ... huge."

"It is. I got this job because I'm bringing this project with me." She sat back and watched me again. As much as I wanted to flip through the pages to learn more, I gave her my full attention.

"How can I help?"

"You told me you're good at developing relationships. That you anticipate problems and make them go away. That people feel comfortable around you. Am I remembering all those things correctly?"

I nodded slowly.

"I think you've been behind a desk for too long."

I took a deep breath, excitement tingling along the edge of my fingers where I gripped the manila. "Where would you like to move me?"

Beatrice pointed at the folder. "All of that is laid out on page two. I'm offering you a huge chance to back those words up, Miss Ward, but I'm giving you twenty-fours to give me an answer."

My eyes scanned quickly, but when I opened my mouth, she interrupted.

"No, I mean, I don't want to hear a yes or a no for at least one day. If you say yes to this, this is your one chance to prove to me that you're not just here because of your last name. Got it?"

Carefully, I forced my immediate acceptance down. "I understand."

Her eyes held mine unflinchingly. "This is a big deal. Working with a company like Amazon opens doors that don't get opened often, Molly. That job description includes a lot of fine print that you'd do well to read through, which is why I want you to take your time."

Returning my gaze to the papers in my hand, I saw a lot of familiar jargon. But there were new phrases as well.

No fraternization.

Morality clause.

My attention went back to her. "I didn't think we had a no-fraternization policy in the Wolves handbook."

"We don't," she answered dryly, "but this one does. I insist on it for anyone who's assigned to something of this caliber and reports to me. I've seen people's careers ruined for a lot less, which is why I take this so seriously." Beatrice held up a hand. "It's for your protection too, if you agree."

"Got it."

She searched my face. "Only say yes if you know, unequivocally, that you can do this job. I don't believe in the three-strike rule, Molly. In life, we get one chance to impress people, and rarely do we get another."

An hour and a half later, I pulled into Logan and Paige's driveway, mind chugging like a freight train. It hadn't stopped since the moment I flipped over to the second page.

I was the first one to arrive for family dinner, which we gathered for every Tuesday night without fail. We held them on Tuesdays because during the season, it was my brother's day "off," if you could call it that. As the defensive coordinator for the Wolves, he still worked what seemed like a thousand hours a week during the season, but it was the one day a week he could get home before six thirty for all of us to eat together.

Before I walked into the house—the same one I lived in from the age of fourteen until I'd officially moved out after college—I took a second to calm my racing nerves.

My family would have varying reactions to this.

My sisters would think it was cool to differing degrees. The twins, Lia and Claire, would freak simply because it was Amazon. Isabel, my middle sister, would want to shadow me day and night because of her obsession with all things related to sports documentaries.

Paige would be excited for me, once she got over the need to punch my new boss in the throat.

And Logan? I groaned. My big brother would hate it. Unequivocally and irrationally. He'd all but command me to say no. Wait for another boss or another chance.

I blew out a harsh breath before I pushed the front door open.

Screams greeted me, as did the smell of garlic and herbs. The screams didn't faze me in the slightest, and the smell had me breathing deeply.

"I'm home," I called over the chaos. "Hide the carbs because I had a day."

Down the hallway in front of me, the one that led to the wide-open kitchen, dining, and living, came the intensified hollering.

"Molly! We're under attack, go! Go! Go!"

Flattening against the wall, I reached an arm out to snag the small body that hurtled past me across the wooden floor. "Slow your roll, soldier," I said into my nephew's hair as I gave him a quick kiss. "Who's attacking us?"

Emmett peered up at me, his blue eyes huge in his face and his cheeks flushed from running. "The zombies," he whispered dramatically. "They already got Dad. He's dead on the couch."

My heart squeezed at his serious delivery, the kind that only an eight-year-old boy could muster for an imaginary zombie attack. "Ahh, okay. Well, I put on my anti-zombie spray before I came in, so am I safe to proceed?"

His skinny arms squeezed me in a tight hug before he took off again. "Yup!" he called over his shoulder, then tore around the corner and out of sight.

My brother, Logan, popped up off the couch when I came into the family room, dropping a kiss on the top of my head, the same way I'd kissed his son, who was really more like my little brother than my nephew. "How'd it go? What's she like?"

I grimaced. "I need wine before this story."

"That good?"

"Just ... unexpected."

He eyed me, more astute than I wanted him to be. But that wasn't a surprise. Logan had been my constant since day one. When I was born, Logan was nineteen years old. That was the kind of sibling age gap you had when our dad married a woman a couple of decades younger than him later in life.

Fast forward fourteen years—our dad had passed away from a

heart attack, and my mom realized that being a young widow of four girls just wasn't the funnest life choice she could make. So she decided not to anymore. The *Eat Pray Love* option suited her better than parenthood, so Logan became our father figure in the legal sense even though he'd had that role for far longer.

"You'd tell me if I need to step in and talk to someone, right?"

I rolled my eyes, trying to hide the irritating flush of embarrassment. His comment was exactly why Beatrice was wary of me. "Yes, Coach."

He bumped shoulders with me as we walked into the kitchen.

"How was your day?" I asked him. "I heard chitchat about some roster changes, but I was too busy with Beatrice starting to really pay attention."

My job was typically pretty far removed from dealing with the players anyway, so it didn't affect me too much.

Or it used to be far removed from the players, I thought, reminded again just how very unhappy Logan would be with this.

Paige, his wife of nine years and the coolest person on the planet, was stirring a boiling pot of pasta. She smiled at me as I poured a glass of white. "How'd it go?"

"Shouldn't I just wait until the other three get here so I don't have to repeat this?"

"No," they answered.

I sank into a stool and took a slow sip of my wine. "She's ... different than Ava. Very ..." I searched for the right word that wouldn't make them hate her right away. "She's no-nonsense. Reminds me of Meryl Streep in *The Devil Wears Prada* but like, at seventy-five percent. Not all the way intimidating, but close."

Paige hummed. "Yes, yes, I'm following."

"I'm not," Logan said, folding his arms over his chest. "Who's the devil?"

"We've made you watch it at least three times," I told him. "The fashion internship movie."

"Absolutely would've blocked that from my subconscious. It's been wiped away by *Captain Underpants* and *Transformers*."

We all laughed about Emmett's current obsessions. Somewhere in the distance, he roared about defeating the undead.

"Do we like her?" Paige asked.

"I think we might," I answered, glancing back and forth between them. "She's actually giving me a promotion. Or the chance at one, if I want it."

Promotion. Test. Whatever.

Logan smiled. "That's great, Mol."

"Seriously great," Paige said. "What is it?"

I swallowed more wine. "She got Amazon to agree to include Washington in one of their *All or Nothing* documentaries."

Paige whistled. "No shit." Logan pushed the swear jar in her direction, and she pulled a five from her purse and dumped it in. "There, I'm covered for the night."

Logan eyed me again. "We weren't told about that. Who are they filming?"

"They're still deciding. I guess Allie and Cameron knew about this," I said, referencing the team owner—Paige's best friend—and the longtime COO. "So does Coach, but they're holding a meeting tomorrow to tell the rest of the coaching staff before they decide which players to film."

My brother was quiet as he processed that, and Paige smiled encouragingly at me, even as she knew her husband would be pissed that something like this might interrupt practice. We were less than a month away from the start of preseason, and while late roster changes weren't out of the ordinary, it was still stressful for the coaching staff.

The Wolves hadn't won a championship since Logan played, even though their record had stayed strong. We'd won our division but failed in the past few years to make it past the playoffs, despite a tough defense and young offense.

"That's big money for Washington," Paige said, "to land something like that."

"It is. And a huge opportunity for more, when you consider merchandising." I set my glass down. "It helps in just about every facet—community relations, social media exposure, and new sponsorship opportunities. Players get exposure to a new crowd that may not know much about them other than their field stats. It's exciting."

Logan nodded. "I get it. I don't have to like it, especially if cameras are tripping my players up during practice."

"They won't, I promise."

His smile was small. "Yeah? You gonna be in charge of them?"

"Sort of?" I grinned. "I have to take a day or two to think about it, but you're looking at the official special projects liaison. I'll be the point person between Washington and Amazon. I'll be in charge of making sure everything runs smoothly; that the film crew has what they need, that the players are protected, and nobody gets in each other's way."

"Molly, that's amazing," Paige gushed. She hurried around the island to give me a tight hug. "She can't be too bad if she trusted you with something like that."

Logan looked thoughtful. Not thrilled, but not unhappy either. "And this is something you want to do?"

I nodded. "I do. And I know, Logan, you loved that I never had to deal with the players, but I'll be fine. I have sixteen years of knowing how to manage stubborn athletes under my belt."

Paige laughed.

My brother rolled his eyes.

"I wonder if the roster shakeup influenced Amazon's decision," Paige said.

Logan stared at the floor but didn't say anything.

"It's possible. Beatrice told me they're looking at a couple of narratives, and one is following the new players as they assimilate into the established culture of a team, college and pro." I shrugged. "But that's just one possibility."

Logan muttered something under his breath. Paige narrowed her eyes at him.

I cocked my head in his direction. "What was that?"

He pinched the bridge of his nose. "I said I think I know who they want to film. Dammit."

Paige slowly pushed the swear jar back in her husband's direction, which he ignored as I stared him down.

"Who?"

Logan slicked his tongue over his teeth and stared me down right back. "This is a horrible idea, and you should turn down the promotion."

"Ummm, no. Why on earth would I do that?"

"Molly."

"Logan." I crossed my arms. "What's your problem?"

"You have worked so hard, kid," he said, and my arms dropped at the sudden seriousness of his voice. "So damn hard, and I'm so proud of you."

Paige glanced back and forth between us, and I shrugged.

"Who did we sign, and why does this freak you out so badly?" she asked.

He rubbed the back of his neck, closing his eyes for a long moment.

I grabbed my phone. "Fine, I'll google it."

"Noah," he said. "We signed Noah Griffin this morning. Press had barely got wind of it by the end of the day."

Paige somehow managed an, "Ohhhhhhh shit," even though her half-open mouth barely moved.

The phone clattered out of my hand, and I sank back down into the stool.

"Like, *Noah* Noah?" I pointed at the house behind ours, the one he hadn't lived in for years. "That Noah."

Logan's look was enough affirmation. Paige covered her mouth with one hand.

My younger sister Isabel appeared around the corner with a half-eaten protein bar in her hand. "What about Noah?"

We all looked at her but didn't answer.

I dropped my head into my hands.

"What about Noah?" Isabel repeated. "I heard Miami dropped him because of some drama in the locker room. Which is weird because he's like ... uber football robot man. I don't think I've seen him smile in three seasons." She whistled. "But damn, his QB sack record is bananas. Off the charts."

Isabel would know. Our resident sports know-it-all.

I thought my mind was racing before. How cute.

"Molly," Logan said quietly. "Come on, think about this. If they're showing up to film him, then taking care of him will be your job. Do you think that's smart?"

I snapped my head up. "I'm not a kid anymore, Logan."

"What in the hell is going on?" Isabel shouted.

Paige pushed the jar in her direction as Logan ignored everything except me.

"Molly—" he said again.

"No," I interrupted. "I'm not turning this down. I was sixteen the last time I saw him. That was forever ago. I'm sure he's forgotten all about it, just like I'm going to."

Paige cleared her throat obnoxiously because we all heard the bullshit in my words.

Like I'd ever be able to forget Noah Griffin.

Former next-door neighbor, the college boy I crushed on for two years before I snuck out, climbed into his bedroom window, and attempted to seduce him before his dad caught us. The same college boy I could've ruined if his dad had walked in much later, and anyone had found out he slept with a minor while on a full ride football scholarship.

Yeah, that Noah Griffin.

Looking around the room, I noted all three of their faces were frozen into variations of *this is a horrible idea.*

"You guys," I stated, "I've totally got this. They probably aren't even coming to film him. We have thirty-one other players to pick from. It'll be fine."

Oh, how very, very wrong I was.

CHAPTER TWO

NOAH

ALMOST NOTHING about my job intimidated me.

A three-hundred-pound offensive lineman could curse me out just before the snap of the ball, threaten my mother and spit through his helmet all the ways he was going to grind me into the turf, and I wouldn't feel the slightest twinge of apprehension.

I didn't become the best at my position by getting scared off easily. I did it by living, eating, breathing football.

Nothing came before it. Nothing ranked above it.

Practice always took precedence over anything I might find fun, which was why my former teammates in Miami used to call me The Machine. I was the first one in the weight room, the last one to leave the film room, the copious notetaker at meetings, and probably one of the only unapologetically celibate football players in the league.

Another thing that didn't come before my job was women, or what anyone around me might think of me.

But when my agent called me two days earlier, and said, "We're sending you to Washington," I felt something foreign lodge behind my chest, somewhere low in my rib cage.

Apprehension.

Nerves.

And worst of all, the slightest, smallest twinge of fear.

Because forty-eight hours later, I found myself standing in front of the closed door of my new defensive coordinator, who was expecting me for a meeting, and I couldn't bring myself to open it.

My hand wouldn't lift to knock, and my feet stayed stubbornly parked in place. I'd clocked in at two hundred and eighty pounds at my last weigh-in, and not one of those pounds, the muscle I'd worked on my entire career, was feeling particularly motivated to move me forward into that office.

My jaw tightened as I stared at the nameplate next to the door, innocuous silver with black letters. *Logan Ward, Defensive Coordinator.*

In the past ten years, I'd only seen him once since I started for Miami, when our teams had played against each other two years earlier. A nod after the game, which they'd won, and that was it.

Prior to that ... I refused to think about. My eyes pinched shut because that one day set me onto a trajectory where nothing, and *no one*, would ever distract me from my goals again.

The door yanked open, and his face greeted me with a scowl.

"Are you coming in, Griffin, or should we yell at each other through the door?"

Whatever trace of fear had been lingering was instantly replaced with annoyance, and I gave him a look of consternation. "Nice to see you, too."

"Let's get this over with because I don't need distractions, and there are already enough of them lining up for the season."

"Are you this welcoming to every guy you coach?" I asked as I followed him into the no-frills office.

"Nope," he answered easily. He sat heavily in his chair and watched me thoughtfully.

His was typical of every coordinator's office I'd ever been in. A desk with two chairs across from it, a whiteboard along the back, and empty walls. Their work took place on the field, their strategies mapped out on clipboards and in the film rooms. And a defensive mind like Logan's, that had been one of the best when he played, had only been honed further now that he coached from the sidelines.

His genius didn't need a fancy office. He just needed players who listened and knew what to do, knew what to look for, and who had that same sense that he did in reading an offense.

"Haven't talked to you in a long time, Griffin."

Just over nine years since we exchanged a single word, but that stayed unsaid, considering my dad sold our house shortly after Logan all but threatened my career in his driveway if I ever looked at his sister again. I crossed my arms over my chest. "I didn't ask to be sent here."

He exhaled a quiet laugh. "Dispensing with niceties, I see."

I swiped a hand over my mouth. This was the part I wasn't very good at. "I guess. I just ... I'm here to work, you know? Yes, you and I used to be neighbors, but it's not like anyone knows that here. I didn't want to leave my team, but here I am. It's not my choice, but I'll be damned if it derails me in any way."

Logan's attention never wavered from my face, and his expression never shifted. It was that razor-sharp focus that every good player had. Every good coach too.

"You've changed," he said quietly.

"In ten years? I hope so."

"Fair enough," Logan conceded. He leaned forward, setting his folded hands on the surface of the desk. "Here's the deal: you've got more natural talent in your pinky finger than most players on my entire defense. And if you tell anyone I said that, I'll deny it until my dying breath."

17

My face stayed unchanged, even as my heart sped up at his compliment.

"But I will not go easy on you because we knew each other. If anything, I'd take great pleasure in seeing you get knocked on your ass a couple of times, simply because it's within my power to make that happen," he said with a grim smile.

I sat back. This was the meeting I'd expected. The warning I'd anticipated. All because his pain in the ass little sister climbed on the lap of a stupid college boy who used to let his dick rule his life.

My thoughts must have been clear on my face because he nodded like he could read every single one.

"I wasn't allowed to knock you the hell out back then," he said. "But I wanted to."

My chin lifted a fraction of an inch. "I know you did, sir."

"I won't now. I've matured in my old age."

If he wanted me to crack a smile and lighten the mood, I didn't give him the satisfaction. Nobody saw me flinch. "You also know I'd hit you back, coach or not."

Logan's smile was slow, but it came nonetheless, because he thought I was joking. When my face still didn't change, the smile disappeared. He shook his head.

"You are one grumpy son of a bitch, aren't you?"

"I've heard that, yes." Then I shook my head. "I'm not grumpy. I just don't take any of this lightly. Football is the most important thing in my life."

"I can respect that." He tapped the side of his thumb on the desk, looked away from me, then looked back, seeming to come to a decision about something. "She works here, by the way."

I tilted my head. "Who does?"

A warning siren started low, somewhere in the back of my brain as he said it, and it occurred to me, just before he answered that maybe this was the reason I felt apprehensive about this change. This was the reason I should've been afraid to come to Washington.

"Molly." He stared me down, daring me to have any sort of negative reaction about her. Any reaction at all.

Over the past nine years, I'd come to think about Molly with a strange sense of detachment, equal parts harbinger of destruction and the symbol of my shifting focus.

"A lot of people work here, sir. What does that have to do with me?"

His eyebrows popped up. "Not much, I suppose. I just wanted to give you a heads-up, in case—"

I held up a hand. "She a trainer?"

"No."

"A coach?" I asked unnecessarily because we both knew none of the coaches in the league were female.

"You know she's not."

"Then it doesn't involve me." I stood from the chair. "I need to get changed and head to the weight room if you're done."

He leaned back in his chair, and I hated the look of disappointment on his face. That face had aged since I last saw him but not by much. It was in the color of his hair, and the addition of a few lines around his eyes. But I'd changed too. I'd gained about seventy-five pounds of muscle since the day I stood in his driveway, humbled and embarrassed and, quite frankly, terrified.

Sometimes, I hardly recognized the man who stared back at me in the mirror. But I promised myself that day that I'd never feel that way again. One stupid slip almost ruined my life. A mistake that never would've been worth the consequences had the wrong person caught us.

"Anything else you need from me, sir?"

It took a second for Logan to answer, but finally, he said, "No, that's it."

I nodded and left his office far more quickly than I'd entered.

As I walked back down the hallway, trying to remember which one led to the elevator that would get me to the locker room and weight room, I harnessed every ounce of mental discipline in my body to ignore what he'd told me.

The absolute last person I cared to see at work was her.

And more than likely, I wouldn't have to. Players rarely saw front office staff unless they made it a point to. I took a deep breath and refocused. The elevator was down the hall and to the right, and that was what I needed to think about.

Someone on the janitorial staff passed me with a polite smile, which I returned just enough that I wouldn't look like a raging asshole. Making the turn, I saw the gleaming metal doors. I punched the button and waited. My muscles bunched in anticipation of a good workout. If I didn't put in a couple of hours a day, minimum, I felt an uncomfortable buzzing underneath my skin. Energy that had no outlet would start seeking one, no matter what that outlet was.

For me, I chose the healthiest. The one that would make me stronger. Make me faster. Make me better.

Some players drank. Partied on yachts. Raced cars. Did drugs. Slept around.

But they weren't as good as I was. To me, all those things were pointless distractions.

The doors opened, and I strode into the empty elevator car. I hit the button for the correct floor and waited. Just as the doors slid shut, a hand popped through the opening, halting their progress.

Like I had a few moments earlier, she surged inside the car, coming to a screeching halt with a squeak of surprise when she saw me leaning up against the wall.

We were frozen there, staring at each other, her mouth hanging open as the doors tried to close unsuccessfully. She stepped forward, and the doors closed smoothly, locking me in the enclosed space with Molly.

"Hi, Noah," she said weakly.

CHAPTER THREE

NOAH

Tilting my chin up, I breathed slowly through my nose.

"This cannot be happening," I muttered.

"Nice to see you too," she said, voice no longer weak and surprised.

Grudgingly, I dropped my gaze, and for the first time in nine years, I looked Molly Ward straight in the face. The last time I'd seen her, my father had marched us over to her house to deliver her back to Logan and his wife.

The last time I'd seen her, I'd pulled her shirt off and sucked on her enthusiastic tongue while she wiggled on my lap. I didn't even have a good reason for doing it, other than being a dumb college football player who didn't question things like hot girls wanting to be with me.

The last time I'd seen her, I was an idiotic nineteen-year-old, completely unaware that the girl with the fantastic rack, the one who eyed me like I was made of chocolate, the girl who climbed into my bedroom window and tasted like Rainier cherries, was only sixteen.

Thank God my dad walked in.

There was a lot about her that hadn't changed. She was still short—or short compared to me even though she was probably around five feet eight—and her eyes were the same bright blue. Her face had slimmed down because the cheekbones were new, while some of the *other* curves she'd had as a teenager were either effectively hidden behind her simple white shirt or had melted away as she grew into an adult. Her hair was the lighter than it used to be, but the stubborn lift of her chin gave me vivid flash-backs to the last time I'd seen her.

I crossed my arms over my chest. "Your brother warned me you worked here."

"I didn't realize I was intimidating enough to require a warning." She smiled, and I had to give her credit for holding it in place as my own mouth flattened into a line. "Welcome to Washington, Noah. I heard about the trade yesterday."

Her polite attempt at conversation almost had me relaxing my stance and softening my tone just a little bit. But as I studied her face again, beautiful and fresh-faced and sweetly smiling, I decided that was the worst damn thing I could possibly do.

The last time I'd been kind to a teammate's wife, giving her a ride home because she drank too much, I was rewarded by her shoving her hand down my pants, a slap on the face when I told her to get the hell out of my car, and the loss of my position on the team when she told her husband that I hit on her.

Just another example that no woman was worth putting my career on the line for.

"It wasn't my choice to be here, trust me."

She watched me carefully, eyes darting over to the elevator panel before she leaned over and slapped the emergency stop button.

"What are you doing?" I hissed. She knocked my hand away when I tried to hit it again.

"Calm down. We have a solid five minutes before anyone in

security is notified."

My answering stare was nothing short of incredulous. "How do you know that?"

"The twins tried it once because they were curious," she said calmly. "Paige was pregnant, and they wondered what would happen if she got trapped in the elevator. We turned it into a labor and delivery drill." Molly tilted her head, smile spreading as she told me. "Logan was so pissed because they disappeared from the practice field with his stopwatch to time it from beginning to end."

Rubbing my temples, I felt the beginnings of a headache blooming behind my eyes. Questions, so many questions, sprang to the tip of my tongue, but I swallowed them down.

"Hit the button, Molly. I need to go to the weight room."

She glanced at a slim gold watch on her wrist. "We have just over four minutes." Then she pinned me with those blue eyes. "What's your problem? You're acting weird."

I pushed off the wall. "You don't know me. You wouldn't know how I act under any circumstances, let alone this one."

Her face pinched briefly. "Fair enough, but I used to know you. You were a nice guy, Noah."

"I was a college athlete who let his dick make stupid decisions. I screwed around and wasted my time on video games and parties and women who I don't remember anymore. Typical player, in more ways than one, and you'd do good to remember that."

The words were intended to hurt. And I saw the moment they hit their mark, as clearly as if they'd drawn blood from her smooth, pale skin.

Molly rolled her lips in, the edges of her cheekbones turning pink, but she didn't reply right away. I expected capitulation. Another kindly spoken request. And for the second time that day, she surprised me.

"I was in diapers when my brother started playing professional football. I've worked here for four years and interned for
two before that. I'm the last person who needs a lecture about
asshole football players. I daresay I've known more of them than
you have."

"Whatever you say, Miss Ward." I shouldered past her and hit
the button.

The elevator chugged back into motion, and she shook
her head.

"There's no reason we can't be friends."

A laugh burst out of me. "There are so many reasons, and I
have no desire to explain any of them to you. You've known a few
players. Good for you. But you don't understand the kind of pressure I'm under, or the way that I operate, so I'll tell you this." I
leaned toward her, gratified when she swallowed roughly, and her
eyes widened. "I'm not here to make friends. You were a mistake
that I narrowly avoided making, and I have no intention of going
down that road again."

For a moment, I expected the crack of another small female
hand against my cheek. But that was not what Molly did.

"What happened to you?" she whispered sadly.

The elevator doors slid apart, the area beyond blessedly
empty. I gave her one last look. "I grew up, Molly. You should do
the same."

I strode past her, and before I was out of earshot, I heard her
mutter, "Dick."

The apprehension and nerves were long gone, but my jaw
clenched at the surprising pang of irritation I felt. I'd been called
worse by women. By teammates. Not by someone like Molly,
though. Someone kind and friendly.

I kept walking, not a single pause in my long strides, because
I was here to do a job, and Molly Ward had nothing to do with it.

CHAPTER FOUR

MOLLY

"Conceited."

Smack.

"Arrogant."

Smack. Smack.

"Little."

Smack.

"Prick."

Isabel raised an eyebrow. "Little, huh?"

"Shut up." I punched the bag again, grinning when it moved her backward from where she was bracing an arm against it. I pulled back one more time and hit the front of the heavy bag with a right cross, then shook my arm out and braced my gloved hands on my knees.

Isabel handed me my water bottle and dropped onto the floor, folding her legs neatly underneath her. The kickboxing gym didn't hold any classes during the lunch hour, so it was empty. Paige used to come here when she first married Logan, and slowly, our whole family became involved in one way or another. Isabel, the showoff, had to one-up everyone by taking over as the manager a couple of years ago when the owner was ready to spend more time with her family.

Perks of being sister of the manager was a private place to work out my lunchtime frustrations when my former crush, minor though it might have been, turned out to be a major league asshole. Flopping onto the floor next to her, I stretched my legs out and hissed at the burn in my quads. "If you do more squats tonight in class, I'll walk out."

"No, you won't," she said. "That's the reason your ass looks so phenomenal."

I sighed. "True."

"What happened?"

No sigh this time, but a deep, tortured, dramatic groan. "Do I have to talk about it?"

Isabel laid down next to me and folded her arms calmly over her middle. "Yes. I'm bored and have no life outside of work, and I'd like to live vicariously through your drama. Just like I always have."

And it was true. I was older than Iz by two years, and she was two years older than our twin sisters, Lia and Claire. The small gap in ages between four girls meant that we were up in each other's business allllll the time.

I shifted, stretching an arm over my chest. "He was so ... mean. And all I did was get onto an elevator. Like I even knew he was in there!"

"And you haven't seen him even once since, you know, the incident?" she asked delicately. Which should've been humorous because it was Isabel. She didn't do anything delicately.

"Nope." I pulled my gloves off and tossed them over by my bag. Sitting up, I wrapped my fingers around my toes to stretch the backs of my legs. Isabel sat up too, tucking her knees into her chest and wrapping her arms around them. "I mean, I knew he played for Miami because I hear his name all the time. It's not like

I was clueless about what he was doing, but"—I shrugged—"he was just the guy I used to have a crush on. I had lots of crushes in high school. He was hardly special."

Isabel pursed her lips.

"Shut up," I said. "I know what you're going to say."

"Do you, though?"

I tugged at the Velcro around my wrist and slowly unwound my sweaty wraps from my hand. "I can make an excellent guess."

Iz set her chin on her knees and watched me. She used to do that as a kid, too. Watch everything around her. Soak it up and process what she observed. It was what made her a good listener because she saw everything.

"So he's, what? Been pissed at you for nine years because you did something monumentally stupid as a teenager?"

"Geeez," I muttered. "Tell me how you really feel, Iz."

She gave me a look. "You climbed through his window, Mol. It wasn't your brightest moment."

Hurt and embarrassment warred for my instant reaction, but I couldn't bring myself to deny it. At sixteen, I'd been boy-crazy, just like all my friends. And it was just my luck that as a next-door neighbor, I'd been given the ultimate gift. A hot college boy who was home a lot during the offseason.

"I was so convinced that he saw me, that he noticed me like I noticed him." I pulled off the other wrap, dumping it into a pile with the first one, then flexed my fingers. "I used to blame Mom, you know? Like her leaving us created this insatiable desire to make sure people liked me enough to want to stick around."

Isabel snorted. "I still blame Mom for a lot. Just ask my therapist."

My head swiveled in her direction. "You go to a therapist? Since when?"

"Eh, I went twice before it pissed me off. She was a whack job who kept asking me stupid questions. If I *knew* why I was so angry with my mother, would I be paying her a hundred bucks an hour?"

Laughing under my breath, I shook my head. That sounded about right. The thought of my emotionally reserved sister spilling her guts in a comfy chair to a shrink did not compute, not in any reality I was aware of. It sounded like something I would do. Allow a perfect stranger to untangle my emotions and figure out why the woman who gave birth to us didn't love us enough to want to stick around.

All four of us bore scars to varying degrees, and over time, they'd all healed differently. Mine was a sense of urgency if I knew someone didn't like me, whatever the reason. A niggling discomfort under my skin to *fix it, fix it, fix it.*

I sighed. "I'm sure that's part of it, but it was him, too. I'd completely convinced myself if I just ... had the chance to really talk to him, he'd fall head over heels in love with me, and I'd have the hottest boyfriend out of all my friends, who played college football."

"Not surprising for a sixteen-year-old."

"No, but it was crazy. To do what I did." My face flushed hot when I thought about it. Something I hadn't really done in years. The moments before his dad walked through the door, I'd never felt more alive. More womanly.

It should have been a blazing red warning light that Noah had no qualms about kissing me like he did or touching me like he had after I climbed through his effing window without so much as a single meaningful conversation between the two of us.

That five minutes after my legs cleared the windowsill, I was straddling his lap. I should've worried that his big, hot hands were underneath my shirt, sliding up my back and tugging it up over my head, when we'd barely kissed. That my hands shook where I'd laid them on his muscular shoulders because when he did kiss me, it felt like I was drowning in something so much bigger than I'd been prepared for.

If his dad hadn't walked in, I would've slept with Noah Griffin that day. And he probably would've never spoken to me again afterward.

It was something I had to come to grips with after it all went down.

After Mr. Griffin marched me back home to face my furious brother and my disappointed sister-in-law, I curled up in my bed and sobbed my sixteen-year-old heart out. The look on Noah's face when he realized how old I was cemented the fact that any happily ever after I'd imagined with him would stay firmly planted in my teenage brain.

"You know how every age you're at," I said, "you feel like, this is the most mature I'll ever be. Right now, I have it all figured out."

Isabel smiled.

"And then a few years pass, and you want to slap your past self for ever thinking something that stupid."

She laughed under her breath. "Yeah. I know exactly what you mean."

"I wish I could go back and handcuff myself to my bed, so I never climbed through that damn window. I wish I could go back and get on the elevator two minutes later so that I never realized what a big, dumb asshole he is now." I shook my head. "I really, *really* wish I could take back the moment I said I wanted to be friends with him."

Her face was sad as she listened. "That doesn't sound like you. You're friends with everyone."

"Not Noah Griffin."

Inexplicably, that made Isabel grin.

"What?" I snapped, well aware that I sounded like the human equivalent of a pout.

"How'd he look?"

I groaned, dropping my head into my hands. "Isabel."

"That good, huh?"

Lifting my head, I glared at her over my shoulder. "You know what he looks like."

"Yeah." She sighed. "Sure as hell do. But seeing him in person, being stuck in an elevator with him, that's a whole different thing, and you know it, Molly. Give me the goods."

How did he look?

Oh my stars, I didn't want to think about how he looked.

Angry.

Big.

Beautiful.

More than likely, Noah would've hated that I called him beautiful, but he was. The symmetry in his features, the bold slash of his lips, the rock-hard angle of his jaw, the shock of dark hair, the icy color of his eyes ... everything about that man's face was a gift of genetics, and it pissed me off on principle.

A face that perfect should be smiling. Kind. Warm.

And he'd been the exact opposite. He took me in, judged me, then decided I wasn't worth a single ounce of his kindness.

What a prick.

I sighed. "It was stupid how good he looked, Iz."

"What are you gonna do?"

I rolled my neck. "I'm not sure. I *do not* want to turn down the new job from Beatrice because of this. There's no guarantee that Noah will be involved anyway. More than likely, they'll follow one of the other new guys ... maybe the new running back."

Isabel's eyebrows bent in. "The guy from the New England practice squad?"

I nodded. "It's not like Noah is the only new contract they signed this week."

"He's just the biggest name," she said gently.

"Thanks."

She held up her hands. "Just saying."

"It'll be fine, even if he is the one they want to highlight." I licked my lips as I thought about the rest of my day at work. "I'm going to go meet with Beatrice before we talk to Amazon, and they start filming at practice. Because I will not let him ruin this chance for me."

"And if they do choose him?"

My lip curled into an uncharacteristic snarl when I considered what that meant for me. It meant my single chance at proving myself to my boss would rest in the hands of the one person in the Wolves organization who hated me.

Awesome.

I bumped her shoulder with mine. "Maybe you can come beat him up for me if he's mean again."

Isabel stood with a grin, holding her hand out for me so she could tug me to my feet. "You got it."

After I'd dumped all my stuff into my gym bag, I slung it over my shoulder. Iz held out her fist to me, and I bumped it as I passed.

"Go get 'em, tiger," she said. "I'd bet on you any day of the week."

"Damn straight," I muttered. Noah Griffin didn't know me anymore either, but he was about to find out exactly what I was made of.

CHAPTER FIVE

NOAH

My reputation as The Machine preceded me, that much was evident. The guys were polite in their greetings but nothing effusive. No violent, back-pounding hugs, nothing outside of reserved happiness that my football talents were now wearing black and red.

There was very little in any greeting about Noah Griffin as a person, and that suited me just fine. Until I got out on the practice field and saw Kareem Jones, outside linebacker and one of my former roommates from U Dub. Before he so much as opened his mouth, I braced myself for the attention I'd been actively avoiding.

He hooted loudly when I cleared the doors, drawing the attention of every damn person on the field. I laughed under my breath as he barreled toward me and lifted me in a massive hug with arms as big as tree trunks. He was two inches taller than me, so my feet cleared the ground for a second before he dropped me.

"Damn, boy, what they been feeding you in Miami?" he said around a wide, happy grin. "The Machine got fat."

I shoved at his shoulder. "You're delusional, Jones. I'd still kick your ass at the line every time, and you know it."

His booming laugh thawed a bit of the icy wall of distance I'd stood behind since arriving. But I still found myself glancing around to see if anyone was watching with suspicion or distrust.

It was ridiculous to think they would. Drama happened in the locker room of every team in the league, and the reason for my hasty departure out of Miami, made up or not, hadn't been fed to mainstream media. What golden boy QB wanted to admit that one of his teammates—bigger, stronger, and more established on the team—had a chance with his *Playboy* Playmate wife? Not the QB I'd left behind, that's for sure.

But still, common knowledge or not, it rankled that anyone might look at me and think it was the truth. It made me wish I could go back and not offer her a ride, that I'd called her an Uber or called her husband or another one of the WAGs who'd been at the event. A drunk woman wasn't my responsibility, even if she'd felt like it at the moment as I came upon her swaying dangerously in the parking lot as she tried to find her keys.

Kareem waved another teammate over to introduce me, and I took a deep breath. No one was judging me. No one was watching with narrowed eyes.

Except maybe Logan, I thought as I caught sight of him at the edge of the field, watching me carefully underneath the brim of his well-worn black cap with the Wolves logo stamped on the front.

Turning my attention to the guys who approached, I recognized a few but not all. They all smiled, made small talk, and joked around with Kareem. The kind of familiarity that typically grew between teammates.

Just not with me.

Sometimes, I hardly recognized that about myself, but I'd

been that way for so long, it felt like a fool's errand to try to change it. Change myself.

"Relax, man," Kareem said quietly as the other guys started talking amongst themselves.

I rolled my eyes. "Yeah, that's what I do best."

"You still a virgin? You know that's your problem, right?"

My whole body froze as he said it far too loudly. I leveled him with a glare, which made him crack up. "Kareem, you asshole. I'm not a virgin—"

His jaw dropped open as he caught sight of my face. "Seriously? You still don't have sex?" His head shook back and forth, slowly, incredulously. "I thought you were just being, like, moody or some shit in college."

"We are not talking about this right now."

He hooted again. "Yeah, we are." One arm came around my shoulders, and we separated from the guys. I wasn't ashamed of the fact that I chose to abstain from women. A woman was a distraction. Sex was not only a distraction but it also came with far too many possible complications. I didn't want kids. Didn't want anything in my life that would fight for the top spot in my life outside of football. "Man, come on, you're killin' me. How do you ... Aren't you *angry* all the time?"

That made me smile, just a little, because the way he said it made it sound like I was attempting an impossible feat. Climbing Mt Everest naked. Bungee jumping over a canyon full of glass with a frayed rope. Jumping from an airplane without checking to see if my parachute was attached to my back.

"And you don't think that helps me?" I asked.

He stopped walking. "I know you're playin' right now. I know you are."

I held my arms out. "Why? You said you'd be angry, right? Where do you think I put all that energy?" I lifted my chin at the field in front of us. "I put it out there."

"You are one crazy motherfucker, Griffin." He shook his head again. "I knew it then, and I really know it now."

Logan—Coach, as I needed to get used to thinking of him as —whistled sharply from the sidelines, and Kareem shoved me hard enough that I stumbled. I shoved him back, which made him laugh, but he was the only one. Coach Ward glared at me.

"Is this how you paid attention to your coaches in Miami?" he asked, arms folded across his chest. Behind him, I noticed a couple of suits—one man, one woman—and a guy holding an expensive-looking camera.

Lifting my chin, I clasped my hands behind my back like a soldier facing his commanding officer. "No, sir."

"It's my bad, Coach," Kareem said on a laugh. "Noah thinks his"—I gave him a sharp look, and he grinned—"his *natural state* of repressed anger means he can beat my ass off the line."

The guys around us laughed, and Coach cracked a reluctant smile. "Yeah? What do you think about that, Jones?"

Kareem slapped a hand on my back. "I think this boy is crazy, and I'm ready to prove it."

The suits and the cameras aimed their attention fully in our direction now, and the cheers and laughter of my new teammates were just enough to distract me from wondering what they were doing.

I shook my head. "Kareem, don't embarrass yourself. Let's just get to work."

In truth, I didn't want to line up like this at my first practice and turn it into a circus. As much as I wanted to be the best, I didn't need the spotlight that came with it. I wanted to break records to prove that I could. I wanted to lift more, run faster, train harder because I was good at it. My body constantly craved that burn, the satisfying edge of pain that told me I was the hardest worker on the field.

But Logan waved at us to do it, so I'd flatten Kareem without a second thought.

Our teammates surrounded us, leaving adequate space in the middle for Kareem and me to face each other. Someone handed us practice helmets, and I strapped mine on while he did the same. The tall, thin woman in the suit pushed some players out of the way so the cameras could see us clearly, and I rolled my neck to ignore them and focused on what I needed to do.

The joke about my natural state of anger fueled the tightening of tension in my muscles as I crouched in front of my former college roommate. He was two inches taller than me and just as wide.

His body held all the same carefully crafted muscles and knowledge of body mechanics for when you were trying to take out an opponent. He kept his fingers loose where they propped him up in the grass, and I did the same, no hint as to where we might move or which direction we might take.

He grinned behind his helmet, and I narrowed my eyes, letting the full blaze of power unroll through my arms and back and legs when I imagined knocking him over. Our teammates heckled and hollered; most cheered on Kareem, but a few voices were saying my name. Coach stood between us, silver whistle in his mouth, which would be our signal.

Movement from behind Kareem pulled my gaze away for a split second.

Molly. On the practice field.

Her blue eyes met mine and widened.

What was she *doing* out here?

The whistle blew, sharp and loud, but Kareem shoved forward a split second before I did. Because, of course, I hadn't fully been paying attention. That was enough for me to have to dig my cleats in and push against him, our shoulders wedged against each other as we fought for the dominant position.

A bright pulse of anger went unchecked that I hadn't flipped him over yet because of her, and that was enough for me to shove him over onto his back.

The guys cheered, some groaned, and Logan watched us with a slight smile on his face.

"Not bad, Griffin," he said.

I held out a hand, and Kareem took it. He slapped my back in a half-hug when he was back on his feet.

"Asshole," he said, but he was smiling.

"Pansy," I returned, which made him laugh.

The crowd dissipated as they started lining up for drills, and when I was about to do the same, the suits and the cameras—and Molly—approached Coach Ward and me.

He looked about as happy as I was at their presence. The one thing he wasn't was surprised. "Can I help you?"

The woman, statuesque and composed and entirely out of place on a practice field, looked me up and down slowly, like I was under a spotlight. I fought not to curl my lip up at her.

"Noah Griffin?" she asked, holding out her hand. I took it. "I'm Beatrice Kelly, Chief Marketing Officer for Washington."

"Pleasure to meet you," I said stiffly. It wasn't. I wanted to be practicing.

As Beatrice introduced herself to Logan, Molly clutched a black and red clipboard to her chest, face blank, and eyes trained on the bright green turf.

"If you don't mind, the crew will be here filming for the remainder of practice, and then I'd like to steal fifteen minutes with both you and Noah when you're done."

Logan glanced at me, then back at her. "And if I do mind?"

She smiled slowly, eyes about as warm as a block of ice. "Then you can take it up with Cameron after practice, and after we've met with Noah."

I saw Molly take a slow inhale, her cheeks taking on a soft

pink color. Personally, I didn't want to meet with this woman after practice, but I'd been playing long enough to know that sometimes, you had to do shit you didn't want to do.

The look that Logan gave Beatrice would've made the biggest, scariest linebacker shrink back, but she was completely undaunted. Even I was glad I wasn't on the receiving end of it.

"I need fifteen minutes, Coach Ward," she repeated. "We can do it now, or we can do it after practice. I'll give you the choice."

He snorted.

I dropped my chin to my chest as he mulled over her offer.

"Griffin, should we get this done now?" he asked quietly.

Pushing my tongue into my cheek, I looked at all the faces in front of me, quick glances as I tried to figure out what the hell this had to do with me. I just wanted to *play*. Was that too much to ask?

The face that snagged my gaze for just a fraction longer than everyone else's was Molly's.

Today, she was in a black shirt and bright red jeans. She matched her boss, matched the field, and for some reason, it hammered home just how much more this place was hers than it was mine.

"Let's get this done now," I said.

Beatrice smiled again, just a touch of thawing to the cold from earlier. "Excellent. Logan? I assume you know where my office is."

His answer was a short nod.

"Great. We'll see you there in ten minutes."

They walked away, leaving Logan and me with our hands braced on our hips and annoyed expressions on our faces.

"What the hell is that about?" I mused.

He rubbed the back of his neck. "Griffin, believe me when I say that I wish there was a way to avoid this."

My face turned sharply in his direction. "That bad?"

"Yeah," he said tightly. "For guys like you and me? It's everything we hate about playing."

Once he'd given some instructions to an assistant coach, we started walking toward Beatrice's office, and I thought about what he said.

Everything we hated about playing. Great.

CHAPTER SIX

NOAH

"THANK YOU FOR JOINING ME, GENTLEMAN," she said from where she sat across a massive, gleaming desk. Her ice gray eyes landed on my face, and she smiled, a completely different kind of smile now that we were on her turf. "How's the transition to Washington going, Noah? It can't be easy to change teams so close to kickoff."

The guy holding the camera in the corner had it pointed straight at my face, and the focus, solely on me, made my skin prickle.

"I'm excited to be here." I answered like I was facing the media and not someone in-house. "And I'm excited to get to work."

Logan sighed. "Exactly. Work. Practice. Which is where we're supposed to be right now."

The grumpiness was so evident that I almost cracked a smile. Only two days into my time at Washington, and I found someone with less people skills than I had.

Beatrice sliced her gaze to the camera and nodded. "A

moment, please. We won't need this. And tell Molly I'll be ready in five."

My jaw clenched involuntarily.

Silence cloaked the office as the camera guy stood and gave us some privacy.

"I'll cut the chase. Amazon is including Washington in an upcoming season of their *All or Nothing* documentary, and you're the player they'd like to highlight."

I sat forward, eyebrows tucked in tightly over my eyes. "What? Why?"

Logan rubbed the back of his neck but didn't say anything.

"The narrative for this season is finding and fitting in to the culture of a team. I've been working on this deal since the day I told Cameron and Allie they should hire me, and we just needed the right player." Her smile softened, and it changed the hard angles of her face, "And that player is you."

"I don't want to have cameras on me all season." I shook my head. "Don't get me wrong, they do a great job. I watched the LA and the Michigan season, and they were great. But being under that spotlight is the last thing I want. I'm here to play football."

She took a deep breath. "Let me rephrase this while it's just the three of us in this office, okay?"

Something about the way she said it made me sit back again and breathe deeply to dismantle the brick that suddenly appeared in my stomach. Logan gave me a quick, uncomfortable glance, and I had a feeling he knew exactly what was going through my brain.

This wasn't a negotiation. It was a courtesy.

"You are the best defensive end in the league. By the time this season wraps up, no one will be able to touch the records that you'll break." Her eyes were so intense, words so coldly delivered that I practically saw frost come from her mouth. Not in a mean way, but in a way that I knew, without a doubt, I'd hate whatever she was about to say next. "But all of that will be overshadowed if people think you got kicked off your team because you hit on your team captain's drunk wife while she was unable to defend herself."

I was out of my chair before I took another breath. "That story is bullshit, and you know it."

Logan stood, laying a calming hand on my back. "Of course, she does. We all do."

My heart was thrashing wildly, every iron shred of my will gone in tatters at the mere suggestion that I'd become a salacious headline. Slowly, I lowered myself back into my chair and fought with white-knuckled grip to gain control of my irritation.

"The story *is* bullshit," she said calmly. "I never doubted it. The people in the front office in Miami know that, which is why there hasn't been a single whisper about it to the media."

"Yet you know about it."

She smiled. "Professional courtesy from someone in their offices who I used to work for."

"What does this have to do with the documentary, Beatrice?" Logan asked.

She watched my face carefully before answering. "One part of my job is to facilitate positive brand awareness for Washington. A documentary like this is priceless for what it allows our fans to see. Normally, they wouldn't get access to meetings, film rooms, trips ... the kinds of things that would never make it on social media. But we can give them that, and this way, we're controlling the narrative. Yes, it's documenting the reality of an established player coming into a new organization, but Noah, this allows you to show people the kind of man you are. Behind the helmet and pads and stats."

My hands, loosely clasped between my thighs, tightened briefly as I dropped my head and processed what she was saying.

"The truth is, I don't think what happened in Miami will be an issue. Not now and not in the future."

I lifted my head. "Aren't you supposed to be convincing me that that's why I should be doing this?"

"Probably," she said with a wry smile. "But I'm not trying to manipulate you. I'm simply stating the truth. You're a compelling person, Noah. Your reputation as a machine didn't come from thin air. But the players who matter to people are the ones who inspire devotion because they're heroes, not just record breakers. Look at JJ Watt or Peyton Manning or Drew Brees. Yes, they've broken all sorts of records, but they are beloved for so much more than that. That is why we'll remember their names and treasure their legacies long after they stop playing."

Logan shifted in his seat. "You're asking him to show the other side."

"Yes," she said. "Show your fans that even for The Machine, it's hard to start over. It's challenging. But you're strong enough to overcome that challenge and find your place in an organization known for its positive culture."

I took a deep breath and closed my eyes. I could already imagine telling my father that I was doing this, could hear the disbelief in his gruff voice.

But my father wasn't here. I looked over at Logan. "What do you think?"

He held up his hands. "This is not my decision. Honestly, I'm not even sure why she needed me here."

Beatrice answered that easily. "Because you're his coach, and this will require your support when we've got cameras on every angle of his life."

Logan grimaced. "That sounds awful."

"Helpful, thank you," I muttered.

He gave me an apologetic look.

The skin on my knuckles turned white when I tightened my

fingers again. She wasn't wrong, but I didn't fully believe she was right either. I didn't need to be adored for all of eternity, but I did want to be the best at what I did. I shouldn't need something like this to prove it. Numbers proved it. Rankings proved it. Wins and losses and trophies. The respect that I earned on the field was subjective, based on who was judging me, but all the things outside of it that could be charted and reported and put into history books were cold hard facts.

But if no one remembered me, no one cared about the man behind the helmet, would the numbers matter?

Not being able to answer that question for the first time in my career made me feel like someone just tossed me into a pool of oil, slimy and thick. I couldn't push through it no matter how hard I tried.

"I'll do it," I heard myself saying.

Beatrice smiled. "Excellent." Then she looked past us to the doorway. "Perfect timing, Molly. Have a seat."

It would've been comical—the way that Logan and I froze in tandem at the entrance of his sister. But it wasn't funny ... it wasn't funny at all.

"I need you to stay in coach mode," Beatrice said to the man next to me. The one who was sitting as rigidly as I was. "Can you do that? Because your sister assures me that your role within this organization has nothing to do with hers."

My eyes narrowed at the way she said it, disbelief rife and heavy in the words.

Molly took a seat next to me, and I caught the slightest hint of peaches as she did.

Fine. I didn't need to breathe by her. No problem.

"Molly got this job on her own merit," Logan said tightly. "And I'm always in coach mode."

Glancing quickly at Molly, she was settling in her chair, focused entirely on her boss. For a split second, her chin tilted in my direction like she knew I was looking but she refused to acknowledge me.

"Good," Beatrice said. "Molly accepted the role of special projects liaison for Washington this morning."

Did the earth just open up underneath me? I actually looked at the ground to make sure it hadn't and that my chair was still on solid footing.

Logan exhaled slowly, audibly. "She told me a little bit about the opportunity you've given her."

"I'm so honored that Beatrice is giving me this chance," Molly said with a loaded glance at her brother. "I'm excited to work with Amazon." She paused, and her eyes flicked to me for the first time since she sat down. "And Noah."

My foot started tapping rapidly. I turned to Beatrice. "What does a special projects liaison do?"

"She'll be your point person. She'll be the one there every day for filming, get Amazon whatever they might need, finalize filming schedule with you, make sure the brand is protected through the process, and make sure everything goes as smoothly as possible. For Amazon, but most importantly, for you, Noah."

Every word was like a tiny slash over my skin. By itself, it didn't open much of a wound, but combine them all and I'd bleed out if I thought too hard about what it meant for me.

I'd be with Molly constantly.

My face was perfectly calm, but inside, a storm raged at the idea, wild and unpredictable. Because all I knew of her was that *she* was wild and unpredictable, something I couldn't or wouldn't even want to control. And *she* would be the one making sure everything ran smoothly.

Beside me, Molly kicked at my foot, a silent warning that her boss couldn't see over the expanse of her desk.

Logan dropped his elbows to his knees and buried his head in his hands.

I pinched the tip of my tongue between my teeth so tightly that I tasted the bright coppery tang of blood.

"Are we excited to get started?" Beatrice asked, as happy as I'd seen her.

"Yup," Molly said.

Logan let out a muffled curse, then lifted his head.

Beatrice stood. "Excellent. Gentlemen, I have another meeting to get to. Molly, please figure out the next couple of days with Noah before he heads to practice." With a demure smile toward the woman sitting to my left, she nodded regally. "Dealing with Amazon is officially your responsibility."

She left, and the thick vacuum of silence at her exit practically pulsed with all the things unsaid.

"This is the worst idea I've ever heard," Logan ground out. "Molly, you cannot be serious right now."

"You don't get a say in it, Logan. Coach mode, remember?" She folded her arms over her chest.

He stood, spreading his arms out. "When have I ever been able to shut off being your brother? Never. And I won't apologize for that."

I leaned forward with a groan. This was my fucking nightmare.

Molly stood and faced him, jaw set mulishly and eyes ablaze. "Logan, outside, now." Then she pointed a finger at me. "You, stay here. I'll be back in thirty seconds, and if you've moved from that chair, don't think I won't hunt you down at practice. Those guys don't scare me."

Logan's eyes were as wide as mine before she grabbed him by the elbow, and even though she was almost a foot shorter and a decade plus younger, she dragged my coach from the office.

CHAPTER SEVEN

MOLLY

Someone from the front office passed us, grinning unapologetically at the way I manhandled my big brother into the hallway.

Logan slicked his tongue over his teeth, ripping the hat from his head with an agitated tug of his hands. "This is a terrible idea," he said again. Like I hadn't heard him the first time he complained about it.

"What would you have me do?" I asked him, not even attempting to keep the heat from my voice. "Beatrice is practically daring me to screw this up. You're not helping me think she's wrong."

His mouth fell open. "I don't think you'll screw it up, Molly."

"Don't you? If you trusted me to do my job, you'd be able to keep all those judgey big brother thoughts in your head." I swirled my finger toward his face, currently frozen in a frown.

Logan groaned, tipping his chin up to the ceiling. "Cut me some slack, okay? It's ... it's him." He gestured helplessly back at Beatrice's office. "The last time Noah was around for any extended period—"

"I was sixteen," I whispered fiercely, my face hot. If he hadn't dropped his eyes apologetically, I would've punched him in the balls. "That's categorically unfair to assume I'd react the same way. You think I don't know how stupid it was what I did? How lucky we both were that his dad walked in when he did? I get it, okay? But you need to check your impulse to remind me of your opinion every single time something big changes in my life."

I was breathing hard, my chest heaving and my throat tight.

It was hard enough to sit next to Noah, knowing he hated me, knowing he wanted nothing to do with me, and knowing that my big shot with my boss was now partially in his grasp. What I didn't need was my big brother treating me like a teenager again.

Logan sighed heavily and pulled me in for a tight squeeze. "I'm sorry," he said into the top of my head.

I clutched my hands around his wide back and allowed myself to relax into his embrace for a moment. Logan might not have been my father, but he was better than the one I'd been born to. And for almost twelve years, he'd been the one assuming the legal role.

"I'm sorry too," I said quietly. Pulling back, I glanced at his handsome face with a shy grin. "Hazards of working together, huh?"

He laughed and slipped the hat back on his head. "I suppose."

"You're lucky you apologized," I told him.

"Yeah?"

"Yeah. I was ready to tell Paige what happened to that picture she bought for the dining room that mysteriously shattered."

His eyes narrowed. "You promised to keep that a secret."

"Secrets have a funny way of coming out when big brothers act like overprotective bullies at work," I said innocently.

"This is Paige's influence," he mumbled. "You four weren't so savage until she showed up."

I laughed.

Logan set his hands on his hips and regarded me carefully for a few seconds. "It's hard for me sometimes, you know?"

"What is?"

"Remembering that you're a grown woman," he admitted quietly. "I was nineteen when you were born, Mol. That's not that far off from how old you are now and ..." He paused, looking a little melancholy. "My world changed when you were born. As much as I wish for you and your sisters that your mom hadn't left, selfishly, I'd never want to give you four back. But it's hard for me to forget what it felt like the day you were born. Even as you're standing here, smart and capable and independent, I think about how little you were, all wrinkled and red and wrapped in that ugly hospital blanket."

"I know, Logan. You're the best thing that could've happened to us." I glanced over my shoulder to make sure we were still alone in the hallway. "But you can't protect us forever."

He nodded slowly. "Doesn't mean I won't want to."

I gave him a smile. "I know."

"I'll bench his ass if he messes this up for you," he promised.

Again, I laughed. "No, you won't."

"No," he admitted grudgingly, "but it doesn't mean I wouldn't want to."

My hands swept down my shirt and straightened the ends. "Okay. I should get back to work."

Logan lifted his chin. "You've got this."

The change in his tone and posture, and the pure respect I saw in his eyes were enough to make my nose burn with unshed tears. "I'll be so mad at you if you make me cry."

"No crying in football, Ward," he snapped. "That's an order."

I rolled my eyes. "Go coach your team, please."

He winked and left me alone in the hallway. Before I joined Noah again, I sank against the wall to gather myself.

Noah wasn't my boss, but it was my responsibility to keep this process as painless as possible for him.

And I wasn't his boss, but he'd need to respect my role, nonetheless. Film when I said he needed to film, cooperate with the crew from Amazon, and trust that he'd be portrayed positively. And more importantly, that he'd be reflected honestly.

Those things didn't always go hand in hand, not in our industry. The best player in the world could be a raging asshole to the people around him. But as much as Noah had rubbed me the wrong way in the elevator, he was still respected by his teammates and coaches. Maybe he wasn't universally adored because of the stoic exterior, but even the iciest person thawed occasionally. And at the end of the day, it was up to me to make sure the world saw that.

Sitting in the too-small chair in my boss's office was a man who had dedicated his life to the same game I'd loved for all of mine.

They called him The Machine because the game of football —brown leather and white laces, cleats and turf and helmets and pads and sweat—was the thing he existed for.

"What's behind The Machine, though?" I whispered.

Before I went back into Beatrice's office, I took a deep breath and let it out slowly. It might take Noah weeks to thaw to my presence in his life, but thaw he would. He'd have no choice in the matter because the cameras didn't lie, and the reason he agreed was to allow a rare glimpse behind the curtain. It reminded me of my favorite movies, *The Wizard of Oz*.

If Noah Griffin was the wizard, all powerful and too big to comprehend for all that he was able to accomplish, then I'd have to be the unsuspecting Dorothy who unearthed the truth, one day at a time, no matter how out of place I felt doing it.

Ruefully, I glanced down at my nude-colored ballet flats and clicked the heels together. Didn't have the same effect as ruby red slippers that glistened in the light, but it would have to do.

When I opened the door, he stood staring out of the window

in the corner, which overlooked the sprawling suburbs where the Wolves training facilities and front offices were located. Off to the southeast, the jagged lines of Mt. Rainier were visible. His shoulders were held so rigidly in place that he didn't give the slightest indication he'd heard me enter, but something at the back of my neck and with the way the hairs lifted on my arms, I knew he was fully aware that we were alone again in the same way I was.

I kept the door open a crack and walked back to my seat. My clipboard was on the corner of Beatrice's desk, and I picked it up so I could flip to the tentative schedule marked out by Amazon. Things they wanted, requests for time and interviews, and insight that they thought would go over well but couldn't be forced.

Setting the clipboard in my lap, I wondered briefly whether I should let him take the lead in this conversation, given he was the one who acted like a giant horse's ass the last time I saw him.

It went against every molecule, every cell in my body not to care what he thought of me. To not try to convince him that I was a safe person for him in this. That our history could benefit us and not make life harder.

But I came to a decision as I sat there in the uncomfortable silence. It didn't matter whether Noah liked me. I just needed him to do his job, and I needed him to let me do mine. We could achieve that whether he liked me or not.

"Beatrice thinks I got this job because of my brother," was the thing that came out of my mouth first. There'd be no filter, not for this conversation. While he and I were alone, honesty was the best thing I could give him.

At the sound of my voice, Noah stilled even further, which didn't seem possible. His massive frame held almost preternaturally motionless. The span of his back was so broad, emphasizing the way his body tapered at the waist and hips. A true athlete, no one would ever look at him and question that he was born to do this.

I knew the kind of dedication it took, and the sacrifices that people like him made to reach that kind of strength and stamina. It was why I did what I did, worked where I worked, and why I'd overlooked his opinion of me and Beatrice's doubts in order to do my job.

"Is she right?" he asked.

I smiled. "I'm sure it helped me get my internship in college. But they never would've given me a job and they definitely wouldn't have kept me around if I sucked at it."

Noah didn't answer, and he didn't turn to face me. I preferred it that way.

"The only way I'll prove to my boss that she's wrong about me is by doing. There aren't enough words in the English language to convince her that I'm not the sole product of nepotism, and this job, this opportunity, is the platform she's allowing me to do that." I stared intently at his back. "To prove that I earned my place here by my actions."

His face tilted in my direction, enough that the light from the window caught the sharp jut to his jaw. The muscles under his skin popped, and I found myself staring at that little square of skin, marveling at how something so tiny could be so potent.

"Why are you telling me this?" he asked.

Leaning back in my chair, I folded one leg over the other and chose my words carefully before saying them. Noah wasn't yelling, he wasn't making a scene, but his annoyance at being in this position was loud and clear, like a blinking sign over his head.

"I didn't pick you for the documentary, Noah. That was Beatrice and Amazon. It's not my choice to be stuck with you. I actually tried to tell her I thought the rookie from New England would be a better choice."

That made him turn. A slow pivot with his hands bracketing his hips. "Why's that?"

Ah, there it was, a bright burst of irritation behind his eyes, probably because I insinuated that someone else would be more interesting than him. If there was one truth in this industry you could take to the bank, it was the competitive nature of these men. God bless their predictability in this single regard.

"My reasons don't matter because they went with you."

He must have clenched his teeth because his jaw did that thing again. I tore my eyes away.

"Sorry to disappoint you," he said.

"You'll only disappoint me if you get in my way."

His eyebrows lifted slowly. "That so?"

My hands shook slightly, and I tightened them in my lap. He couldn't see the frantic bouncing of my foot, but if he had, it would have betrayed whatever badass version of myself I was trying to portray.

I had one shot. I thought about what Beatrice said in our very first meeting. That we rarely had the chance to revisit someone's first impression of us.

One chance to rework whatever definition he had in his head about me.

One shot at this conversation that would set the tone for us to work together.

To prove Beatrice wrong.

"You think you're the only person who understands pressure?" I asked. I stood from the chair and dropped the clipboard onto the desk with a sharp slap of sound. He didn't need to tower over me like an overbearing ... whatever he was trying to be right now. "I'll forget our interaction in the elevator yesterday because we were both taken by surprise." I lifted my chin. "But it's been almost ten years since you've seen me, Noah. I'm not the same girl, and you are not tempting enough to risk the opportunity that's been given to me. If I can get over what happened, then you need to too. It's not like I'm ripping my shirt off and begging for another chance."

Those eyes flicked down my body, an intentionally derisive motion that took my measure in no more time than a single thud of his icy chunk of a heart.

"Sweetheart," he drawled, "it wouldn't matter if you were."

Heat burned my cheeks, but I refused to drop my gaze. "Glad to hear it."

Noah's eyes narrowed slightly, but he didn't say anything else.

"If you're free after practice tomorrow, my office is two doors down on the right. We'll meet with Rick, he's the Amazon producer, and go over our filming schedule for the next couple of weeks. We'll need on-field and off-field access to you."

At that, he made a sound that could almost be confused for a laugh, if he wasn't a soulless robot with no emotions.

Scratch that.

Noah had emotions. They just seemed to be slight variations of irritation.

"Off-field access to me will be pretty boring," he admitted. "But they're welcome to film it all the same."

"Good." I held out my hand, but he didn't move closer. If he wanted to shake on it, he'd have to come to me, and based on the dangerous gleam that entered his eye, he knew it. "See you tomorrow?"

For a second, my hand was frozen in the air, and I worried that he'd let it stay there. But then he took two steps and enveloped my hand with his. My whole arm tingled, chills slipping up my skin at the dry, hard calluses on his fingers. It had been a minute since a man had touched me, and I hated that he was the one to elicit the reaction.

"Don't make me regret that I agreed to this," Noah said, still gripping my hand tightly in his.

I smiled, and for some reason, the sight of it made his face darken like a thundercloud. "Right back at ya."

CHAPTER EIGHT

NOAH

"Hope this doesn't bite you in the ass."

I grimaced, tightening my grip on the weight ball under my palm, then lowered slowly toward the ground in a push-up until my muscles shook. When I straightened my arms again, I rolled the ball and caught it with the other hand, setting that on top of the rubber surface for another rep.

"It won't," I told him through clenched teeth as I did another one.

"I thought you wanted defensive player of the year again. It's been two years since you won it. Why split your focus on something unnecessary?"

That was my father for you. I couldn't see his face since we were on the phone, but I knew damn well what his facial expression was doing. Stern set of his wrinkled brow, hard slash of a mouth that rarely ever smiled.

He loved me, but he wasn't a warm man. But in his concern, and in the way he had always shown it, I'd learned to glean the words he wasn't saying.

I love you, and I'm worried about you.

Another push-up and I sat back on my haunches, rolling my shoulders as the light outside my apartment started dwindling to a bluish purple.

"Because the front offices don't see it as unnecessary," I told him.

"Yeah, well, they're not the ones who have to suit up every week, are they?"

I smiled unwittingly, wondering if the grumpiness he injected into his voice was a hereditary trait. If it was, I'd inherited it.

"No, they're not. But I don't think they're wrong either. In the end, I think it'll be a good thing." I couldn't believe I said it without choking on the words. More than that, I could almost believe that I meant them. "I met with the crew from Amazon today after practice. I like what they're trying to do. They're not sensationalizing what life is like for players or creating drama or fake story lines. It's just a clearer look at what it's like for us."

He harrumphed.

"You tell your mother yet?"

I lay back on the ground and stretched my body out as long as it could go. Something satisfying popped in my back, and I groaned. "Not yet. Haven't talked to her in a few weeks."

My parents divorced when I was in high school, old enough to decide that I'd rather live with him in Seattle than move with her and her new husband to where he was stationed in Germany. My relationship with her was ... fine. Neither parent was overly effusive when it came to their emotions, and I was the byproduct of a lifetime of that reserve.

In high school and college, it had been my goal to be the opposite.

I'd be fun because my parents weren't.

I'd enjoy life because they sure as hell weren't.

I'd be able to do both of those things while succeeding at football because my dad hadn't been able to.

But in the end, whether through circumstances out of my control or the sheer force of my genetic makeup—probably a little bit of both—I was my father's son, through and through.

What mattered was my performance.

What mattered was that I did things the right way.

What mattered was that I was the best.

Everything else got shut behind a door that I'd prefer stayed closed.

Somehow, though, that door got cracked open, and I couldn't ignore what was behind it as easily as before.

All I could do was hope that doing this documentary would show that the man I was when the helmet and pads came off was just as driven and focused. I didn't know how many teammates were home alone on a weeknight during offseason, working out more than the four hours of practice I'd done. More than the three hours of workouts I'd completed at the facilities. But I was doing those things.

My dad said something, and I adjusted my earbuds in my ears. "Sorry, I missed that," I told him.

"Wasn't important," he said easily. "Just asking about your new place."

"It's got a bed and a kitchen. That's about all I need for the time being." I glanced around. My agent had found it for me as soon as he got the call from Washington, a sublet from another player he represented. It wasn't my taste, the lines of the furniture sleek and modern and impersonal. I liked dark wood and leather couches, dim lamps and bookshelves and deep chairs that I could actually fit in. The views were amazing, though, with floor-to-ceiling windows that overlooked Seattle, even if I didn't have my telescope yet.

Watching the stars was my only real hobby outside of football.

"Well," he said, "that's good. Anything else?"

Because I knew it would be exactly a week, down to the minute, before we spoke again, I tried to think of anything he might actually care about. When I came up empty, I shrugged. "No, I can let you go."

"Talk to you next week."

He disconnected the call almost immediately, like he was relieved that we were done catching up. My dad was that way with everything. If his quiet, simple life bothered him, you'd never know it because he didn't dwell on it. The door holding all of that for him had never even been unlocked, let alone opened. I braced my hands on the floor behind me and looked around. Wasn't I similar, though? This was my exciting football player life, and I never stopped to worry about how little it contained.

Working out more than I already had because I was bored, and my weekly phone call with my father.

Amazon would tire of me before the week was out.

With a furrowed brow of my own, I stood and stretched my arms over my head. It was easy enough to recognize the direction my thoughts were going in. I'd agree to do this.

Therefore, I'd do it better than anyone else. If they wanted to follow a player trying to fit in to a new team, I'd show them what the prototype should be.

All the lights were off in my apartment except a small one in the kitchen, and I wandered over to the wall of glass. The oblong shape of the Space Needle gleamed in the distance, and I wished that I'd brought my telescope so that I could look at it more closely.

The skies beyond the city were dark, but I knew with the right equipment, like I had back in Miami, I'd be able to see so much more than met the naked eye. My former assistant was waiting to send me my furniture until I found a place to live, someplace that felt like me, but as I stood there, I found myself wishing I had just a few items to make me feel more at home.

A thought occurred to me, and before I could think better of it, or wonder what in the hell I was doing by contributing to this craziness, I pulled my phone out and found the number I'd saved in it earlier.

Me: Do you think they'd be interested in "Noah goes house hunting"?

Not even a heartbeat past before the gray bouncing dots appeared on the screen.

Molly Ward: YES! That's a great idea. I'll add it to the agenda for tomorrow.
Me: The sooner the better.
Molly Ward: Got it. Don't you have a place to stay now?

I sighed, leaning my shoulder against the glass.

Me: Yeah, but it's not my style. The chairs were made for someone half my size.
Molly Ward: I'm not laughing at you, I swear.
Molly Ward: If he says yes, and I can't imagine he wouldn't, send me a list of what you're looking for. I can help narrow the search.

That pulled my face down into a frown.

Me: Is it your job to help me search for a place to live?
Molly Ward: It's my job to make this process easier. If you want to send me some search filters, I'll compile a list and you can pick your favorites. I'll reach out to the listing agents.

Something about it made me uncomfortable. I didn't want to feel like Molly was at my beck and call. I didn't want to be working with her in the first place, but when I'd shaken her small hand, fingers so much colder than mine, I meant the gesture for what it was. A truce.

Me: Needs- 3 bed/3 bath, outside of downtown preferred, large yard w/ privacy, space for home gym, pool is a plus but not a requirement. I'd like to stay under 1.5M
Molly Ward: You got it.

I took a deep breath and sent another one.

Me: Thank you. I appreciate your help.
Molly Ward: Careful, Noah, I'll mistake that for being friendly...

I shook my head slowly, but as I tucked my phone away and stared at the stars again, I had to force away the smile that threatened.

CHAPTER NINE

MOLLY

"You are a badass, and you can do this," I whispered fiercely. Her lips were petal pink. Her hair was pulled back into a braided ponytail, and the white shirt made her eyes pop. She was me, and she was about to slay her first production planning meeting with Amazon and the big, scary football player who hated her.

I groaned. Not the kind of thought I wanted in my subconscious before I channeled my inner boss bitch.

Honestly, it was time to revise that statement anyway. The text thread on my phone proved that maybe Noah didn't hate me after all. Spending a couple of hours of my night at home searching for a house for him was bizarro but also nice ... in a twisted way.

The search history on my laptop, now inundated with three-bedroom, three-bathroom houses, had kept him at the forefront of my mind.

When my alarm went off, a gentle chiming of bells, I woke from my dream with a start, searching the bed for the warmth of someone else's body because it had been so vivid in my mind that he'd been lying next to me in bed.

Not doing anything, mind you. Just ... there.

Big and warm and solid. If I closed my eyes hard enough, making my own reflection disappear, I'd still be able to feel what I felt.

The complete absence of him in a tangible way.

My forehead wrinkled thoughtfully. Dreams about warm, sleepy Noah were not what I needed in my life, but at least it had been on the platonic side. Like I could have been sharing a bed with a golden retriever and achieved the same thing, if I thought about it critically.

Perfect. I nodded resolutely. Noah was a golden retriever, and he needed a home, and I was helping him because for the time being, my ship was tied to his.

Then I burst out laughing.

Noah as a cuddly, shaggy, sweet dog was just about the worst comparison in the entire universe of comparisons.

There was nothing unassuming or average about him.

The thing I noticed most, as he towered in the corner of Beatrice's office and as he moved through practice earlier, was that he never relaxed. Never allowed the tension to leave that massive body. His eyes were alert and searching, picking apart weaknesses in his opponents, whether that opponent was a teammate he was lining up against or little ole me.

An alert went off on my phone, the reminder I'd set for our meeting, and I took a deep breath.

It didn't matter how I tried to lessen the impact of Noah, he'd always take up more space—physical, mental, and emotional—than the average man.

I left the bathroom with a renewed sense of purpose because if he could reach out with an olive branch, then I could train my brain to view him with the necessary sense of detachment.

He was just a regular football player.

I didn't actually know him, no matter what happened between us.

And because of that, I'd be able to do with my job without any interference.

The small conference room across from my office was empty, so I flipped the lights on and set the stack of folders down, one in front of each empty chair. Beatrice was off-site for the day working on media stuff, so I didn't need to worry about her lurking in the hallway to judge my performance. Which was good because my pep talk was waning a little bit as the hands on the clock ticked closer, and no one had shown up yet.

The watch on my wrist showed the same time as my phone, as did the digital clock on the wall of the conference room.

Didn't these men know that ten minutes early was on time? Being on time was as good as being late.

Taking a seat, I impatiently crossed my legs. Then crossed them again. My feet already hurt because I'd decided that a couple of extra inches wouldn't hurt for one day. Inner badass and all.

I glared at those inches, encased in shiny black patent, innocently pinching and creating pain and suffering as it wrapped around a foot that'd never done anything to deserve such treatment.

"Screw this," I muttered. I sent a text to Paige to make sure I wasn't crazy for wanting to chuck my shoes across the hall into my office.

Me: A boss bitch can be a boss bitch while wearing sedate ballet flats, right?
Paige: Abso-effing-lutely.

"Abso-effing-lutely," I repeated and stood resolutely. The

heels were off in the next instant, and even though I shrank, my entire body sighed in relief.

"We go barefoot here?"

I jumped, clutching the shoes to my chest when I saw Noah in the doorway. His eyes were trained on my toes, then they moved slowly, oh, so very slowly up my legs, past the gray pencil skirt, and over the white V-neck shirt to my face.

"You guys were late," I said.

Because that explained everything perfectly.

One eyebrow lifted slowly. "I'm three minutes early. How is that late?"

He was also freshly showered in addition to being three minutes early-which-was-actually-late. I could see it in the dampness of his dark hair and smell the sharp, clean scent of soap that filled the room.

Taking a deep breath, I fought against the urge to fan my hot cheeks. This was already going swimmingly, wasn't it? "It's ... whatever. I need to grab some different shoes before everyone else gets here."

"Excellent idea."

Yet he stood there, blocking the exit. Noah looked at me expectantly.

"You don't make a very good open door," I told him.

His head tilted.

"Move, please," I said slowly. "I need to go across the hall."

That jarred him out of his stupor. "Oh, sorry."

He shifted to the side, and when I brushed past him, I heard his slow, steady inhale.

Lord have mercy. If we could get through this first meeting without further incident, I'd be the happiest girl in the world. Down the hallway, I could hear the indistinct chatter of Rick and Marty, the main camera operator. I shoved my feet into my Tieks and met them just outside my office.

With a smile, I held my hand out toward the conference room. "Rick, Marty, good to see you. We're over here."

Noah was waiting in the corner with his hands tucked into the pockets of his dark jeans. Rick and Marty introduced themselves, and I watched covertly at how Noah handled himself. I'd yet to see him smile. Each time we'd run into each other—the elevator, the practice field, Beatrice's office, and now—his face had been in the same determined, stony expression.

It was almost like he never removed his helmet, that thick layer designed to protect him from the outside world. How were the cameras supposed to capture Noah Griffin, not just the man in the uniform, but the man as he really was, if that never came off?

We took our seats, and Rick looked at me with a smile.

"Rick," I said, "why don't you start and talk a little bit about what you and your crew will be looking for from Noah? We have some ideas, but it would be helpful to get some direction from you first."

He nodded. I liked Rick. In his late forties, he had shaggy gray hair, a big nose, and an even bigger smile. He was easy to talk to, and that probably made him a natural at making people feel comfortable even though they were being filmed constantly.

"My direction," he said to Noah, and then with a deferential nod at me, "will be to be normal." He shrugged. "Go about your day as you normally would. Practice, watch film, eating boring meat and veggies and no pizza."

We all laughed. Well, except Noah. There a slight warming behind his eyes, but damn the man, he still didn't crack a smile.

"My life isn't very exciting," Noah admitted. "I still can't understand how this will make for compelling television."

Rick nodded. "You'd be surprised. The business of football is as fascinating to our viewers as the emotional piece. We've found success with this series because it balances both. There are dynamics at play in each arena, the personal and the professional, and it's my job"—he nodded to Marty, the camera operator, who threw up two fingers in a laid-back gesture—"and Marty's job, in my absence, to capture those dynamics, no matter how they play out."

Noah looked at me, then nodded thoughtfully.

Right. My turn. "If you guys look at your folders, I have a tentative schedule laid out, based on when the defense is practicing and when Noah has meetings that you can attend," I said. "This covers the next three weeks, and we've got a few open gaps in that schedule because I think what we're missing is the personal piece." My smile was small because I wasn't trying to beat Noah over the head with *why don't you have more friends, give us something to film.* "Noah had a great suggestion yesterday that maybe we could tag along when he's house hunting."

"Absolutely," Rick agreed. His pencil flew across the top of the paper. "If you've got someone who can come with you, a parent or a teammate, that's even better."

Noah shifted in his seat, face blank. "Not really."

From the corner of my eye, I noticed Marty shift the camera on his shoulder. Had he been filming this entire time? I guess it made sense if he was. No telling what was worth catching and what wasn't. That was what the editing process was for. Cut the shit and focus on the good stuff.

"No one?" Rick asked.

"Kareem Jones and I played together in college," Noah answered, "but we're not close. Normally, I wouldn't ask a teammate to help me pick out a house."

Rick tapped his pencil thoughtfully, and I chewed on my lip as I flipped through a mental Rolodex.

"Can't I just ... do it by myself?" Noah continued. "No offense, but it's not like anyone else's opinion matters when it comes to what kind of house I live in."

At that, I smiled.

"What?" he asked me. He sounded like a grumpy teenager.

"Nothing." I shrugged. "You're just so certain. Usually people like having another person to bounce ideas off. Help them figure out what they want to do."

Noah looked genuinely perplexed. "Why would I need someone else to figure out what I want to do? I told you what kind of house I want, right? So if I was someone else, would I have asked you, how many bedrooms do *you* think I should have?"

It was probably the worst thing I could have done, and I tried desperately to keep the wide smile hidden. His entire countenance—the set of his jaw, the line of his lips, the downward slash of his eyebrows—was mystified at the idea that some people invited guidance or could possibly want someone else's opinion.

The battle was officially lost when he narrowed his eyes at my trembling mouth.

My chin tipped up, and I laughed helplessly.

"It's not funny, Molly."

Rick wiped a hand over his mouth, hiding a smile of his own.

"It's a little funny," I said between peals of laughter. "You look like I suggested you walk naked through Pike Place."

"Glad my decisiveness is so entertaining," he mumbled, crossing his arms over his chest.

I breathed out slowly, finally getting control of myself. "I'm sorry."

He lifted his hand in a gesture of dismissal. "It's fine. As long as you guys aren't going to make me pretend I'm friends with someone, we'll be okay."

"You can absolutely film by yourself." Rick kept tapping his pencil, now that the moment was over. "We can do some voice-over stuff. We'll have to do that anyway. As long as we're getting your thoughts, whether it's through dialogue with someone else or through interviews, we'll be good to go."

I was flipping through the printouts of the houses I'd found for Noah when something occurred to me.

"Doesn't your dad still live in town?" I asked before I thought better of it. "I thought he loved it here."

Every eye in the room swiveled in my direction, and my throat turned to sticky sand.

Well, shit.

Rick's pencil was frozen, hovering over the surface of the paper. "You know his dad?"

I shifted slightly, refusing to meet Noah's steady, unrelenting gaze. "I know he *has* a dad. Doesn't everyone?"

What a blatant non-answer, and Rick knew it. He wasn't good at his job for nothing.

When I felt Noah's eyes boring into my profile, I turned and met them head-on.

Sorry, I mouthed. Those eyes closed briefly as he sighed, and that was as good as permission in my book.

"Noah and his dad used to be our next-door neighbors," I told Rick and Marty, who suddenly looked very interested in what I had to say.

"How long ago was this?"

"I was in high school when they moved somewhere else," I said.

Oh, and how complicated that explanation was. For months, I hadn't caught a single glimpse of Noah or his father, and then one day, a For Sale sign popped up in their front yard. At sixteen, it all felt very dramatic. It made me feel like a horrible person; that what I'd done was so bad that they'd moved away. In retrospect, I couldn't really blame his dad even though it had caused more than a few dramatic tears when I thought I'd never see him again.

"Didn't like the neighbors?" Rick asked Noah with a smile.

He was saying it innocently, but it caused my neck to go hot regardless. Noah, to his credit, kept his face completely impassive when he answered. "Neighbors were just fine. The house was too big for us."

I pointed at Rick and Marty. "It's not a big deal, so don't make it one."

Rick held up his hands. "I'd never."

I gave him a look. "Okay, so I'll schedule with a few of these listing agents and make sure Marty is available to film. Do you need to be there, Rick?"

He shook his head. "I'll only be around about half the time. Marty is fine on his own for most of it, and you'll pick up fast what works and what doesn't in my absence. I'll be going back and forth between here and Tampa. We've got a rookie down there that we're filming right now too."

I nodded. "Besides house hunting, do we need anything else off field?"

Rick looked at Noah. "That's up to him. What do you like to do when you're not here?"

Noah folded his hands on the table and shrugged. "I work out. Watch film. Go for runs. Swim if I can."

"So, you work more," Rick supplied.

I smiled again.

Noah grimaced. "Nothing I do is all that interesting, trust me."

"They call you The Machine, right?" I asked.

His eyes sharpened, landing hot and fast on my face. "Yeah."

"Even machines need to be refueled. There has to be something you do, somewhere you that recharges you." I kept my gaze on him. "No one here is going to judge you, no matter what it is. But there has to be something that you keep for yourself, that isn't about football. Everyone has something like that."

"Your brother did?"

"Sure. He had us." I shrugged. "My sisters and I were his life, and it was a part of his life he kept private for a really long time. But once the stadium lights were off, and he'd showered off the sweat, he was back home, picking up toys and watching Disney movies and learning how to braid hair. His family refueled him."

Noah worked his jaw back and forth. The way he looked at me, it felt like it was just him and me in the room as he tried to decide if this was a place he could be honest. "The stars," he said gruffly.

"What about them?" I kept my voice gentle, like he'd spook at any second.

"I like astronomy. I would've minored in it if my dad had agreed." He cleared his throat. "My assistant in Miami will send my telescope as soon as we find a house."

Now this is a surprise, I thought pleasantly. This was the layer we needed to peel back, even if it took us the entire time to show what was underneath. "Where's your favorite place to go? To look at the stars."

"Here?"

"Anywhere. If you could go anywhere to look at the stars, where would it be?"

Noah let out a slow breath, his eyes taking on the hazy look of someone who'd just mentally transported somewhere else. Somewhere they wanted to be very, very badly. "My grandma's cabin in the Black Hills, South Dakota."

Rick nodded at me, just a tiny lift of his chin. *Keep going.*

"How come?" I asked.

"It's so quiet. So ... open. The mountains are different there than they are here. Less people. Less lights. Less pollution." He closed his eyes, and every line in his face disappeared as he imagined whatever it was that he was seeing in his head. Suddenly, I wanted to be there too, to see what it was like. "The sky is bigger there than anywhere else. It's the one place where I feel small."

Noah opened his eyes, and I felt a strange snapping on my heart. Like someone had pulled a rubber band, tightening that statement into place around the thing that pushed the blood through my body.

Without looking away, I knew there was a three-day window in the practice schedule just before preseason started.

"Does our budget include a weekend in South Dakota, Rick?" I asked, eyes still lasered in on Noah.

He smiled, and I saw his head move from me to Noah and back again.

"It does now," he answered.

CHAPTER TEN

NOAH

"You cannot be serious."

When I tried, unsuccessfully, to duck my head through the opening, her answer was a helpless bout of laughter. It reminded me of a wind chime at my grandma's cabin, the light tinkling sound of the wind moving through the glass. I used to love that wind chime. Now it would remind me of Molly Ward's laughter. The thought made me frown. Which made her laugh even harder.

"This house was built for someone a foot shorter than me, Molly."

"Short people need places to live too," Marty reminded me, half his face hidden behind the ever-present camera.

I glared at him. "Aren't you supposed to be a silent observer?"

He grinned. Or half-grinned. "Everything that doesn't serve the narrative will end up on the cutting room floor anyway. Don't you worry about me, Griffin."

Serve the narrative. That kind of PR jargon made me want to rip through the drywall with my bare hands just so I didn't have to get it stuck in my head.

I leaned toward Molly. "If I start saying things like *serve the narrative*, punch me in the throat."

She nodded seriously. "Please say it now. I'd like to practice if that's okay."

"Hey. We agreed on a truce."

"Yes, yes," she said lightly. "We did, didn't we?"

It took me a moment to realize that the cameras were on us, like it had been ever since we arrived at the first house of the day. It was about thirty minutes east of Seattle, close to Seward Park. From the outside, it looked promising. Trimmed landscaping and a Frank Lloyd Wright architectural style that appealed to me. A little pricey, for just me, but it was close to the water and had a pool.

Then we walked in and realized it was built for someone probably a foot shorter than me. I'd hit my head on three door-frames already. Each hit took my mood from ambivalent, to annoyed, to fully irritated.

She crossed her arms and surveyed the kitchen. "I like it."

"You would," I said. "You can walk through all the doors without getting a concussion."

Her lips, red today, twisted up in a smile. "Isn't that view worth it?"

I didn't even glance at the wall of windows. "No."

Molly rolled her eyes. "Fine. Do you want to go to the next place?" She gave me a winning smile, and her left cheek showed a hidden dimple that I didn't remember. "It's got tall ceilings."

She was handling me. Managing me because I sucked at this. It made my skin feel too tight and my head pound at the base of my skull.

Yesterday, somehow, she got me to confess something that I'd never planned on confessing. And I did it in front of a camera crew.

I'd underestimated Molly, that was for sure. Because as she

aimed that sunny smile at Marty, who ate it up with a spoon, I vowed I wouldn't do it again. Her ability to herd me in whatever direction she wanted was like a kitten backing a grumpy tiger into a cage.

I was the tiger.

And this short-ass kitchen was my cage.

"I need to get out of this house," I muttered, brushing past both of them. Marty turned to follow, and because I was cognizant of the camera trained on me, rather than where I was going, the smack of my skull on the frame of the door echoed through the room. "Fuck," I yelled, rubbing the top of my head.

Molly slapped a hand over her mouth. This time, she wasn't laughing when she dropped it. "Are you okay?"

Instead of answering, I strode out of the house, only taking a full breath when I was outside again. The skies were overcast, the threat of rain heavy in the air.

The sudden turn in my mood surprised me, but I didn't want to analyze why.

It probably started when they made the uncomfortable realization that my personal life from an outsider's perspective was about as fun as watching paint dry. That nagged, all night. Even if my dad still lived in town, inviting him to come look at houses would've been a terrible idea. Our relationship was as warm as the highest peak of Mt. Rainier off in the distance.

Behind me, I heard Molly approach. When she walked, she barely made any noise. Something I'd noticed in our meeting. She always wore those shoes ... the ones that looked like glorified slippers. And because of that, her steps were just slightly above a whisper of sound, which made me hyper aware of her movement.

"What was that?" she asked.

Today, she was wearing jeans and a long-sleeved Wolves shirt that fit her too well.

I didn't want to notice that she was wearing a shirt that fit her too well.

It pissed me off.

"None of this feels natural," I growled. I speared my hands into my hair and stared out to the line of blue water in the sound. "And even though I've heard all these reasons it's fine, and why people will find it interesting, I don't understand how I'm supposed to just ... wander around these houses and it'll help the team. Or help me be a part of the team."

Molly took another step closer, sighing softly as she did. Her face, delicate and sweet and pretty, was bent in a thoughtful frown. "It's not supposed to help the team, Noah. It's not about winning or about making them better," she said haltingly.

"Then what's the point?"

Her eyes searched my face. "The point is showing the truth. This is the reality of being a player in the league. Sometimes you change teams, and sometimes it's hard when you do."

I clenched my jaw and caught sight of Marty in my peripheral vision. The little shit was even sneakier than Molly, creeping around without anyone noticing.

"Aren't you supposed to be out of the shot too?"

She didn't take my bait, and I felt a moment of shame that I swiped at her in the first place.

"No, I'm not supposed to be doing anything other than this," she said quietly. "I'm helping you find someplace to live because that's what you need. You need a place to feel like home, to have chairs that fit you and walls around that you that make you feel like this is where you're meant to be. And if you're upset because you don't have anyone else to call to help you with this, then fix it. If you don't like it, then do something about it."

At that moment, I realized that you didn't have to yell or be the biggest and loudest to infuse your strength into an important moment.

So few people in my life took me on head to head. She was the last person I'd expected to be willing to step up to the plate and do it, this petite woman who barely reached my chest with the top of her head, who I could lift with one hand.

"You're not my friend, Molly," I reminded her. My voice was low, so Marty couldn't hear us. "I don't need this from you, so stop trying to psychoanalyze me."

Her eyebrows bent in. "That's not what I'm doing."

I leaned down toward her. "Yeah, it is. You keep trying to make me more interesting, more fun, more friendly, and maybe that's the version of me you want the world to see, but that's not what I am. Quit trying to turn this into something it's not." I straightened, ignoring the hurt, speculative look in her eyes. "I'm done looking for today. I'll take care of this myself."

They wanted to film The Machine, and that was what they'd get. Starting now.

CHAPTER ELEVEN

MOLLY

"THAT HOUSE MUST HAVE BEEN WORSE than I thought," I muttered. "It's like that last hit to the head knocked his personality into a coma."

Standing in the kitchen of Noah's temporary apartment, Marty and I watched carefully as Noah did his best impression of a man ignoring everyone around him.

By that, he was sitting on the couch with headphones on and watching film on his iPad, occasionally pausing the film to jot notes into a massive notebook.

"So we just stand here?" I asked.

Marty sighed, checking the position of the tripod that held his smaller camera. "Yup."

"He's not doing anything."

"Nope."

His unperturbed tone had me glancing at him. "How often do you get bored doing this job, Marty?"

He chuckled. "Rarely. Even at times like this."

"Seriously?"

What he lacked in height, Marty made up for in his huge

smile. "Seriously. You don't go into a job like this because it's exciting all the time. It's about finding the moments of interesting in the mundane, you know? I've done six-month shoots tracking wolves in Yellowstone, and it's not like you're constantly filming them on the hunt, right? They're sleeping half the time, pissing in the grass, tugging at a pile of old, dried-out bones to find a last scrap of a meal. If you get lucky, someone fights over a female, and you manage to catch it. But most of the time, it's quiet."

My eyes trailed back to Noah, sitting quietly on the couch that was painfully out of proportion for his large frame. In my mind, I couldn't imagine him as a wolf. He was too large, his frame too dense and weighted down with muscle. He was a bear, tall and broad and ominous, big enough to blot out the sun if he stood over you.

"And you're never tempted to force action?" I asked.

"What do you mean?"

"Like they do in reality TV." I held my hands up when his face pinched with distaste. "I'm not suggesting it, trust me. Just ... trying to understand the process is all. How doing this serves the narrative."

Marty leaned over to check the camera again and changed the angle to account for the setting sun. "Things like today were perfect or would've been if he hadn't had a tantrum at the first house. It's something real and true, something he needs to accomplish to get settled now that he's here." His eyes, astute and keenly observant, moved back over to the man in the other room. "But this is real and true too. He's retreating to something that's safe, something he's good at, and this is just as important to capture."

I nodded, glancing at my watch. We had about an hour left in the filming schedule, and it was about as fun as watching paint dry.

"But if you want to ask him some questions," Marty said, leaning toward me and speaking quietly, "I wouldn't tell you not to. You get a reaction out of him that no one else seems to. And that's good on film. As long as his reactions are his, are true, it's never going to be a bad thing."

The laugh huffed out easily. "But that's not forcing action?"

"It's not. You know we can edit you out of the shot if that's what needs to be done, but look at him," he said. We both did, and my face felt flipped upside down at what a sad picture it was. "He's alone, by choice, in this place that clearly doesn't fit him or make him feel comfortable, and he's supposed to make it feel like home."

"Seattle was home to him," I corrected. My eyes zeroed in on my shoes as I felt a flush of heat crawl up my neck. "I just mean, it's not like this is new to him."

"How well did you know him?" Marty asked the question just a little too smoothly.

I gave him a look. "Not well. I knew of him. Knew he played football. It's almost impossible to be a sixteen-year-old girl and not be aware of someone like that living next door." I shook my head. "But I don't remember him being like this."

"Is that hard for you?"

"Hard how?"

He shrugged. "Guy's pretty closed off. I hope we can get enough good footage off field, you know? Make it worth it to keep his storyline in the final cut."

A flash of discomfort turned my stomach over, imagining Beatrice's face if that were to happen. How that would reflect on me if it did. "It'll make the final cut. I saw the way he tore up practice this morning. You guys won't cut his footage."

"It's happened before." Marty clucked his tongue. "Be a shame, since Washington put all their eggs in his basket. One he doesn't seem very motivated to hold onto, if you ask me."

"Oh, you are a dirty, dirty cheat," I muttered under my breath, which made him grin unrepentantly. "I'm motivated enough for the both of us, trust me."

He nudged me with his shoulder and started unhooking the camera from the tripod. "I think your boss is banking on that too, Ward."

So many people called me by my last name, a hazard of working in the industry that I did, but for some reason, it reinforced why I was in this position and what was riding on it.

My last name held weight in the halls of Washington and even more on the field. When I walked into a meeting with someone new, there was an undercurrent of established respect. One that I'd be a fool to ignore, no matter how much it rankled that Beatrice didn't think I'd earned my place honestly.

I had earned it honestly. But it also came with undeniable perks. And one of those perks was a knowledge and respect of the game of football that stretched back my entire life. Maybe I hadn't lived with Logan until I was fourteen, but I grew up watching him play. Some of my earliest memories include standing in the stands and cheering him on when he was in college, then more than a decade of him playing professionally.

I could throw down with any man about this sport, no matter how much of a die-hard fan they were. No matter if they were a player either. Marty's words echoed through my head as I approached the couch. It was long and black, low to the ground, with sleek oblong pillows flanking each arm.

Noah pretended he wasn't aware of me coming closer, but I saw the tightening of his jaw, and the way he shifted the iPad away from my gaze. Inexplicably, it made me smile.

That he noticed because his eyes flicked briefly from the screen, over to my mouth, then back. His frown intensified.

It was amazing how, only a couple of days after seeing him again, that frown had lost some of its ability to intimidate me. I folded my legs under me on the couch and leaned close enough that he sighed irritably. It wasn't film of Washington.

It was a game he played at Miami against an opponent we'd be facing in week two and on the road as well. Their stadium was a hostile place to play. Loud and open and unforgiving for any team that didn't call it home. I nodded when he backed up the cursor to watch something for a second time.

"What?" he snapped.

I tapped the space over my ears, and he obliged, pushing the headphones off. "That was week three last season, right? Not the season before?"

His eyebrows curved in. "Last season."

I nodded. "I could tell."

Boom.

Noah didn't want to be interested. That was why his jaw snapped tight, and he closed his mouth after it popped open to ask me a question. But interested he was. That was why his eyes darted back and forth between me and the screen.

"How?"

I shuffled just a couple of inches closer, snatching the headphones from his head so I could turn them off. The sound popped up instantly, and I pointed a finger at the screen.

"Well, last season, their O-line was better, so their QB was able to hold onto the ball about a second and a half longer than the season before."

Noah's mouth sagged open before he snapped it shut. Inwardly, I pumped my fist in the air so violently, it would've been obnoxious.

"Then there's you," I said, letting my voice trail off.

His whole frame went still again, and I was starting to recognize it for what it was: a warning.

You know how the air feels before a tornado swoops down? Everywhere you look, there was a perfect, ominous stillness.

Even the color of the sky was different, rosy and warm and pinkish yellow.

"What about me?" he asked, voice all low and grumbly and delicious. I felt that grumble in the soles of my feet, and it made my toes curl up in my shoes.

Deep breath in, deep breath out. "You changed the way you pivoted around the tackle to get to the quarterback. Before, you used to duck more, lower your body mass, which made it harder to move as fast because your momentum wasn't helping you." I pointed at the screen. "And see, right there, that's how I know it was last season. That's when you started spinning around them, like Freeney and Mathis used to do back in the early two thousands for Indy. You broke the single season sack record last year because of that change. You should have won defensive player of the year. I always thought you got robbed."

Noah's finger punched the screen, pausing the video. He took a second to breathe deeply, and I risked a glance at his face. He was staring at me with such an arrested intensity that I fought not to squirm away from the force of it.

"You—" He stopped, then shook his head as though I'd punched him.

What was it about him that was so entertaining when he was off-balance? Smiling at him, laughing at him, it would be the last thing he'd want from me, especially given his earlier mood. And even more surprising was that it wasn't hard to fight the impulse. I didn't want Noah to think I was laughing at how hard it was for him to adjust to this thing we were doing. I wasn't the one being filmed all the time.

"How do you know that?" he finally managed. "About Freeney and Mathis. You couldn't have been older than ..." He stopped to do some mental calculations.

"I was in middle school." I grinned. "Come on, Noah, my brother was a second-round draft pick the year I started kindergarten. What do you *think* I've been watching every Sunday my entire life?"

Behind the couch, Marty moved on silent feet, but Noah paid him no mind. All his attention was on me, and something about that unwavering focus raised all the little hairs on the back of my neck.

Maybe it was because I'd shocked him or maybe it was because he had to come to terms with the fact that he'd underestimated me, but Noah Griffin was staring at me like he was contemplating ways to devour me whole.

"You gonna tell me how I can improve now, Coach Ward? With your endless wealth of football knowledge." The edge to his voice wasn't unpleasant, not in the slightest, and it was taking me some time of my own to realize that I'd underestimated how mercurial his moods were.

If I could anticipate them, it might have felt less dangerous somehow, less like I was standing in the middle of a thunderstorm with a giant metal pole in my hand.

This time, because of that shift, I let my lips curl up in a smile. "Yoga."

"Yoga," he repeated.

"You're strong, and you're fast, but when you lose your balance, you lose the sack."

Noah sat back like I'd shoved him with both hands. "You're serious."

"As a heart attack."

"I work out for hours every day, Molly."

"I know, trust me." I let my eyes wander over the curves of his shoulders, down the vein that traced his biceps, the muscles bunching like I was touching them with the tips of my fingers. "But weights and strength training and the stuff you do in practice aren't the same thing as yoga, and I'd bet you a hundred bucks that if you practiced something like that regularly, it would help you."

His eyes sparked, and for the first time, I saw a teasing glint in those depths. It changed every aspect of his face, and it was hard not to want to curl my hand around his skin and feel the change for myself. "A hundred bucks? That's a steep bet."

I exhaled a laugh. "Not all of us have multi-million-dollar contracts, hotshot."

"Deal."

My eyes shot up. "What?"

"It's a deal." The edges of lips almost curled up, and I found myself holding my breath.

"You're going to go to yoga with me?"

"No," he said firmly. "But I can hire someone. Or if you send me something on YouTube. I'll try it at home where Kareem can't see me."

I bit down on my lip because the smile threatening was so big and so overwhelming that I felt my heart pinch. "Okay."

"Okay." He lifted his iPad. "Can I get back to work now?"

CHAPTER TWELVE

MOLLY

"It's probably a really, really stupid idea."

"I couldn't say one way or the other."

No matter what my sister said, I knew it was as I us drove to Paige and Logan's house for our Tuesday night family dinner. But as I took the exit, I couldn't stop thinking about Noah sitting on that friggin' black couch, his legs too long and his frame too bulky for him to be comfortable. I thought about his fridge, full of boring food filled with vitamins and minerals and zero good carbs.

Good carbs like the bread kind of good carbs.

I thought about the fact that his telescope was being shipped from Miami, and how he never sat at the clear dining room table because he was always eating by himself.

"I'm just going to do it."

Isabel glanced at me from the passenger seat. "Molly, if you keep overanalyzing, I'll jump from this moving vehicle just so I don't have to listen. For the love of all things holy, make a decision."

My thumb punched the Bluetooth button on the steering wheel.

"Call Noah Griffin," I said.

Stupid, stupid, stupid.

Iz sighed and shook her head.

But there were no cameras to be found, and maybe it would be a good way for him to just ... relax. The phone rang and rang, and with each one that went unanswered, I felt even more resolute that he needed someone to step up and be in this role for him.

Noah needed a friend.

He needed someone who could see past whatever trappings were entailed in being The Machine.

After a prolonged beep, the disembodied voice of his phone told me to leave a message after the tone. I debated hanging up but didn't end the call when it came through the speakers.

"Noah, it's Molly. Umm, I know it's last minute, but if you ... if you're hungry, or bored, or whatever, we always do family dinner at my brother's house on Tuesdays. I mean, we do dinner. Sometimes non-family members show up too. Not often, but they do. Lia always brings her friend. I know it's not *your* family, but you're welcome all the same." I pinched my eyes shut. "You know where it is if you want to join us."

When the call ended, I blew out a disgusted breath.

"I can't imagine why he wouldn't want to come," Isabel mused.

"Screw you. Drive yourself next time."

"We live together, Molly. That's a gratuitous misuse of fuel." She wedged her sneakered feet up onto the dashboard before I knocked them down. "Hey, they're clean."

"So's my car. I'd like to keep it that way."

"Don't you think Logan would have an issue with one of his players showing up unannounced?"

That made me sigh. "Probably."

"Yet here we are. For all you know, Noah's going to show up like a grumpy lost puppy on the front porch in twenty minutes."

As I glanced in the rearview mirror, I caught my gaze, feverish and bright with excitement.

Stupid, stupid, stupid.

"No, I don't think he will," I admitted. "Yesterday was better, though. Sort of. One minor snag, but it's understandable that it would take him time to adjust. I know I'd feel off-balance in his position."

"And how do you feel in your position?" she asked pointedly.

"I don't know, Isabel. I think this is a really weird job, and it's putting me in a strange position because no matter what I do, Noah could still wake up tomorrow and decide to quit."

She pointed a finger at me. "*That* is highly unlikely, and you know it as well as I do. These guys are so freaking competitive. They can't play Scrabble without it hitting Super Bowl level of intensity."

I laughed. "Remember when Logan flipped the board because he thought we were cheating?"

"I sure do."

"Okay fine," I conceded. "He won't quit. But Amazon could decide he's not worth the film they're wasting on him. I don't know whether Beatrice would be upset at me about that or not. I don't know her well enough."

She sighed. "Wouldn't it be nice if we could read our bosses' mind?"

The way she said it had me looking at her twice. "What's wrong with Amy?"

Even though I'd just pulled the car into the driveway, neither of us made a move to leave. Isabel unhooked her seat belt and shrugged as she thought about the longtime owner of the gym she managed. "Nothing that I can pinpoint, per se. But she seems ...

scattered. Like she's not as present when she is there. In some ways, it's fine because she's definitely not micromanaging me, but our membership is dipping more than usual, and I don't feel like I can put that onto her plate."

I hummed. "Well, maybe it's just a phase. Everyone goes through them."

"True. And maybe Noah is in a grumpy loner phase, which is not your responsibility to fix." Her eyes, just as blue as mine, stared unblinkingly in my direction.

"I know," I said on a groan. "I know it's not mine to fix."

"Just remember that when that alpha asshole thing turns out to be some emotional wound that you desperately want to take care of." At my eye roll, she clucked her tongue. "Don't even deny it. Women go stupid over that bullshit, when, in reality"—she punched a finger in the air—"they should take their asses to therapy."

"Didn't you think therapy was a waste of time?"

"Yes, but I'm not the one taking on the responsibility of someone else's happiness." She laid a hand on her chest. "I happen to think if Noah is bored and lonely on his too-small couch, then he should take his millions of dollars and buy a dog and a new couch. He doesn't need you to kiss his boo-boos."

A sister's logic was so wildly ill-timed, pretty much at any given moment. I was about to tell her what she could do with her opinion when Lia knocked on the driver's side window.

I rolled it down.

Lia grinned in at us. "What are we doing?"

"*We* are about to come inside," Isabel said. "Because *we* have nothing more worthwhile to do with our time than to eat a family dinner and focus on our own issues."

Lia's pretty face scrunched in confusion. "A little heavy on the subtext, are we? I feel like I'm missing something."

Because that was not something I felt like getting into, I

waved at Claire and Finn, Lia's best friend, who were hanging back while Lia leaned next to my car. Finn, tall and lanky and the kind of nerdy cute that always made me hope that he and Lia would hook up, waved back.

"Gawd, when are you two gonna do it already?" Isabel muttered.

Lia's face blazed red. "He is my friend," she whispered, just shy of a hiss.

I grinned. "He got bigger over the summer," I mused. "Didn't he, Iz?"

"Someone's working their arms, that's for sure."

Lia's face stayed even, which was annoying, because if you lost the ability to bait your little sister, were you even living your life right?

"I'm hungry," Claire yelled from the driveway. "Can we go in, please?"

"Oh, did your legs stop working when you got out of the car? No one is making you wait," Lia said over her shoulder. Finn tucked his hands in his pockets, but I saw his cheeks lift in a wide grin.

Isabel ignored the exchange between the twins. "He's got that Clark Kent thing going that I am not mad at."

"Don't think I won't make you suffer if he hears you say that."

I dropped my head in my hands. Probably good Noah didn't come. The front door of the house opened, and Emmett whooped loudly.

"Hey, Finn! I saved you a seat by me! We can almost beat the girls in numbers now!"

Isabel climbed out as Lia, Claire, and Finn made their way to the door. I took a second to watch them shuffle into the house. Chaos was so ingrained into the normal ebb and flow of my life in various ways. It was hard for me to understand it any other way.

Even the apartment I shared with Iz, small and cute and

tucked in an affordably safe building downtown, was never quiet. We always had music playing, the TV on, or an audiobook going while I cooked. If we were home more, we probably would've had a dog or two that I could take on walks and snuggle on the couch with.

Maybe that was why thinking about Noah made me sad for him, causing a slow, unfurling ache in my chest that I wanted to rub at until it went away.

I didn't want him to be sitting alone in the dark, and it wasn't because I wanted to heal any emotional wounds.

Liar, a voice in the back of my head whispered.

I didn't want that man sitting alone in the dark because I liked him, and there was no earthly reason I should've. He was snappish and grumpy. His moods shifted faster than the weather, and for some reason, he refused to acknowledge that there was another side to him than The Machine.

Stupid, stupid, stupid.

This was my curse, apparently. Something that made me good at my job when my own feelings weren't on the line, but horribly inconvenient when they were. Without trying all that hard, I had a sixth sense that jangled like a bell when it came to the people I was forming relationships with.

Noah needed warmth and laughter. He needed someplace where he didn't need to be perfect all the time. Where he could just be Noah.

My phone, still connected to the Bluetooth, rang loudly through my car's speaker, and I took a deep breath when I saw Beatrice's name flash across the screen.

"This is Molly," I said.

"Molly, it's Beatrice." Wasn't it fun when we all started our calls like we didn't have caller ID? "Sorry I'm calling at dinnertime. Do you have a minute?"

"Sure, go ahead." Paige opened the door and held up her

hands questioningly. I held up my finger, then pulled my hand to my ear to signal a phone call. She nodded and went back into the house.

"I just got off the phone with Rick. He's on his way back from Tampa."

My fingers tightened in my lap. "Yeah, he told me he plans on being there for filming tomorrow. We've got everything set up for a defense only practice and some stuff in the weight room."

She hummed. "Yes, he told me that as well."

Something about her voice pricked uncomfortably. "Did something happen, Beatrice?"

"He's thrilled, you know, with how it's going with Noah."

"That's ... good. Right?"

She kept talking as if I hadn't said anything. "Marty sent him footage from Noah's apartment last night, raving about your ability to draw him out. Get him to lower his guard."

I rubbed my lips together and fought the irrational impulse to flee the car. "We were just talking about football. I didn't do anything special."

"Molly, I wish you'd been honest with me about knowing him."

My whole body went ice cold in an instant. "Beatrice, I ..."

"Both Rick and Marty were thrilled that you had previous history with Noah." She paused meaningfully. "Not something I appreciated hearing from them as opposed to my own employee."

"I'm so sorry, Beatrice," I said in a rush. "I should have told you. I didn't know Noah was even coming to Washington when you offered me the promotion."

Because she couldn't see me, I leaned forward and dropped my head in my hands again.

"Is this going to be a problem?" she asked. "Your history with Griffin."

"No," I answered instantly.

The question was jarring to just about every part of my brain, like a cloth that was ripping off center away from the main seam. Whatever I was feeling toward Noah, I knew without a doubt it wouldn't be reciprocated. He had one relationship in his life, and that was football, and I'd do well to remember that.

What mattered was doing my job.

What mattered was keeping my eye trained on that, no matter what instincts he was pulling out from inside me.

"I know I'm being tough on you, Molly." Her tone had softened, which had my shoulders relaxing slightly and the nauseous tumbling of my stomach settling down just a little. "I'm only hard on the employees who I think have potential."

That had me sitting up. "Th-thank you, Beatrice. I kind of thought you gave me the promotion as a ... I don't know ... a test you expected me to fail."

"I'm not as awful as you think," she said wryly. "And if that were true, it's not a very good use of my budget, is it?"

"Probably not."

Would this be a problem? No matter how quickly I'd told her it wouldn't be one, I still had to be honest with myself. It was Noah. And if I closed my eyes, I saw him as he'd stared at me the night before. That look that had singed me straight through. But that look could've meant a thousand different things. Maybe he was pissed that I noticed something he'd done poorly before he fixed it. Maybe he was impressed that I knew what the hell I was talking about.

"You don't have to worry about a thing," I told Beatrice firmly.

"No?"

Isabel was right. Noah's issues weren't my responsibility. I could do my job and still maintain a professional level of distance. Because if I couldn't, then what right did I have to feel frustration at Beatrice's reservations?

"No," I repeated. "I hear you loud and clear."

"Good." She sighed. "Now, I have one more call to make, and if I remember correctly, you have a family dinner to get to."

My eyebrows popped in surprise that she remembered. "I do."

"Enjoy it. Thanks, Molly."

"Thank you," I told her. I meant it too. Her call was a timely reminder that I needed. Noah wasn't mine to fix, no matter how he'd looked at me, and I'd do well to remember that.

CHAPTER THIRTEEN

NOAH

NORMALLY, I didn't think of myself as a slow thinker. Just the opposite, in fact. A defensive player should have the ability to see possible scenarios play out before they happen, in the twitch of a finger, the shift of body position, or the pivot of a foot. But when it came to Molly Ward, I was a little slow on the uptake.

It took me two days of actively avoiding her while we filmed to make the connection that I was not, in fact, the ignorer. I was the ignored. And because it was me, I had to mentally break down, in detail, how the hell that had happened and how I missed it.

Three days after she schooled me on her football history, the crew was at practice, and for the two days prior, I kept my eyes off her at all time. Yes, I cataloged what she was wearing within fifteen seconds of her walking in my peripheral vision, but that was it. I did not give her a second of full eye contact as she tilted her head toward Marty's, and they discussed filming for the next day, and Marty said something that made her laugh. That tinkling, wind chime laughter that made me want to do something ridiculous, like shove my fingers in my ears so I didn't have to hear it. It was the latter part of day three when the wheels started falling off, and it was all Kareem's fault.

They decided to haze me since I'd had over a week to get used to the rhythm of practice and let my guard down a little bit. That was when he started sending the rookies over to me—one by one—each one asking me for a selfie, an autograph, and a ridiculous question that they would've known their freshman year in college.

About cleats.

Then favorite stain remover for the grass stains.

How to avoid athlete's foot.

I was slow on that uptake too, my irritation rising exponentially with each one who approached me throughout the four hours of practice. By the fourth rookie, and his question about which jock strap I preferred to keep my balls in place, the rein on my temper snapped.

"Jones," I roared, seeking him out between the snickering faces. "Kareem Jones, get your ass over here."

The camera was pointed at me, but I couldn't care less.

When Kareem sauntered over to me, wearing a wide-ass grin on his face, I had a moment when I wondered whether Molly would step in and try to cool me down.

"How much did you pay them?" I asked.

"Oh, watching the look on your face has been priceless enough, Griffin," he said.

I crossed my arms over my chest. "So they get nothing out of it?"

He wiped under his eyes. "No, I told them that if they did this, we wouldn't duct tape them to the field goal after practice."

"I'm too old for this shit," I said, pointing a finger at him. "If you want them to earn their freedom, use someone else. I'm here to work, not run a daycare for rookies."

He knew me too well to be fazed by my temper, but a few of

the guys who didn't, rookies and veterans alike, shifted uncomfortably, their laughter dying down to throats that suddenly needed to be cleared.

Kareem whistled, rocking back on his heels like I'd pushed him. "Hear that, rookies? I think he said the magic words, didn't he?"

"What magic words?" I snapped. "Kareem."

"Don't you back out now," he said, glancing carefully into the faces of everyone around us.

Our quarterback, a young guy in his third year with a rocket arm, grinned at me, then looked over his shoulder. "You heard Jones. Get him."

Before I could blink, every rookie on the Washington roster had me pinned, no matter how much I thrashed, threatened, or shouted. The coaches laughed. Even Logan had a wide smile on his face, and if I hadn't been betrayed by my entire defensive line, who sat back roaring with laughter, I might have thought it was funny too.

"You nice and sweaty, Griffin?" Kareem asked as he approached.

"You asshole." I tried to pry my arm away from where three rookies held it. I was pinned to the turf, on my knees with my hands behind my back, and I finally gave up.

"I'd close my eyes if I were you." That was the only warning I was given before they proceeded to dump black and red glitter down the front of my shirt, then snap my shorts away from my waist and dump it down there too. The cleaning crew would hate them, and I'd be planning retribution for the rest of my life, but from the tear-inducing laughter from every person present, it must have been worth it.

Behind the camera, Marty wiped at his face, and as I stood, shaking as much excess glitter as I could from my body, that was the first that I noticed Molly was avoiding me.

If she'd watched what had happened to me, she wasn't watching the fallout. She wasn't approaching me with that big, bright smile on her pink lips, trying to suss out how I felt about what they'd done. She wasn't eyeing me curiously through my anger. She wasn't eyeing me at all.

It crossed my mind, as I showered off the mess and changed into clean clothes after practice, that I'd forgotten to return her call from the day before. She had invited me to dinner at Logan's house, a message I hadn't received until hours later because I often didn't check my cell while it was charging. By the time I saw it, by the time I'd listened to it, it was well after eleven, and I wasn't sure what to say.

Thank you, but your brother would sooner poison my dinner than have me show up with you.

I don't know how to do family dinners, so I'd sit there like a freak.

Their family was big and loud and had probably only gotten bigger and louder in the years since I lived behind them. Not my scene, even if I'd wanted to go.

Molly had made no attempt to hide that she was puzzled by the way I acted with the people around me. That "The Machine" was a moniker she didn't deem appropriate, even if everyone else thought it was. I'd had glitter down my ass crack to prove how appropriate the rest of my team thought it was.

But Molly wasn't wrong either.

If I was well and truly a machine, with no pulse or heartbeat or complex emotions, it wouldn't have bothered me that she wasn't speaking to me.

Which was why I sent her a text, late on day three.

Me: I apologize for not returning your phone call. It was late when I got the message. Thank you for inviting me, though.

An hour or so later, I received my reply.

Molly Ward: No problem, it's fine.

A reply like that from a person such as her was telling, and it still didn't click in my head that something was wrong.

Day four was no better, and that day had been free of pranks, free of tempers, free of anything that could have upset her. Even the fact that I was still pondering what I might have done to inspire this type of reaction in her should have been a warning sign.

I lifted weights, had a meeting with the coaching staff, and watched some film. Between those things, I talked with Rick, giving them something they could use later for voiceover work. And Molly stayed placidly behind the camera, face either pointed at her phone or at the back of the camera screen.

In fact, she was doing such a good job of not looking at me that I was now an expert in the top of Molly's head.

Rick cleared his throat, and I looked back at him. There was a knowing glint in his eye that made me want to punch him.

"Does glitter make you feel like part of the team?"

"Yeah, it's really magical that way."

He smiled. "You weren't too happy, though?"

The tip of Molly's pencil slowed as she was writing, and something warm flashed bright inside me. She was still aware; she just didn't want me to realize it.

"Would you like to be held down by seven football players and have them dump glitter all over your sweat-soaked body?'

"No."

I rubbed my jaw. "No, I wasn't happy." I paused and started thinking about what Molly would have asked me if she wasn't doing a such a good job of ignoring me. She'd want me to flip up the lid on why I felt that way, why my anger at that moment was so hot and so high, instead of being able to laugh it off like a lot of my teammates would. "It's probably a control thing," I admitted slowly. "Why I got so mad."

Her pencil stopped moving over the surface of the paper. Her whole frame froze, to the point where I wasn't even sure she was breathing.

"Everything about switching teams reminds you how little is in your control in this league." I propped my hands on my hips. Trying to unearth the right words for what this reminded me of when I was little and used to dig in the dirt around this bush in our yard. I'd find something that felt small, that I could pull up easily, but inevitably, it was part of a larger, more stubborn root. I'd tug and tug, and only a little bit would give way before I needed to stop. "I can't control my teammates, no matter where I am. My coaches. My opponents. None of it."

"What can you control?"

For a second, I stared at the top of Molly's head, her shiny hair, and willed her to look up at me. But she didn't, and the pencil in her hand shook for a second before she started writing again.

"I can control how prepared I am," I said. My eyes moved back to Rick. "I can control how in shape I am. What I eat. How I sleep. What I allow as a distraction."

"That seems like a pretty good list," he commented.

I laughed humorlessly. Normally, I'd avoid dwelling on this at all because even that felt like wasted energy. Energy I could harness elsewhere.

It was a trait I inherited from my dad. If it didn't serve my goal, it was a waste of energy. Keeping the door closed to things I couldn't control was the best way to protect myself.

Slowly, day by day since I'd gotten here, this ragtag group of people had turned the knob, but I was the one who had to do the rest of the work. Conversations like this were because I was opening that door.

"If I had a normal job, that list would go further. In this league, doing what we do," I said, "it's a fraction of the whole picture. There are a million things that are out of my hands."

"Like your teammates pouring glitter down your shorts."

"Like that," I agreed dryly. "Even if it's meant as a joke, it's hard to be reminded of the fact that, at the end of the day, the only thing I can control is me."

"A flawlessly working machine," he said quietly.

I nodded. "Yeah."

"Makes sense."

"That's why I almost never stop working on those things," I told him. "Why going out is less important to me than watching film. Why eating right is more important to me than drinking." I took a deep breath and let it out slowly. "Perfecting my craft is the best way for me to spend my time."

"You're good at it, so you're doing something right."

The only way I could explain why I shifted the subject, with a camera aimed at my face, was that part of my personality that refused to back down from a challenge. I allowed one side of my mouth to hook up in a quick smile. "Someone smart told me recently that I could be better, though."

Her pencil froze again.

Rick glanced at her, then back at me.

"So I'm gonna try yoga," I announced.

The pencil fell out of her hands, and her head snapped up.

For the first time in four days, Molly's eyes were on mine. How was it possible that I'd forgotten that color already?

Her mouth gaped open, and I saw Marty smile behind the camera.

"Yoga?" Rick repeated.

"Yup. I like a challenge." I held her astonished gaze until she blinked. "Do you think you could help me find an instructor? You said you'd come with me, right?"

Molly snapped her mouth shut, just then realizing that Rick, Marty, and I were all staring at her.

Then the strangest thing happened. I expected a smile, a laugh, maybe even a joke about a guy like me actually trying yoga. But as she studied my face, I saw her pull down the hypothetical shutters.

Her expression was blank, and the brightness of her blue, blue eyes dimmed.

"I can send you a link for a YouTube video for beginners. You'll be fine on your own."

She nodded at Marty and mumbled something about a meeting, then Molly fled like the hounds of hell were nipping at her heels.

My eyes narrowed on her retreating figure, and to someone like me, she'd just thrown down the most irresistible kind of gauntlet. Something had changed in her head when it came to me and whatever tenuous friendship we'd started forming, one that had been undaunted by my mood swings and prickly nature.

"Uh-oh," Rick said under his breath. "Trouble in paradise?"

I gave him a look, which made Marty snicker.

"Just ... trying to figure out what I did to piss her off."

"Good luck," Marty said with a chuckle.

I didn't need luck. She was about to find out just how stubborn Noah Griffin was when he wanted something, and just then, I wanted to figure out what was wrong with her.

CHAPTER FOURTEEN

NOAH

It took a lot for me to get nervous to make a phone call. But there I was, pacing the length of the apartment as the phone trilled ominously in my ear. I should've made the call as soon as Rick agreed to do this in the first production meeting. But I'd waited until right now.

"Hello?" the voice barked.

"Hi, Grandma."

Silence.

"I think I've finally lost my mind."

A reluctant smile ghosted over my lips. "You haven't, I promise."

"I must have. Because I used to have a grandson who loved me and called me regularly, but that grandson just *texts* now, like that's good enough."

At the sound of her voice, my pacing slowed, and the nerves settled. "I'm sorry. I'm not ..." I scratched the back of my head. "I'm not the best at making phone calls."

"No shit, Sherlock."

A laugh burst out of me, and the muscles it used to make such a sound were so atrophied from disuse that it almost hurt.

"How are you, half-pint?"

"Good. Busy."

"Eh, busy is used as a badge of honor these days," she grumbled. "Doesn't impress me much. I want to know how my grandson is doing in this thing we called life."

Before I knew it, I'd sprawled back on the too-small couch to soak in the sound of her voice. My grandma Pearl, my dad's mom, was one of my favorite people on earth, and the fact that I'd gone months without talking to her made me feel like a giant sack of shit. Yeah, I was busy. So what?

"I'm playing in Washington again," I told her.

She hummed. "I heard that on *SportsCenter* last week, I think."

I smiled again. "You watch that?"

"How else am I gonna find out what's going on? My son has the conversational skills of a yo-yo, and you're not much better, half-pint."

The nickname she gave me at three had stuck this long, and even if I gently reminded her that I was a foot and a half taller than her, she'd still use it.

"Well, I'm hoping I can make up for my lack of phone calls."

"Yeah? How so? You gonna buy me another house?"

It was the first thing I'd done when I cashed my signing bonus from Miami. I flew to South Dakota and paid cash for the place I knew my grandma'd had her eye on for a couple of years but would never be able to afford on her own. She hated that I'd done it. And she loved the house. She'd cried the entire time we walked through after she got the keys. Anything I'd sacrificed for this game was worth it at that moment. Every-fucking-thing.

"Mind if I come visit my investment?" I asked her.

She was quiet, but I heard the quick, sharp inhale of surprise.

When she spoke, her voice wobbled just enough that I knew she was fighting tears. "After the season? Or sooner than that?"

"This weekend, actually. I have a couple of days off before preseason."

It was quiet. Then she sniffed. And sniffed again.

I shook my head. "Come on, Grandma, don't cry. I'll think you don't want me to come."

"I'm not crying, you dingbat," she said in a watery voice. "Just caught a frog in my throat."

"Is that a yes?"

"I think I could have the guest room ready," she answered.

"Good." I blew out a breath. "I'll, uh, have a couple of people with me, if that's okay."

"A woman? Oh Lord, please say it's a woman. Or a man. I don't care who, as long as it ends with me having a great-grand-child before I die, which is probably going to be soon."

Molly's face flashed through my head, there and gone in the same breath, and it occurred to me that introducing her to my grandma was a big deal. A really big deal. Because the only conclusion I'd been able to come to in light of the realization that she was ignoring me was that it bothered me that she was ignoring me. And it bothered me because, in my head, Molly and I had started forming a tentative friendship. Besides Kareem and his glitter bomb, I didn't have any friends in Seattle. I didn't want her silence or her professional distance. It quickly went beyond wanting to know why she was doing it to wanting to fix it.

I explained the Amazon documentary to Grandma, who immediately fussed over the fact that her home would be on film, and simply because it was easier, I glossed over Molly's role in the weekend.

"There will be four of us. Me, the producer, Rick, the camera guy, Marty, and someone who works with me here in Washington. She kind of oversees everything."

"She your boss?"

The smile was there again, imagining pint-sized Molly bossing me around. To the rest of the world, she probably wasn't so pint-sized, but she was to me. "Not my boss. Just a coworker, I guess."

Grandma hummed. "Okay. I'll put you in the basement room since you don't need impressing. The camera guy and the producer, you said? Yeah, Marty can go in the bunk room across from mine, and what's her name?"

"Molly."

"Molly can sleep in the main guest room."

That had me rubbing my forehead. The king bed in that room was the one I always slept on. She'd look tiny in the middle of that bed by herself. Under the sheets and underneath the down plaid comforter that I loved because it was soft and light but kept me warm even on the coldest South Dakota winter night. "Right."

Even to my own ears, my voice sounded rough.

A text notification dinged in my ear, and I pulled the phone away. Inexplicably, my heart sped up when I saw it was from Molly.

Molly Ward: This was just emailed to me. Just FYI.

I clicked on the link and found myself scrolling through the pictures too fast because I loved what I was seeing. My thumb hovered over the map, and I zoomed in. It was on the east side of Lake Washington, the same place that the Wolves owner, Allie Sutton-Pierson, lived with her husband, retired QB Luke Pierson.

"Grandma, I have something that just came through my phone that I need to look at. I'll email you my itinerary, okay?"

"Sure, sure. You'll fly on one of those fancy private planes?"

I smiled. "Probably. You know I need the extra legroom."

She harrumphed. "Whatever you say, half-pint."

"I'm excited to see you too, Grandma."

"Oh, hush. You know I love you best."

I rolled my eyes. I was her only grandchild "Love you too."

After I tossed the phone down, Marty shifted from the corner, and I bit back a curse, sending him a glare instead.

His smile widened behind the camera, but he didn't say anything.

"I actually forgot you were here, you creep." That made him laugh. "Am I going to get in trouble if I talk to you?"

"Nah. We can edit around anything, you know that."

I sat up on the couch and grabbed my phone again. The house that Molly sent me was ... perfect. Absolutely perfect.

A little bit more money than what I wanted to spend, but it checked every other box. Tall ceilings, warm tones, a massive kitchen, and sprawling views of the lake and the mountains, greens at every height in the trees that surrounded it. Trees meant privacy, and I liked that too. It was set back from the road, but the house itself wasn't a behemoth. Four bedrooms and three baths with a fully finished basement and a home gym already installed. A pool for laps in the morning before practice.

It was a space I could actually live in, not just exist.

Me: Marty is here already. Want to come with us if I can get a hold of the listing agent?

The fact that I held my breath as she started typing was akin to a blaring airhorn in my ear.

Danger! Danger! Abort!

Molly Ward: I can't tonight. The twins are here

**hanging out. Just wanted to pass the house along, it
looked like you.**

She started typing and stopped. Then once again. No other
text popped up, and before I realized what I was doing, my jaw
popped from grinding my molars together.

"Molly meeting us?" Marty asked lightly. Too lightly.

I cut him a look, then pulled up the number for the listing
agent. Something about all of this, the past few days, had me
feeling edgy and restless. There were too many circumstances out
of my control, and it had my skin humming in relentless buzzing.

It would have been convenient to blame that for how the next
two hours of my life unfolded.

The listing agent for the house filled my silence as I walked
around all four thousand square feet of the home. Each stretch of
wood floor, each reflection of the lights in the granite lining the
massive kitchen island, every corner of the large, light-filled
bedrooms fell prey to my notice, even if I didn't say much
about it.

She must have had a sixth sense for the way I studied each
inch of the place.

It did look like me.

It felt like me too. And Molly had known it.

If her inbox was anything like mine, I'd had a dozen houses
emailed to me, most of which had only earned a cursory glance
because I was too damn tired most nights to try to go see.

The space was large enough for someone my size, the furniture in the home big and comfortable with hefty wood frames
and room to spread out. Sprawling views of blues and greens
and glinting water. In my bones, I knew it was meant to be
my home.

It was one of those times when I never questioned how
quickly I came to a decision. It was a trait that served me well on

the field, acting on instinct, because I knew my instinct wouldn't steer me wrong.

This place was mine.

If Marty was annoyed by my lack of commentary, he didn't prompt me to say something that would serve the damn narrative. He simply followed me around as we both ignored the mindless chatter of the woman who was about to make a huge-ass commission off me.

"It's been on the market for a little over a month," she said, trailing red-tipped fingernails along the custom trim on the windows overlooking the lushly landscaped backyard. "I know I'm not supposed to say things like this, but I'm sure my clients would be"—her eyes trailed deliberately over my chest and arms —"flexible."

I held her gaze and saw exactly what she'd be willing to give me.

Nothing about her tempted me. Not her long legs or curvy hips, the nipped in waist and generous bust, or the curly dark hair spilling down her back. Most guys on the team didn't believe me, but it's entirely possible to flip the off switch when it comes to the desire to sleep with a stranger.

She was beautiful. Incredibly beautiful.

And the last thing I wanted was to see the look in her eyes at how much she'd let me do to her. It was every cliché that I hated about being a professional athlete. Because I did what I did, I was desirable. Because I wore a recognizable jersey and had a familiar face, she'd let me flip her flat on her back with no more than a nod of agreement on my part.

Nothing about that appealed to me, and so, no part of my body reacted.

Instead, all I wished was that she was someone else. Someone shorter with lighter hair and brighter eyes and a bigger smile. Someone who found my temper mildly amusing and schooled me on football. Someone who looked at me and wanted to dig beneath the surface, not worship the façade.

"Could I have some privacy to make my decision?" I asked her.

She glanced at the camera and back at me in question, like she couldn't tell whether I wanted her or Marty to leave the room.

"I'd like to be alone," I said more firmly. Her eyes shuttered in an instant, and she gave me a nod of deference.

"Of course," she purred.

Marty stayed by me, a strangely comforting presence as I braced my arms on the ledge and stared ahead.

"You find a house, Griffin?"

All that restlessness from early uncoiled slowly, sinking into something comfortable. "I think I did, Marty."

He gestured on the ground, just behind the couch. I didn't see what it was at first until I crouched down and pulled it out by the edge. A smile lifted my lips when I saw them stacked on top of each other.

I called the agent back in the room.

"I want it."

Her eyes flared with a different kind of excitement. "Excellent. I'd be happy to present an offer to my clients."

"I'll offer their asking price, but I want a two-week close date so I can move in before the season starts." And I lifted my hand, letting her know I wasn't done. "I also want to film a segment here tonight if they'd be so kind as to not return home just yet."

She lifted her eyebrows. "They're out of town, so that should be fine."

"And I want to borrow these." I lifted the other hand.

If I thought her eyebrows were high before, they shot up even farther.

"You ..." She shook her head. "That's what you want?"

"Do we have a deal?"

"I-I'll call them right now," she said cautiously. In her eyes, I must have lost a bit of my appeal and replaced it with a healthy dose of insanity.

Marty chuckled. "You're serious, man?"

I looked at my hands. "As a heart attack. She won't say no to this."

CHAPTER FIFTEEN

MOLLY

"Do you think Paige would think it's weird if I write a paper on the maternal impact she had on older children who have no biological tie to her?"

My hand froze, the bottle of wine suspended mid pour over my glass. "Umm, no?"

Claire typed furiously on her laptop before slapping it shut. "I can't figure out what to do with this paper, and I have to get started."

Isabel came down the hallway of our apartment and glared at Claire's computer like it kicked her in the crotch. "Do you have to type so loudly? You sound like a chicken pounding a mallet on that thing."

Claire flipped her off.

From my perch on the couch, I smiled at both of them as I took another sip of my wine. It was drier than I usually liked, so I grimaced as I swallowed. Lia and Claire were huddled together on the other end.

Their faces were mirror images of each other, but our family could tell them apart with no problems. It was in the angle of

Lia's jaw and the slope of Claire's nose. Not to mention, the second they opened their mouth, it would be a dead giveaway to anyone who actually knew them.

Our mom—or as Isabel affectionately referred to her, that selfish bitch who birthed us—might not have won any parenting awards, but she passed down a helluva gene pool because all four of us bore a striking resemblance to her. I could see her easily in the dark, thick hair, high cheekbones, and shape of our blue, blue eyes.

Isabel's smile was more like our dad's, more like Logan's, and she had the same lanky, athletic build that Emmett promised to have as he grew up. My curves had lessened into adulthood, but the twins still maintained a curvier figure as they tiptoed quietly into their twenties.

"Why wouldn't you write your paper about Paige?" Lia asked, handing Claire a half-finished glass of wine. Claire took it without a word and finished for her. "She basically was our mom."

In the kitchen just around the corner, Isabel slammed the cupboard door shut. "There's no basically about it," she called.

I smiled at Claire. "Which class is this for?"

She was graduating from college with a major in developmental psychology and a minor in sociology with plans to start her master's in the spring after a winter graduation. Dropping her head back on the couch, she sighed. "Sociology of families. I should have taken it earlier, but"—she shrugged—"I was kind of dreading this part of it."

Lia took the empty wine glass from Claire and set it on the end table. "Our family isn't that dysfunctional."

"No, but trying to discuss the structure of it is a bit confusing." She started ticking off fingers. "We had married heterosexual parents with an unconventional age difference. One died, followed a few years later by one voluntarily abandoning us to an unmarried heterosexual male relative. A couple of years after that, he married a single heterosexual female for legal purposes. Neither adopted us, and Paige never had guardianship rights installed, so technically, she's just a cool sister-in-law who helped when she didn't have to." Claire shook her head when Iz slammed something else around in the kitchen. "For all intents and purposes, she was the main maternal figure in our life, but our mother is still around. Just not ... around us."

"Isn't she in fucking Bali or something?" Isabel muttered from the kitchen. "That's what her last bullshit email said, what? A year ago?"

"India, I think," I corrected. "She lives at that center. The weird guru guy who wrote all those books on mindfulness and blah, blah, whatever."

The wine had me feeling pleasantly fuzzy, not drunk, not even really buzzed, but just happy enough that I didn't even care that we were talking about Brooke—that selfish bitch who birthed us. Even she was a pleasant distraction from the fact that Noah had invited me to come look at the house. Saying no had been hard. Really, really hard. Like Noah's biceps hard. Noah's rock-hard ass hard.

Not that I knew what his ass felt like, but I could imagine. I'd watched him lift weights all week. Do squats. Bend over on the field when he lined up against the offense. I'd touched a few things on Noah's body back in the day, but his ass had not been one of them.

What a freaking tragedy, I thought through my wine haze.

Isabel stormed into the family room, a bottle of tequila in her hand that had me blinking owlishly at her. Were we at tequila level? I missed it. "Paige deserves to have a paper written about her."

"She does," Claire said diplomatically.

The tequila bottle waved like a flag. "She stepped in when no one could handle you two little hellions."

Lia rolled her eyes. "Like you were a walk in the park, Miss Angry Girl."

"That's the point of this class, though," Claire interjected when Iz opened her mouth with what promised to be a scathing retort. "The structure of the family, as we know it, has changed dramatically. Even the phrase family structure itself holds different weight than it did twenty years ago. The rise in single parent families, homosexual parents, even saying things like *nontraditional* implies a bias that we need to be careful of. Our family history didn't meet any sort of definition of 'traditional,' even when our parents were married. Dad was so much older than her, but they still fit the definition of a traditional family structure as it's been historically defined. It implies there's something wrong or nontraditional about Paige and Logan raising us when they filled the parental roles to much better success."

We all stared at her for a beat.

I poured more wine.

Iz unscrewed the top of the tequila and disappeared into the kitchen.

Lia spoke first even though she'd probably be able to stare at Claire and communicate what she was thinking. "So why are you questioning what to do your paper on?"

Claire licked her lips, and her gaze darted to the kitchen. "Because I'm wondering if it's too easy to write about Paige. I could argue that Mom, and her absence in our life, had a greater impact on us. On how the structure of our family changed, and how that played out on our emotional growth and maturity."

Isabel stormed back in. Her hair, unbound and tumbling past her shoulders, flew behind her like a flag, and her eyes were blazing in her pink-cheeked face. "No way, that bitch does not get papers. She doesn't deserve papers written about her."

"Isabel," I cautioned quietly. "It's not your decision."

"Then why is she asking us for our opinion?"

All four of us fell quiet. Claire, as wild as she'd been as a child, had mellowed more quickly than Lia had once they reached high school. She was an observer of life, of the people around her, like Isabel was, while Lia still held that boundless energy that had been a hallmark of their youth. She was like a live wire, always bouncing, always tapping her foot, always seeking an outlet for the force bound behind her skin. Yet despite that, she was quietly watching our middle sister, eyes bright with unshed tears at how quickly she turned to anger at the topic of Brooke.

"I'm asking your opinion because I love and respect you," Claire said.

Isabel relaxed, her shoulders losing a bit of their tightness.

Lia looked at Claire and smiled sadly. "But opinion is different than permission, isn't it? You don't need our permission to do this."

Leave it to those two. The thought had flowed from Claire to Lia without skipping a beat. Claire nodded. "It is."

My eyes fell shut because we all knew what that meant.

"What do you think, Mol?" Claire asked.

Words crowded my throat because as much as I knew moments like this required me to act as the firstborn, I didn't feel like that was me. But I *was*.

I'd always been content to let Logan assert his role as first-born, the big brother and father figure we'd so desperately needed when we were younger. So even though I was the oldest of my four sisters, my feet had never filled those shoes. Not really.

I didn't want to tell Claire what to do because what if I steered her wrong? What if agreeing that doing the paper on Brooke's impact on our family structure was equivalent to setting off a nuclear bomb in our tight-knit little circle? That was the last thing I wanted. Our family kicked ass. I loved our family. Tuesday nights were the highlight of every single week for me.

The idea that Brooke's ghost, though she was still very much alive, could punch through that, filled me with dread. But it wasn't my place to lay the mantle of my opinion on my younger sister's education.

Because it was only that. My opinion.

"I think I've had too much wine for this conversation," I admitted weakly.

"Cop out," Isabel said.

I glared at her. Claire sighed.

"Did you ask Logan?" Lia asked.

"Why does he get an opinion?" Isabel shot back. "Brooke is our burden to bear, not his."

Claire straightened on the couch. "You know, your anger on this particular subject gets really fricken annoying after a while."

I held up my hands. "Knock it off, you two."

"Logan is the head of this family," Lia said. "That's why he gets an opinion."

I rubbed my temples, where the beginning of a headache was starting to bloom. To think, I could have been wandering around a big, beautiful house and helping Noah spend all his money on it. But no, I chose my sisters because family came first.

Around me, the noise increased from all three of them. Lia and Claire joined forces, which they always did, and Isabel squared off in the doorway to the family room, not intimidated in the slightest by the two-against-one odds, like always.

No one even noticed that I sat there, eyes closed and wishing I was anywhere else. I didn't want to talk about Brooke. I didn't want to listen to my sisters argue about which woman had the greater impact in our life and why Claire's paper somehow changed the definition of that role.

"You guys," I interrupted. "Could you stop, please?"

No one listened. Lia had stood from the couch. "You know, I'm so sick of you acting like you carry around some different wound than the rest of us. Brooke left all of us, Iz. Just because you haven't worked through your own shit doesn't mean your opinion counts more."

Claire rubbed her forehead. "Let's just drop it. I have a couple of weeks to make the decision."

They ignored her too. The two hotheads went at it, and I gave Claire a commiserating smile.

"I don't think my opinion counts more," Iz yelled. "I'm pissed that that woman is somehow getting credit for the way we turned out. It had nothing to do with her."

"Ohhhh yes," Lia drawled. "Look at you. You're the picture of someone who's unaffected by your childhood."

"Hey," I snapped at her. "Watch it."

Her face pinked, but she didn't move her flinty gaze from Isabel.

My phone buzzed, and I sighed heavily before flipping the screen to face me.

Noah: My savings account just took a pretty massive hit thanks to you.

The tone of his text, the fact that he texted me at all, pulled a smile onto my face. I missed him, which made no sense. I could talk to him, be friendly with him, and it wouldn't be fraternization, right? In my wine and family drama haze, I shifted through my mental checklist of why I'd decided to pull back from him all week.

Maaaaybe because when I was around him, my entire body tugged in his direction like he was pulling on a string. The only way I felt like I could combat it was to snip the cord clean through.

But that hadn't really worked either.

All week I was forced to watch him, and think about him, and wonder what he was doing when we weren't filming. All week, I struggled with the feeling that he noticed my distance, and that it bothered him.

My fingers flew across the screen before I could talk myself out of it.

Me: You got the house?! I KNEW it was perfect for you.
Noah: It was. I'm glad you sent it to me.
Noah: There's one problem, though ...
Me: What?
Noah: The yoga mats that came with it are too small for me. Either that or I'm less flexible than I realized and need massive amounts of help.

He attached a picture that had me laughing out loud. Marty must have snapped it, which had me smiling so big it threatened to split my skin open. Noah was attempting a downward dog, but his feet were a solid foot past the end of the bright pink mat. His form was terrible, and I couldn't see his face, but it was, hands down, my new favorite picture of all time.

Me: Oh boy. Yeah, you're in trouble.
Noah: Will you come help me? I think Marty misses you.

My face flushed warm and happy and pink, and my chest expanded on a heavy inhale.

Me: Does he?
Noah: He said I was boring to film when I'm by myself. Just think of how embarrassing it will be

when I do my first yoga session in my new house, and because I have no guidance, I fall and break my hip, which will put me on the bench for the rest of the season.

His next text included the address, and I clicked on the map. If I requested an Uber now, I could be there in twenty minutes. The desire to go was so strong, especially when I factored in the chaotic state of my living room.

Two angry sisters arguing about Brooke, or a football player who made my tummy flip upside down when he looked at me?

Tapping my Uber app, I requested the ride before I could talk myself out of it. This was the impulsive Molly I didn't let out often, but in this situation, I wasn't going to second-guess it. Why he was still at the house, I had no clue, but I wasn't second-guessing that either. All I knew was that ignoring him was stupid because we still had to spend a lot of time together. Ignoring him was pointless, actually.

When a driver accepted the trip, I stood and sent Noah a quick text, telling him I'd be there. Instead of waiting to see what he said, I tucked the phone into the side pocket of my leggings.

"I need to go to work," I proclaimed to anyone who would listen.

And just like that, their arguing stopped. Like magic.

"Now?" Isabel asked. "You've been drinking."

"I have an Uber coming."

"Why do you need to work so late?" Claire asked.

"I just ... do."

Isabel's face softened in understanding.

"Quit fighting, okay?" I said gently. "Let Claire do her paper on whatever she wants. It's not up to you two, and it's not fair to make it harder on her than necessary."

Claire pushed up from the couch to wrap me in a tight hug. I kissed her cheek when she whispered her thanks into my ear.

Isabel wiped a hand over her weary face. "Sorry, Claire."

I cleared my throat.

"And sorry, Lia," she mumbled.

"I'm sorry too," Lia added.

I pinched my cheeks and looked down at my Wolves tank top and white sneakers. My hair was pulled back and anchored into place with a few hair pins. I shrugged.

"Be careful," Iz told me.

"I'm just going for some filming they're doing of his new place." When she lifted an eyebrow in disbelief, I propped my hands on my hips. "I am."

As I skipped down the steps outside our apartment to my waiting Uber, I thought about her warning and had a moment of pause.

"Ready?" my driver asked.

I blew out a breath. No second-guessing. "Yup. Let's go."

CHAPTER SIXTEEN

MOLLY

A BRIGHT FLURRY of nerves popped and bubbled like champagne as I approached the house. The pictures didn't do it justice. As I walked up the covered front porch with solid wood beams holding up the peaked roofline, I got the distinct impression that this house had been built for someone as strong and intimidating as Noah was. Someone tall and strong, who'd fill the space and not be dwarfed by it.

Looking at the massive wood front doors, flanked by custom cut glass windows and artfully dimmed porch lights, I couldn't help but feel a little dwarfed myself. I lifted my chin and knocked, though, because the whole point of this—my job, the promotion, showing up to prove that I could be unaffected by Noah—was to prove that these things wouldn't and couldn't overwhelm me.

Beyond the door, I heard his deep voice tell me to come in, so I tested the door handle carefully. It opened, and I couldn't help but gasp when I walked into the house.

"Holy shit," I breathed. It was stunning. Even though the skies outside were dark, the soaring ceilings and crisp white walls made it seem bright and airy and welcoming. Rugs covered the floor around the solidly built furniture, and windows facing Lake Washington sparkled with the lights of nearby houses and buildings across the water.

"Thanks for coming."

I jumped, slapping a hand over my chest when I saw him round a corner. A ghost of a smile graced his lips, and my fingers itched to push it further, see how the motion would transform his already handsome face.

"It's ..." I shook my head, eyes still trying to take in the space. "It's amazing, Noah."

He approached slowly, hands hanging loosely at his sides. His legs were covered in black track pants with the bright red Wolves logo near a pocket, and stretched over his chest was a white T-shirt so worn, it was practically indecent.

Underneath it, I could see the shadows and lines of his upper body, and a hole in the neckline gave me an extra glimpse of tanned, smooth skin. My entire body swayed toward him. That same tug I always felt.

I guess I was a bit more tuggable after a bottle of wine.

His forehead creased. "Have you been drinking?"

"A little," I heard myself admit.

Why was his face doing that thing? The swirling, ominous thundercloud thing that made him look like lightning was about to crackle from the surface of his skin. The mental picture made me grin, and his face pinched further.

"You were drinking and then drove here? Are you insane?" he said, voice low and dangerous and deep as he took another step toward.

"What?" I blinked away from his mouth. "No."

"You could've killed yourself, Molly." His volume increased, the thundercloud face getting darker and darker, and I watched in abject fascination as he came even closer still. "What were you thinking?"

All I'd have to do is reach out, not even fully extend my arms, and my palms would land somewhere in the vicinity of his pecs. Underneath that white shirt, they were the size of dinner plates.

"You need to calm down," I said. Was I talking to him? I think I was. But maybe I was talking to me. I needed to calm down too. My fingers, in the haven of my mind, tracked over the entire topography of his chest, memorizing it for future use.

"Calm down?" he roared.

My hand reached out and almost settled on his chest. He snatched my wrist before it made contact.

His fingers were so, so warm.

"I took an Uber, you psycho," I murmured. "Your hand is so much bigger than mine. Isn't that funny?"

Noah sighed, eyes falling shut as he dropped my hand. *Boo.* "Why didn't you say so?"

"You were kind of busy yelling at me." I turned and hummed in appreciation when I saw the kitchen. "And you had your thundercloud face on, which makes it hard to interrupt you."

"My ... what?"

Walking along the length of the island, I let my palm glide just above the surface of the granite. "When you get mad, you look like a thundercloud."

Noah was quiet, and I felt his eyes on my back as I opened a few cabinets.

"Where's the listing agent?"

His footsteps started following mine as I wandered through the dining area and into the main living space, staring through the sprawl of glass windows facing the water even though I couldn't see anything other than the moon glinting off the far side of the bay.

"We convinced her to give us a couple of hours to film."

I smiled over my shoulder. "And she said yes?"

"She was very willing to accommodate, given my offer."

My smile felt brittle. "Ahh."

"Ahh, what?"

I shrugged. "Nothing."

He let it slide, and I was oh, so thankful for that.

"How was hanging out with your sisters?"

The laughter that escaped my lips was harsh and tired and all sorts of tangled emotions. Amazing how much you could wrap up in one puff of air. The argument about Claire's paper was easier to ignore when I was trying to escape it, when their voices overlapped each other and I just wanted it to stop, stop, *stop*.

But it was quiet in Noah's house, and he wasn't searching to fill the silence with meaningless words. Behind me, he was a solid, steady presence, and it was exactly what I needed.

There was just enough wine in my system, loosening my brain and allowing honest words to roll from my tongue.

"We fought," I told him. "Or they did, I guess."

"What about?"

"Family structure," I answered with a sad smile. His eyebrows bent in, but he didn't say anything. The arm of the couch was close enough that I could sit back on it and still stare out the window into the inky darkness. "Ours is nontraditional even though I'm told by my sister who's minoring in sociology that's not a term you should throw around lightly. And the structure we had before this one was sort of traditional but incredibly dysfunctional."

Noah shifted so he could see my face, his big shoulder braced on the wall just on the other side of the window.

"Claire—the one in school—has to write a paper on maternal influences in nontraditional family structures," I explained.

"Logan's wife?" he guessed.

"That's where we started the discussion, but ..." My voice

trailed off. How much of this did he actually want to hear? "Where's Marty?" I asked, suddenly very aware that we were alone in the big family room.

He tilted his head. "On the phone downstairs. I think it's Rick, but I'm not sure."

I nodded.

"The paper," he prompted.

"Are you asking to avoid your yoga lesson?"

"Absolutely." His face was all harsh lines and angles in the dimly lit room, and I laughed at his answer. Another flash of a grin appeared, but it was gone just as quickly.

I moved off the arm of the couch and onto one of the end cushions, my hands clasped lightly in my lap. This didn't feel like the kind of conversation you had while sitting in a pseudo-seat. "Paige is the obvious answer," I said quietly. "She and Logan got married when I was sixteen, the twins were twelve, Iz was four-teen, and since then, she's been our mother in every way that matters."

With each word, and each moment of precious quiet he gave me to process, I felt the effect of the wine drain slowly from my body.

"I remember when she showed up," he said.

"I'll bet," I said wryly. "You know it's really her fault that I climbed through your window."

His eyes sharpened. "Is it?"

I wondered how long we'd tiptoe around this, and now seemed like as good a time as any.

"Of course, she didn't know how literally I'd take her advice, but at that time, I had such a desperate craving for a person like her in my life. To hear her tell me to take the bull by the horns and go for what I wanted—someone I viewed as smart and strong and feisty and successful and beautiful and just ... everything I wanted to be as a sixteen-year-old. Her words were as good as gospel, you know?"

He took in a slow breath and let it out before he walked toward me and took a seat on the coffee table that faced the couch. Somehow, he didn't doubt it could hold his weight, but it did, and he spread his legs so that his hands dangled between them.

"I always wondered what prompted it." His eyes never wavered from mine.

I grinned. "Besides a raging crush on the boy next door?"

He exhaled a laugh. "That part was clear enough," he forced out. I had to close my eyes at the sound of his voice, rough and raw and low.

If I reached back far, so very far, into my memories, I could still remember what it felt like to kiss him. I'd kissed dozens of boys, even slept with a couple who I thought would be something to me, but the memory of Noah Griffin's lips still haunted me the most.

Slick tongue. Strong hands. Muttered curses as I climbed onto his lap.

My eyes popped open because those thoughts wouldn't bring me anywhere of value.

"What prompted it." I sighed. "That would have to be maternal influence in a nontraditional family structure."

His laughter came instantly, loud and surprising, a sharp burst of sound that had me sitting up straighter. There it was. His elusive smile. Perfect, straight white teeth and lips stretched wide across his face. The lines bracketing his mouth made it look like he smiled often, instead of the reality, which was that it was rare and fast and made you feel fortunate to see one.

"So that's why you left? Talking about Paige's role?"

"No," I said immediately. "No, it was the discussion of how our own mother influenced our family structure by her leaving."

His smile faded. "How old were you when she left?"

"Just turned fourteen. We were so young, you know? And having three younger siblings to look after, plus an older brother who was just getting his footing in his own way, it was almost like ... I couldn't dwell on how much it hurt me that she left because I had so many other things to worry about. I had my sisters to worry about, and they were so much more important than Brooke."

His eyebrows popped briefly. "I never really ... I never thought about why you guys lived with Logan. Where your parents were."

"Most people didn't know. He did such a good job of protecting us. And because he did, we could just be kids. Teenagers who got into trouble and played pranks and were allowed to make normal mistakes because we had him."

"Sounds like you protected your sisters, though, too," he said. The look he was giving me, searching and intense, reminded me of the night on the couch when he was watching film. Like I was something worth studying, like picking me apart would help him understand.

That knowledge was like someone pressed their foot on the gas pedal, but I was stuck in neutral until I could explain something to him in the right way.

"I think what I used to do then, and still do now," I said, leaning forward, my knees almost touching his, "is try to take responsibility for how they feel. And that wasn't my job. I didn't want to impose my will, you know? It wasn't like I wanted them to feel what I felt. I wanted to make sure that everything stayed okay, even if it was to my detriment."

"Even if it hurt you," he said slowly.

"Maybe. I don't know. I wasn't the teenager who threw tantrums for attention, but if I went too long trying to keep the peace among my sisters, I'd just ... burst. Do something stupid."

His eyes drifted to my mouth. "I can't imagine what you mean."

"Liar."

His grin flashed bright again, and it made my skin tighten deliciously.

"I still do it, and that's a big part of what's made me good at my job, yes, but... some of it isn't smart for me," I admitted, tucking a stray piece of hair behind my ear. "I was doing it with you."

That had him straightening. "What do you mean?"

It was so hard for me to say things like this and risk what he might think of me, so I stood nervously from the couch and went back to the window. The coffee table creaked when he stood and followed.

"I found myself worrying about how this process, this move, this change was affecting you. Affecting your game, your mood, your frame of mind."

Noah breathed deeply behind me, and I felt his exhale ruffle the hair on the back of my neck. In my mind, I imagined the string connecting us, wound tight around my hips when I turned slowly to face him.

"Is that why you pulled away this week?" he asked.

My eyes stayed focused on the line of his throat and jaw, sharp as a knife's edge. He swallowed roughly at my unwavering attention. "Yes. Because I need to worry about how this is affecting me too."

"H-how was it affecting you?"

Had he moved closer? Or was that me?

I didn't answer, probably because my mouth went tumble-weed dry at his nearness. My eyes fell shut; my head spun dizzily. No alcohol in the world could've affected me like Noah Griffin's body next to mine.

"Because I can tell you what it did to me," he continued.

Opening my eyes, I had to tilt my chin up to see his face. "What?" I whispered.

"You became the most unreadable offense I'd faced, and you knew something like that would drive me insane. All I could think about was what I'd done wrong or how I'd upset you to make you shut me out like that."

The protestation was on my lips instantly. "You didn't do anything wrong."

"So quick to defend me," he said, his mouth curving in a smile. "And I've done nothing to deserve that from you."

My hands lifted, like an invisible puppet master raised them into the air, and I forced them back down. Touching him wouldn't help. None of this was helping him or me but neither of us seemed motivated to move.

"Why did you invite me here?" I asked.

Maybe Noah had a string wound under his skin too because his hand lifted, and he watched it like he had no control over where it was going, his shaky exhale hitting my forehead in a sharp burst.

"Because you ..." He stopped and swallowed, and so very, very carefully, he slid his hand along the line of my throat until he was cupping the back of my neck. My entire body vibrated danger-ously at his touch, like the tines of a tuning fork struck with too much force. "You were the first person I thought of to share this with."

He dipped his head, and I sucked in a quick breath. We both froze when my breasts brushed the front of his chest. Noah's eyes searched mine, and I lifted my hands, laying them lightly on his chest. In the span of a heartbeat, I thought about pushing him away, but my fingers curled into the soft fabric instead.

With a tug and a lean, his lips were a mere inch from mine.

Suddenly, Noah shoved away from me, and I swayed forward

dangerously. It took me a second to realize why over the roaring pulse in my ears.

"Hey, Molly," Marty said, ascending the stairs with light steps, camera perched on his shoulder like it always was. "Nice place, huh?"

"Hey. Umm, yeah. I l-love it."

Noah rubbed the back of his neck, a safe distance separating us now.

If Marty suspected anything, he didn't show it. "Ready for some yoga?"

"Ready as I'll ever be," I said weakly.

CHAPTER SEVENTEEN

NOAH

IT WAS rare for me to think to myself, *this was a terrible idea*, but in the first three minutes of starting our yoga lesson, I thought it at least seven times. The first was when Molly rolled out her yoga mat and started stretching forward, brushing her fingers along the ground. Marty was getting his main camera settled on a tripod, his small handheld on his shoulder so he could catch more than one angle at once, and I fought to keep my eyes off the rounded curve of her ass. The way her eyes closed as she breathed deeply. The way her chest lifted on an inhale and the way her waist curved up from her hips.

Muscles I'd never noticed on her before popped in her arms as she moved through her warm-up. When she noticed I wasn't moving, she straightened carefully and gave me a curious look.

"Are you going to join or just watch?"

I swallowed. "Sorry. I'm joining."

This was a terrible idea, I thought again when she laid her hand on my back and guided me to drop my hands to the ground.

"We're just going to doing a basic series here before I start the video I found, then she can guide us through. It's specifically for football players, so I don't think anything will be too challenging for your first time."

I didn't answer. Mainly because I didn't trust my voice not to betray the thoughts tumbling through my head.

I almost kissed her.

I almost kissed her.

If Marty hadn't walked up the stairs when he did, I would've had Molly Ward pressed against the windows and my mouth on hers. I tried to focus on what she was saying, but I couldn't mute the mental images flashing, one after another, after another. My hands on her. Her hands on me. How soft her lips would've been. The way she tasted.

So easily, I'd slipped from a desire to understand her into just plain old desire. Except there was nothing plain or old about it.

"Noah?"

I blinked. "Yeah. Sorry."

"Tuck your chin and push your weight into your heels."

Once I followed her direction, Molly moved to the mat next to mine. Her toenails were purple, and it pissed me off that I noticed. She exhaled slowly and mirrored my pose.

"Set your hands on the mat and move your legs back into downward dog."

"This is what got me into trouble in the first place," I mumbled but did as she asked.

She laughed. "You probably tried to shift your hands around if it felt uncomfortable, but you should keep your butt in the air and move your feet. Hands stay planted."

Huh.

"Better," she said.

Following her lead and the patient instructions she gave me, we spent about five minutes doing some basic stretches. A few things were clear in those five minutes, and only got clearer as she cued up the video on her iPad that she set up in front of us.

Molly was much better at yoga than I was.

Molly was much more flexible than I was.

And Molly looked like sex on legs as she moved through each position.

Every time she moved, I found myself cataloging a new part of her body, something I'd never noticed before.

Her ears, for example. Even though her hair was almost always pulled back, I'd never noticed Molly's ears. They were dainty and stuck out just a little bit, which I found oddly endearing.

Her second toe was just a hair longer than her big toe.

When she arched her back, she let out a breathy exhale every time. I wanted to hear it in surround sound while she dug her fingernails into my back.

I had to pinch my eyes shut when that one crossed my mind because I hadn't allowed myself to enter that headspace in so long, and it felt like I was doing something wrong.

When she laughed at me because I couldn't stretch as far as she could, the skin around her eyes crinkled up. It was adorable.

Her neck, long and graceful and as I know, as soft as satin, made me want to drag my teeth along the edge when she tilted her chin up to the ceiling when we were in Upward Dog.

"Fuck," I whispered.

She sat up and gave me a concerned look. "What? Did you hurt yourself?"

Yeah. There was a part of me that was hurting all right, and it needed to friggin stop because I had a camera pointed at me.

Was I sweating? I swept my hand along my forehead, and sure enough, a few minutes of simple poses, and I was sweating.

"No, I'm fine," I said from between gritted teeth.

A smile trembled on the edge of her lips as the woman on the screen told us in a soothing voice where to position our legs.

Goddess pose or something like that. All I knew was that Molly's legs spread wide, and she lowered herself easily.

She was strong.

"Did you know that Dallas started bringing in a yoga instructor for practices?"

I glanced over at her. "Seriously?"

Molly arched her arms and pushed her legs into a different position, and when I followed a few seconds later, she grinned at my obvious delay. "Seriously. Helps avoid injuries because the players are more flexible. One of their linemen had back surgery, and when he wasn't working out during the off season, his PT suggested yoga to strengthen his back and core without risking more injury. It worked so well for him that their coach brought someone in for the whole defense to try it. Now they do yoga twice a week as a part of practice."

For the first time since we started, my mind flipped back into its natural default. Football.

"I never even considered it," I said, then grunted when I was asked to do something entirely unnatural with my legs. Molly caught a glimpse of my face and laughed, her belly shaking as she laid flat on the mat.

I hated to admit it, but it was harder than I thought. We were supposed to lay there and keep our legs in the air for eight minutes.

Eight minutes.

Molly held her legs straighter than I did. Her fingers wiggled on the mat, and not an ounce of tension existed in her body anywhere I could see. Actually, it looked like she could've fallen asleep for how relaxed she was.

Pressing my lower back firmly against the mat, I tried to breathe through my chi or harness my inner sunrise or whatever the instructor was talking about on the video.

"Are we almost done?" I asked.

"Nope."

I sighed.

"You watch," she said, eyes still closed when I turned my head to look at her, "this'll be the season you break the sack record, and when you do, you better thank me."

I smiled and directed my gaze back up to the ceiling. "You got it."

My movements were jerky when we shifted position again, whereas Molly looked like her joints were made from water.

"You're terrible at this, Noah."

In the kitchen, I caught a glimpse of Marty smothering a smile.

I narrowed my eyes at her. "I'm not terrible."

She folded her body in half. "Yes, you are."

"Fine, you come to practice tomorrow, and we'll see how you do in my world."

"No, thank you," she demurred. "Enough of my life is taken up by football. I don't need to add time on the field into it too."

"Too much football," I said quietly. I lifted my arms over my head and mimicked her movements. "Is there such a thing?"

"Maybe not when you're in the thick of it." She exhaled slowly through her mouth. "But you can't play forever. What are you going to do when you're done?"

A wry smile bent my lips as I straightened and propped my hands on my hips. Whatever the pose was in the video, my big ass body did not bend that way. "They'll have to drag me kicking and screaming off the field when they want me to retire."

"Yeah?"

"As long as my body cooperates," I said, "I'll be out there."

"Maybe you can set a new record. Oldest defensive player of the year."

She pointed at my mat, and I sighed, dropping down to do what she was doing. Cat or cow or cobra. I couldn't remember.

"Yeah, in ten years, maybe."

"You think you'll still be averaging a sack and a half per game in ten years?" she teased. "Yeah, right. You'll be limping around by that point unless you do some more of this."

I glared at her, but it didn't dim her smile. It got brighter. Everything else around her faded.

Why didn't that terrify me? That everything in the room except Molly's face became blurry and unimportant, but the way her lips stretched into a smile, how that smile lit up her eyes, was vital and precious. I didn't intimidate her in any way, and that suddenly felt like something I needed to protect. Something I should wrap my arms around and cocoon from the outside world so nothing and no one could change that about her.

It was the only reason I could think of for why I didn't see her reach out to tip me over.

Balancing like I had been, I fell like a freaking oak tree.

She collapsed into helpless laughter while I flopped onto my back.

"Dirty cheat," I groaned.

Molly wiped tears of mirth from under her eyes and balanced on her knees over me. "Are you okay?"

"Oh sure, pretend you care now. You could've injured me."

"Who knew The Machine was such a crybaby."

Narrowing my eyes, I felt my body tense to pounce, but she scrambled backward, laughter coming out in short puffs of air. Before I flipped around to my knees to take off after her, I froze. What was I doing?

Every second of this was on film. And if I laid my hands on her now, I'd be lost. Molly saw the change of mood on my face, and those bright blue eyes softened in understanding. How could she read me as well as she did? It made no sense.

"That was pretty good for your first lesson," she said quietly.

Standing, I stretched my arms over head, then held out my

hand for her. She slid her palm against mine, and I pulled her up easily.

Her fingers didn't drop right away, and the impulse to tug her closer was almost overwhelming. I stepped back, and our hands dropped.

"Thanks for coming over to show me." I looked around. "And to see the house. I suppose we should clear out soon anyway."

She nodded and leaned down to roll up the yoga mat.

Marty flipped off both cameras and groaned like he'd just done the video with us. "That was great, guys. Rick will love it."

The way Molly fidgeted as she stood with the yoga mat and the way she didn't make eye contact with Marty meant she must have felt the same way I did after talking to my grandma. It was disconcerting to forget that he was there, but I still found myself doing it more and more.

"We didn't do that for show, Marty."

In surprise, I glanced over at the defensive tone in her voice.

Marty was giving her the same look. "I know. Just saying that it was a good segment. We needed some more stuff like this after a week of filming practice and Noah glaring at his iPad screen while he watched film."

That brought a smile to her face.

"I don't glare at my screen," I argued.

He pointed at Molly's iPad. "May I?"

"Go right ahead."

Marty lifted it and did this weird squint face frown that had Molly laughing out loud.

"I do not look like that," I said.

"Trust me, buddy, you do." He grinned, handing the iPad back to Molly.

As he packed up, the two of them chatting easily, trying to figure out if it made sense for Marty to drive her back home or if it was out of his way, I had a strangely settled feeling.

Was it sad that these two people—the guy who was being paid to film my life and the woman I should want nothing to do with—were now my closest friends?

They didn't look at me and see The Machine. I was Noah to them, and it had been a long time since that had been the truth for anyone.

Molly said goodbye to Marty as he hefted his camera bag over his shoulder, and I walked through the family room and dining area to make sure all the lights were turned off. Neither one of us spoke as she watched me tidy up and return the rolled yoga mats behind the loveseat where I found them.

I straightened and faced her, very aware of the quiet house, and how it was the first time we'd truly been alone since our moment in the elevator. No one would be coming up the stairs. Down the hallway. Through the front door.

It was just me and her.

Judging by the deepening pink on her cheeks, she was just as aware of it.

Her breath left her in a rush, shakier and louder than when we'd done the video, and I saw her punch some buttons on her screen almost frantically.

"Can I take you home?" I asked.

She shook her head, and a few stray chunks of hair that had slipped from her updo fell around her neck and shoulders. "I just called my Uber. It'll be here in about five minutes." Molly looked past me and stared at the lake again. "I think that makes more sense."

"It probably does," I agreed.

Me taking her home was a slippery slope. We were already going to spend the weekend together at my grandma's, and that was complicated enough. In one evening, I felt like Molly took a wrecking ball and knocked down every wall that had been constructed around my life, and she'd done it unknowingly.

Offering to take her home went in direct opposition to everything I'd promised myself after I left Miami, but I couldn't even care because it was her.

I realized with stunning and simple clarity that I trusted her. This was not someone who'd betray me. Who'd use me or derail me or undermine my career.

And I wanted her.

Those two things, true and real and important, were why I moved toward her.

Admitting that I wanted her was so much easier than I thought it would be. All week, I'd used an array of excuses as to why I fixated on her so much and why her distance from me was so bothersome.

All those excuses fell away quietly, easily. My brain clicked into place, another decision made, one that I knew instinctually was right.

I wanted Molly Ward.

For the first time in years, football wasn't the first thing on my brain. It wasn't even the second. Not at that moment. At that moment, the only thing I cared about was knowing more about this woman. About how she felt in my arms and what her skin smelled like underneath the ears that stuck out from her delicate face.

Molly, oblivious to the seamless thoughts in my head, had turned toward the door.

I snagged her wrist before she could.

"Wait," I said, turning her back to me.

Her face was full of pleading and yearning, the kind that I felt hammering behind my chest in the empty spot under my ribs.

"Noah, I—" Her voice came to a halt when my hand slid up the smooth length of her arm. Her eyes fluttered shut. I cupped her face in both hands and only let out a breath when her hands came to rest on my waist, her fingers curling into the material of my shirt. With that arching of her fingers, she anchored me in place. I'd only leave if she let go. I'd stop the second she asked me to. But as long as she held me to her that way, she was mine.

My mouth was on hers, my face tilting to seek out the taste that had eluded me earlier, the one that made my mouth water and my skin tighten over my frame. Our lips sipped, tasted, and tried, hers were soft and warm and delicious, and I bit gently on the full curve of the middle of her lower lip. Then tugged.

Her sharp inhale punched me squarely in the solar plexus, and my arm tightened around her small frame, clutching her to me desperately. It was the first moment that I realized the magnitude of allowing myself this kiss with her.

For years, I'd chained up the sexual desire for anyone.

Until right now, with her. My hands shook as I touched her because suddenly, it wasn't enough.

Faster, more, harder, my brain screamed, and my whole body shook from the effort it took not to follow that instinct.

I wouldn't feel this with any woman, not after so long of not having the press of soft breasts to my chest, the natural way her hips cradled me, the rocking of her pelvis against me. It was Molly.

We kissed and kissed and kissed before she pushed up on tiptoes to get closer to me, and it wasn't enough.

My hands trailed down the supple line of her back and gripped her bottom so I could boost her up in my arms. Her legs twined around my waist, and with one stride of my legs, her back was against the door.

We groaned in unison, the sounds lost in each other's mouths as our movements got messier and the kiss got deeper. My tongue pushed harder against hers when she caught the tip of it with the sharp edges of her teeth.

Her hands dug into my hair and pulled me harder against her. I couldn't get any closer to her, not if I tried. I rocked, pleasure gathering in a ball of flames at the base of my spine, so I gritted my teeth and pulled away from her.

She whimpered when I did, and I smiled against her mouth.

"Patience," I murmured between artless kisses. Whatever I lacked in finesse, I made up for in sheer fervor because she tasted so good and felt so good, and my hands were up underneath her shirt in the next heartbeat.

I wanted to feel the thrashing of her heart under my palm, I wanted to rip her leggings off and know how much she wanted me, I wanted to mark her chest with my mouth and stay with her like this for the rest of the night.

Molly froze completely, her hands pushing against my chest.

I did the same, my mouth hovering over hers as I took in the wide eyes and flushed cheeks and mussed hair.

"Noah," she whispered. "We shouldn't do this."

Four years of playing professional football and four years of college before that honed my discipline into something that was iron sharp, and I had to use every single ounce of that discipline to let her feet drop carefully to the ground.

"Right," I said.

"We can't, Noah," she said apologetically. "You know we can't."

I nodded, swiping a hand over my mouth. I wasn't sure I knew that, but I'd respect her all the same.

"We-we have a whole weekend together after this. It's important," she continued. I wasn't sure who she was trying to convince —me or herself. "And Beatrice would kill me."

Like I cared what her boss thought. But Molly did. I pinched my eyes shut and leaned forward to press a kiss to her forehead.

"It's okay," I told her. "It's okay."

For a moment, she leaned into me, letting her face fall into the center of my chest as I wrapped an arm around her back.

"It'll be all right."

Molly nodded shakily.

"It'll be all right," I repeated.

I just broke a woman-free streak that had lasted years, and I was about to spend the weekend with her. And a camera crew. And my grandma. And I was supposed to keep my hands off her now that I knew exactly how she tasted and the noises she made when she sucked my tongue into her mouth.

No problem.

CHAPTER EIGHTEEN

MOLLY

A FEW THINGS became clear to me over the next eighteen hours since I walked on Jell-O legs out of Noah's new house.

1- Noah could still kiss

2- I was an idiot

3- I needed an intervention because I tossed and turned the entire night afterward, replaying that kiss like he'd just served me the best sex of my entire life

Number two was the one I needed to focus on the most. It should have told me everything I needed to know that it wasn't in the number one spot in the first place. Rick and Marty wanted to do some editing before we left for South Dakota, and Noah had a big practice before the weekend leading into preseason, so we didn't film the next day.

Work provided a meager distraction, but not enough to quiet my screaming thoughts. The whole day at my desk, my thoughts had done this basic dance.

Did kissing count as fraternization?

No.

Yes.

Maybe, because there was a lot of tongue action.

But probably not.

Fraternization was probably just P into V. Actual intercourse, like the way they'd taught us in middle school. Nothing else counted.

Would Beatrice demote me for making out with him?

No.

Yes.

Maybe, because holy shit there was a *lot* of tongue action.

I called Isabel as soon as I left the parking lot because I knew she was working, and I knew there were no classes scheduled that night.

"Can I come do a training session with you?"

On the other end of the phone, I heard the thumping bass and the mic'd up voice of one of their instructors running a class. She must have closed the door to her office because it quieted considerably. "Sure. I need to be here anyway because Amy is doing a one on one with a client, and we always make sure neither of us is alone when it's someone new."

"Good," I exhaled gustily. "I need you to beat the thoughts in my head into submission."

"I'll see what I can do," she promised.

By the time I got there, Claire and Lia decided to join too, and I grinned on my way into the building. The mirrored doors swung open, and I saw my sisters stretching in the empty square that was surrounded by steel frames and swinging chains holding heavy one-hundred-and-fifty-pound bags.

Isabel's hands were wrapped in black, her hair slicked back into a sleek ponytail at the top of her head, and her tall, lean body was covered in black leggings and a black halter top.

I'm nicer after kickboxing her shirt proclaimed in big block letters.

145

It was hard for me to recognize sometimes exactly how my little sister turned into such a badass.

Amy, the gym's owner, was in the back corner by the racks of free weights, medicine balls, and jump ropes. She was stretching too, and she waved at me as I joined my sisters.

"Will her client care that we're here?" I asked Iz as I plopped on the ground and started tying my shoes.

She shrugged. "I can't see why. He's still getting a personal training session."

"You don't think Amy could handle some new guy alone?" Lia snorted. "Amy could beat the shit out of Logan on a bad day."

We all laughed.

Isabel smiled. "She could, but that's not the point. It's a safety thing. When we don't know the client, male or female, we make sure we're not here alone with them."

Claire laid back on the rubber mat floor. "I'll just relax here. Someone wake me when you're done."

Lia nudged her as she stood. "Slacker. Come on, we're here for Molly."

When Lia glared at me, I held up my hands. "Don't blame me. I didn't invite you."

"You didn't have to," Claire said. "In lieu of a golden retriever, younger sisters must act in an emotional support assistance capacity."

"We really do need a dog," Isabel said. "Because you two complain too much."

Lia kicked her leg out, which Iz dodged nimbly. Then she shoved her hands into the focus mitts that I'd end up punching the shit out of and slapped them together sharply. It sounded like a gunshot in the gym, and Claire jumped. Isabel chuckled. "Come on, lazy ass, get up. We're not here to waste my time; we're here to work. Let's go. Two laps around the gym, then back to your bags and give me a side lunge into a side kick. Each side five times. If that heel isn't higher than your toes when you kick the bag, you owe me a burpee."

We all groaned but did as she asked.

Thirty minutes later, my mind was clearer, my shirt was soaked in sweat, and my arms and legs were burning.

I loved how yoga improved my flexibility and core, but sometimes, I just wanted to beat the shit out of the bag.

Trying to decide what to do after making out with Noah and dry humping him against his front door was one of those times.

I flopped onto the ground when I was supposed to be doing push-ups and watched with an exhausted grin as Isabel yelled at Lia to move faster.

"I'm done," gasped Claire as she joined me. "Next time you need emotional support, please go to a dog shelter or something, okay?"

That had me laughing, though it quickly dissolved to a groan when that hurt too.

"Why are we supporting you again?" she asked.

I gave a quick side-eye at her phrasing. "Just ... it's a big weekend. I needed to clear my head before I'm stuck in a cabin with Noah."

Stuck in a cabin. Imagining his hands. And lips. And oh, my stars, how big and strong and hard and ... big ... and hard ... he was.

Thank goodness my face was already bright red from the beatdown Iz was giving us.

Isabel came over and frowned at the two of us. "You're not done."

"Yes," I said. "We are."

"I need to be able to walk tomorrow, Iz."

She blew a raspberry with her lips. "Walking easily is overrated. How else will you appreciate the body you have if you don't feel every single ... muscle." Her eyes went laser sharp, and her voice trailed off as someone walked into the gym. I sat up and turned, and Claire did the same. "Holy shit," Isabel whispered.

Holy shit was right.

New client was tall and dark and handsome. New client had muscles on muscles, and a dark, forbidding expression that sent a shiver down my spine.

"I know him," Lia murmured as she came to stand next to Isabel. "He was an MMA fighter. Finn loved watching his fights."

Just before he approached Amy, he glanced at us, eyes touching briefly on Isabel, before he dismissed us completely.

I heard Iz suck in a breath. "Yeah, he was. His wife just died, so he retired to take care of his daughter."

That cast a quiet hush over the four of us.

"You okay, Iz?" Claire asked.

She blinked. "Yeah. We're done, right?"

I exchanged glances with Lia and Claire, who gave me identical shrugs. "Yeah, we're done. I should go home to shower and pack anyway."

"When do you leave?" Lia asked.

"I have about three hours. But we're taking a private plane, so I can get to the air strip right before we take off and be fine."

"Baller." Claire grinned.

"Ha. Yeah, I am."

Isabel started picking up around the bags, and her cheeks were bright pink.

"What's her deal?" I whispered.

Lia shrugged again. "Who knows. I'd ask but ..." Her voice trailed off, and we all knew why.

We could ask, but unless Isabel wanted to share, she wouldn't tell us shit.

"Maybe she was a fan of his," Claire said, pointing at Mr. Tall, Dark and Scary-looking.

"Maybe." I sighed. "Okay. Tell me that I'll be fine this weekend."

"You will," Claire said. "No matter what happens, you'll be fine."

Lia grabbed my shoulders, serious face in place. "You can do this. He's just a big dumb football player who won't remember you when he's gone from Washington, which will probably be soon since players are traded all the time."

Claire's mouth fell open. "You are terrible at this," she told her twin.

My mouth screwed up like I had sucked on a lemon. "Thanks."

I gave all three of them hugs and made my way home to shower and pack.

As I did those things, Lia's poorly delivered words banged around my head like it was an empty crate.

She was wrong. He wasn't dumb, and he wouldn't forget me.

But she was also right. He could leave at any time, given his abrupt exit from Miami.

That still wasn't justification enough to put my job on the line. But it did add a certain edge to my thoughts, an urgency that I couldn't deny as I packed my suitcase.

My history with Noah had started off with a poorly thought out decision, one that was made without heeding any possible consequences, and ended—for me, at least—in humiliation and tears.

We were both older and wiser, but I couldn't say we were any less stubborn, not in the ways that counted.

Noah was decisive and self-controlled. His journey to making a choice, no matter how big or small, was quick and instinctual. It was why he was a great player. All the great players had that in common. If you took the time to pause and second-guess, someone else would move past you.

In his new house, he'd decided that kissing me was his next course of action, and he never wavered. Kissing him back had felt amazing, but there'd still been a niggling sensation in the back of my head, a voice that I hadn't quite been able to mute.

I zipped up the side of my suitcase slowly.

Could I walk into this weekend and not allow that voice to hold me back?

What I wouldn't do was be a typical football groupie, begging for whatever scraps he'd allow me.

And I wouldn't ask him to sacrifice something he wasn't ready to sacrifice. I respected his drive more than that. Just as he respected me enough to stop when I'd asked.

The choice was mine.

I could take this weekend and own the opportunity for what it was. A chance, even if it was my only one, to finally bring this tangled history with Noah full circle. I could clearly, and deliberately, take a step into action and understand the weight of what I was doing, if he got on that plane and wasn't shutting me out completely.

Noah's career, my career, was so much bigger than anything we were working on that weekend. I wasn't even sure that this Amazon documentary would make a highlight reel by the time he retired. Which also meant my time with him was short within the context of his career.

A window to finish something we'd started a very, very long time ago.

The comparison had me smiling because a window is what got us into this mess in the first place. His behavior back then had guided my own, and as I finished up, I knew I'd treat this weekend no differently.

I arrived at the airfield in jeans, a black zip-up hoodie, and my black Chucks in place on my feet. He smiled at them when I approached.

"I'll take your suitcase," he said and lifted it up for me so I could ascend the narrow steps uninhibited.

"Thanks," I told him. He let me go up into the plushy decorated plane first. A smiling flight attendant stopped and asked if I wanted a glass of champagne. "Oh, just water, please."

No more wine for me, not in the presence of cameras and Noah Griffin. Marty and Rick had their heads bent toward a laptop screen, and I waved at them before taking a seat in the wide captain's chair covered in soft, buttery leather.

"You ready for this?" Noah asked as he sat opposite of me. His eyes were warmer today than I'd ever seen them, and I liked the way he studied my face, like he could absorb the details on my skin without so much as a single touch.

"I'm excited to meet your grandma," I told him.

The way he smiled melted something inside me. If his behavior was going to be my guide, then I was slowly, slowly sinking into an ooey gooey puddle of *I want him.*

"My grandma is the best woman I've ever known." He shook his head. "Just to warn you, she'll probably call me embarrassing nicknames and fuss over me."

I smiled. "There's nothing wrong with that."

"No," he admitted. "There's not."

He glanced over at Rick and Marty and shook his head again. "I should probably interrupt them to say thank you."

"For what?"

When he glanced back at me, his eyes glowed. This was Noah happy. That was why he looked so unfamiliar. It wasn't that driven, hyper-focused man who kept blinders on to everything outside of the game. It wasn't the man who frowned at the screen when he watched film. Because no matter what he said to Marty, he did do that. Or who worked out simply because he was bored at night.

This was Noah. The version of him I'd never met before.

I wanted to tie him to my bed and mount him like a cowboy on a bucking bronco.

"For picking me," he said. "If nothing else, I'm glad I did this documentary thing because it's getting me out to visit her again. It's been too long." Noah shrugged. "I miss her, you know?"

If this was my first glimpse of a carefree Noah, and we were on our way to his happy place, free of the distractions of work, I was completely and utterly screwed, and we hadn't even taken off yet.

CHAPTER NINETEEN

NOAH

As WE LEFT the small airstrip about forty minutes away from my grandma's, it was hard for me to make polite conversation with the three people riding with me in the car. Molly had taken care of all the logistics of getting us from Seattle to Custer, South Dakota, and the stoic driver of the large black Escalade was about as talkative as I was.

Our reasons were different, no doubt, but nobody riding in the vehicle questioned either of us.

As he maneuvered the car along the winding roads toward my grandma's, I stared out the window and felt a foreign pang of melancholy. And guilt.

For the second time in the past week, I couldn't shake the feeling that I'd made a sharp turn in the wrong direction of my life. It was unsettling, and I didn't like to feel unsettled in this place that I loved so much.

I wanted to plant my feet and know that where I was heading was right, was correct, because that was how I did things.

If you weren't sure about what you were doing, then you

probably made the wrong decision. And in my eyes, making the wrong decision was the same as failing.

But the problem with that was too much had caused me to second-guess things lately, stemming back to offering my team-mate's drunk wife a ride home because it was the right thing to do. That was minor even though it had major consequences.

What wasn't so minor was kissing Molly. Even worse was that I was struggling to feel any sort of guilt or regret over it, except for the fact that I didn't know how *she* felt about it.

That was what made its impact so much bigger than the impetus to my presence in Washington. One kiss with her wasn't just one kiss. It was more than knowing how she tasted or how soft her lips were. It was a simple motion that had not so simple consequences because it could undermine everything I'd cultivated.

I woke up earlier that day in Seattle, and the first thought that crossed my mind wasn't about workouts or practice or preseason. I found myself wondering if Molly drank coffee. If she was a morning person or a night owl. If she slept sprawled across her bed like I did mine. And how tonight, I'd go to bed under the same roof as her.

That was why that kiss mattered.

But as difficult as it might be, I had to put it out of my head. At least for the day.

The green hills and black tree-covered mountains rose every-where, a totally different kind of landscape from Seattle, but to me, it was just as beautiful. And I hadn't been here in years.

Large log cabins set back from the road on generous plots of land gave me something to focus on as the view blurred from the speed of our car. The driver's GPS told him when to turn, which was good, because enough had changed in the three years since I'd visited that I would have missed the turn had I been driving.

I tilted my head when I saw the green metal roof come into

view. She was at the base of the foothills, so the gentle curls of smoke coming out of the chimney had a lush green backdrop as the mountains pushed their edges into the skyline.

Molly said something under her breath to Marty, and he laughed, cutting into the thoughtful silence I'd immersed myself in.

"How long has your grandma lived out here?" Rick asked.

My eyes closed briefly because I knew I'd need to shift my headspace. This wasn't just a grandson paying a long overdue visit to his grandma. This was intentional, to show a side of me that no one believed existed. Thinking about the public intruding on this moment, when I already felt guilty enough about not coming to see her more, I had to keep reminding myself why this was a good idea. Why I'd agreed.

"Her whole life," I answered. "But this house specifically, for the last four years."

"When you started in the league." His statement left no room for subtlety.

I glanced back at him. "If you're going to ask something, Rick, just ask it."

He grinned.

Molly's eyes were covered in blue-mirrored sunglasses, and I wanted to rip them off her face because I couldn't tell what she was thinking or if she was even listening in the first place. Instantly, I flipped my attention back to Rick as we approached my grandma's because I shouldn't even be worried about whether she was paying attention.

"It's a beautiful place," he mused when the driveway appeared, as did the sprawling cabin with a massive wraparound porch. Two black and white horses grazed in the fenced-in area north of the house. Who knew where the goats were, probably in the barn that was partially obscured by the house. "Big, just for one woman."

"She didn't want to feel cramped," I said, the edges of a smile starting on my mouth as the car pulled over the gravel driveway. The porch was covered with all shapes and sizes of potted flowers and plants. Along the east edge of the roof, a line of wind chimes swayed in the breeze.

The driver parked the car, and as I unfolded out of my seat, I heard the screen door bang shut.

"That you, half-pint?" she called.

Every head swiveled in my direction.

"I'm so glad I got that on camera," Marty whispered, and Molly dissolved into giggles.

When I cleared the front of the car, my grandma stood like a sentinel at the top step of the deck. Her curly gray hair was shoved down around her face by a straw gardening hat, and the frayed red ribbon told me it was the same one she'd always had. At the sight of me, her face broke open into a huge smile. I felt that smile clear down to my toes, in a way I probably should have been embarrassed to admit.

I met her halfway when she started down the steps, and her delighted laughter when I wrapped her in a bear hug and lifted her tiny frame off the ground made me feel like the Grinch on Christmas Day.

Two, three, four uneven chugs of my heart, and it quadrupled in size.

"Goodness, you're big," she said, tightening her arms around my neck. "Now put me down. I'll break a hip if you drop me from this height."

Chuckling, I set her down, making sure her feet were firmly planted before I stepped back from the inevitable grandmotherly inspection. Her eyes narrowed thoughtfully.

"They're certainly feeding you enough, aren't they?"

"Yes, ma'am."

She nodded, and her eyes were suspiciously bright as she

gently patted my chest. "Good, good. Now, who are your friends?"

Rick and Marty shook her hand, and when Molly appeared from behind the car with her small silver suitcase, I saw my grandmother study her from head to toe. Her gaze never darted back to me, but it might as well have.

It shouldn't have felt so important to introduce Molly to this woman, the one who meant the most to me in the world, but it did.

"I'm a hugger," Molly said with a wide smile, "if that's okay with you."

My grandma laughed and opened her arms. "So am I, sweetheart."

As they embraced, I felt my newly enlarged heart do something strange, and without realizing what I was doing, my hand rubbed at my chest where it was drumming a little faster than necessary.

"Come on in, come on in," Grandma said, waving us up to the house. "I have supper ready to go. Figured you'd be hungry."

"Starved," I said. "What'd you make?"

She winked at me. "Grandpa's roast and my mashed potatoes."

My blissed-out groan made everyone laugh again.

The cabin hadn't changed at all since the last time I'd been there, and I took comfort in that. The couches and chairs, all faded brown leather, still had the same blankets folded along the back. The fieldstone fireplace and long oak mantle held the same photos in shiny silver frames of varying shapes and sizes. That was my grandma for you. If she found one thing she liked, whether it be pots of flowers, crocheted blankets, or picture frames, she'd fill her space to the brim with every variation.

The floor-to-ceiling windows at the far end of the house

ushered in a hushed silence as our guests caught the view of the sun setting over the foothills.

"It's so beautiful here," Molly said. "I can see why you love it."

I glanced at her because I couldn't tell whether she was speaking to me or Grandma. My grandma was the one who responded, and that was probably for the best. "I'll stay here till I die, that's for sure. Can't imagine watching the sunset anywhere other than right here, even when there's snow as high as my head and the wind cuts right through your bones." She patted my arm. "That's what I told Noah when I saw it for the first time. This is the one, and if you don't mind, bury me in the back by the pine tree grove. Keep your funeral costs down."

I shook my head when Molly laughed.

"Where should we bring our stuff, Miss Griffin?" Rick asked.

Grandma showed Rick and Marty to the upstairs guest rooms, leaving Molly and me alone in the family room.

"You bought this for her, didn't you?"

My exhale was slow and steady. There was no real point in denying it, and at least I could be glad she didn't ask when Marty was around with his camera. When I turned my head toward her, though, she wasn't looking at me. She was studying the photos on the mantle, smiling at the varying phases of me in my youth.

"Yeah, I did." I approached the fireplace and reached past Molly, the inside of my arm brushing her shoulder as I plucked one of the smaller frames. It was of my grandpa and me, and I couldn't have been more than six. It was a few years before he died, and he'd just taken me fishing. It was the first time I caught a smallmouth bass on my own. It was tiny, and I barely kept it on the line long enough for my grandma to snap a picture, but my grandpa smiled so proudly, you would've thought I'd snagged a six-foot marlin.

"When I got my signing bonus from Miami, I came straight here and paid cash for it. My whole life, I'd heard my grandma say she wanted a little plot of land at the base of the foothills, with two horses and some goats to keep her company. The house didn't need to be fancy, just big enough to hold her family when they came to visit." My voice got rough by the time I'd forced the last sentence out.

When Molly turned, her big blue eyes full of so much understanding, I had to look away.

How did she know me so well already, that she could instantly see my guilt in what I'd just admitted?

I was setting the photo back when her cool, firm fingers wrapped around mine and wove our hands together.

"You're here now, Noah," she said quietly. "That's what matters."

My jaw clenched tight, and I found myself nodding. Briefly, I allowed my fingers to tighten around hers, an anchor I hadn't asked for nor had I expected, but still had a hard time letting go of.

As I extricated my fingers from hers, the brush of skin on skin had me breathing unevenly.

Ridiculous.

That was the problem with choosing a celibate life, wasn't it? One small touch of her skin on mine had me desperately trying to rein in every caveman impulse galloping through my flimsy veins.

Carrying her suitcase for her, I showed her the main guest room across from the family room but was smart enough not to follow her in. My eyes landed briefly on the king-size bed as she laid her suitcase on it.

And still, I closed the door to give her some privacy as I brought my own things downstairs to the bed my grandma had assigned me for the next two nights. It wasn't as big, and it wasn't as comfortable, but I couldn't help but feel a small sense of relief that there was an entire flight of stairs separating me from Molly.

By the time I came back upstairs, they were all sitting down at the long wood table as my grandma served up fragrant spoonsful of tender roast and gravy. It was the kind of home-cooked meal that I never got unless I took the time to make it myself.

Upon her firm instruction, Marty had set the camera aside for our first meal. *No gadgets allowed at the table,* she'd said. The way Rick smiled, I knew they'd already planned to give us this one meal of un-filmed interaction, but at least they were kind enough to let her believe it was her idea.

The evening sped by quickly, despite how late the sun started setting in the summers. The five of us talked and laughed easily, my grandma telling stories of what I was like as a child when I visited in the summers and over spring break with my dad.

Rick asked questions, and even though I knew he was doing it for the purpose of the documentary, whether the camera was rolling or not, nothing felt forced or uncomfortable.

The whole meal, and the cleanup afterward, when Molly insisted my grandma go relax on the couch so the men could pull their weight in the kitchen, had a warm, steady feel to it. Like we were sitting on a docked boat on a calm lake.

There was a gentle ebb and flow to the conversation, instilling such a drowsy sense of comfort that I felt weigh my eyelids down once the kitchen was cleaned and I was able to sprawl out in the recliner that used to belong to my grandpa.

"Who's getting up with me in the morning to feed the horses?" Grandma asked.

Molly grinned. "I will!"

My gaze sharpened on her face, something I'd hardly allowed myself to do all night. "Seriously?"

"I love horses," she said earnestly.

"Do you love getting up at sunrise?"

She grimaced, and we all laughed.

Grandma got up out of her chair and kissed Molly on the top

of the head. "If you're up, you're up, but I'll forgive you if you decide to sleep in, sweetheart."

The easy show of affection surprised me, and it clearly surprised Molly because her cheeks pinked as she glanced up at my grandma. "Okay."

I got up and wrapped Grandma in another hug. "G'night."

She patted my chest again, probably because she was too short to reach my face. "G'night, half-pint."

Marty snickered under his breath, and I quelled it with a glare.

Rick made his way to bed too, leaving me, Molly, and Marty.

Molly got up and walked to the windows, where my first telescope was still sitting. She glanced at me over her shoulder. "Yours?"

Nodding, I joined her even though I kept a safe distance between us as much due to Marty's presence as my own sanity. *Mainly my sanity*, I thought as I caught a whiff of her fruity shampoo. I wanted to bury my entire face in that head of hair.

"She bought it for me when I was twelve." I leaned over and lined up with the eyepiece, then pulled back to adjust a few knobs on the side to fix the focus. More than likely, it had stayed untouched for years. When I looked through again, I hummed. "Come look. You can see Virgo."

"Really?" She hurried over and leaned down. "How do I know what I'm looking at?"

"The brightest star, Spica, is the starting point along the bottom. Then you follow one more star up to Parrima. That's another easy one to spot."

She hummed. "They all look pretty sparkly to me."

I laughed. "I'll show you what it looks like on a diagram. Once you know the shapes, it's easier to pick them out."

Molly straightened and gave me a curious look. A silky chunk of her hair slid out of her ponytail and curled down her neck.

Before I knew what I was doing, I picked it up with two fingers and rubbed the edge of my thumb against her hair. Her mouth opened with a jagged inhale, and her eyes darted past me to Marty.

Right.

I dropped her hair and stepped back.

"I'm pretty tired," she said carefully. "And I really do want to help your grandma tomorrow with the horses."

My hands curled into fists to keep from reaching for her. My mind wouldn't even allow itself to process what I'd do once I did. As she said her good nights, I turned back to the window.

In one short evening, it felt like this place had ruthlessly dismantled every mental barrier I kept tied tight to myself.

"Feels like we're in another universe, doesn't it?" Marty asked. He was clueless as to what was going through my head.

"It does," I agreed. "I needed this more than I realized."

He got off the couch and patted me on the back. "Good."

Marty bid me a good night as well, and I stood by the window, watching the stars get brighter and brighter as everything around it continued to darken.

Except I wasn't trying to place the stars or follow lines or find the patterns that I knew as well as the lines on my hand. All I could do was think about Molly in the room just to my left.

The water turned on in the bathroom, and I pinched my eyes shut as I imagined her washing her face, then changing into whatever it was that she slept in before she slid between the sheets of the bed that was normally mine.

Nothing here felt normal.

And most disconcerting of all was how much I wasn't bothered by it.

There was no checklist and no schedule.

No rules to follow, other than the self-imposed ones. That

lack of structure should have made me feel uncomfortable. But instead of discomfort coursing through me, it was restlessness.

An edgy sort of energy that had no outlet. It was the way I felt before a game. On those days, I could strap on pads and my jersey, tape my fingers and tie my cleats, knowing I'd work myself to exhaustion on the turf. I'd tackle and run and hit and find a safe place to put everything that I kept locked down so tight during the week. And those sharp bursts, like a gunshot going off, kept me calm and steady once I was done.

But this ... this was torture.

At least thirty minutes had passed before I heard the slow turn of the doorknob.

My heart took off, and I held myself as still as possible. Maybe she wouldn't see me standing in the dark, given only one small lamp was still left on over the stove.

I tried not to breathe, tried to meditate or calm my energy or whatever that one yoga video tried to teach me to do to relax. Because if Molly saw me, she'd speak to me. If she spoke to me, if I spoke to her, I might touch her.

And if I touched her, I'd lose the tiny, fragile grasp I had on my control.

When had she frayed it down to nothing?

I was around for all of it, every interaction, and I'd hardly noticed her severing each individual strand.

Her soft footsteps padded toward the kitchen when she inhaled sharply.

"Noah," she whispered. "I didn't see you at first."

I dropped my chin to my chest and breathed deeply. "Sorry."

Go back to bed, go back to bed, go back to bed, I wished feverishly in my head. I couldn't turn. I couldn't look at her. Not even for a second.

My whole body tensed as the sound of her bare feet came closer.

"I-I couldn't fall asleep."

What strange intimacy was created in moments like that one. Something about a dark room and whispers. Knowing that no one could see us, knowing that she had already stripped herself of the confines of the day, ratcheted that tension coursing through my body higher and higher, something bright and fierce.

My eyes were pinched closed so tightly as she stopped next to me that I saw bursts of white behind my eyelids.

I probably looked ridiculous.

"Don't you want to know why?" she whispered. "I could hardly sit still wondering if you were out here, if you were alone."

"Molly," I begged. I didn't even know what I was begging for.

Touch me.

Don't touch me.

Give me permission to do this thing.

Lock the door on your bedroom so I'm not tempted to splinter it to shreds for getting between us.

"Look at me," she begged right back.

Slowly, I peeled open my eyelids and looked down at her. Her face was bare, and her hair, that glorious hair that I loved so much, was in messy tumbles around her bare shoulders. Bare, save for thin straps of a white tank top. Her legs, bare, save for impossibly small white and pink shorts.

She wasn't wearing a bra.

My lungs, they'd stopped working properly at the sight of her.

"Doesn't it feel like ..." She stopped to lick her lips. "Like this is inevitable?"

"What?" I rasped. She was so beautiful in the dim light that my vocal cords stopped working too. I wanted to devour her.

"You and me," she answered quietly. Her eyes were huge in her face, and they searched mine so deeply that I felt it in the slow turn of my heart. "Even if it's just ... here."

I blinked. "Here?"

She laughed quietly. "This may be the dumbest idea I've ever had, but I was tossing and turning in that bed, trying to figure out a way to make this make sense in my head. You and me, thrown together like this. And now, in this place that's so far removed from every complication. I can't stop thinking about that kiss, Noah, and whenever you look at me, I know you can't either. I don't see how it's possible to leave it at just that. Not with how good it was."

My hand lifted slowly, and I slid it against the silky skin of her neck, allowing my fingers to tangle in her hair as I cupped the back of her slender neck.

"What are you saying, Molly?"

Molly lifted her chin and hit me with the full force of her gaze, the full force of whatever decision she'd come to before she walked out the door.

"I want you to come back to that bedroom with me. I want us to have these two nights, to get whatever this thing is between us out of our system. I feel like ... like we pushed a wheel into motion ten years ago, and we need this to make it stop."

If I'd grabbed the frayed edge of a live wire, it wouldn't have had as powerful of an effect on me. My whole body shuddered from the force of it.

"These two nights," I repeated.

She nodded slowly. "What happens in South Dakota, stays in South Dakota."

That she could make me smile at that moment should have terrified me, but it didn't. It felt right. And as she'd said, it felt inevitable.

Molly tilted her chin, inviting my kiss, but I shook my head. My thumb pulled at the generous curve of her lower lip.

"If I kiss you here, I won't be able to stop long enough to move to that bed, and if I get an entire night with you ..." I dropped my forehead against hers and took a shuddering breath. "Then I need room to work."

Molly whimpered.

It was the last shred unraveling, the final cord splitting with an audible snap.

Slowly, leisurely, with a measure of control that I did not know I had left, I slid my hand down her shoulder, her arm, her wrist, and wove my fingers through hers. Then I led her back to the bedroom.

CHAPTER TWENTY

MOLLY

EVERYTHING TOOK ON A FILMY, hazy, decadent quality when the door clicked shut behind me. Like someone changed the filter through which I saw everything, and it shut my brain off in the same motion. My hands didn't even seem like they belonged to me when I pivoted and pushed Noah up against the door.

His expression was forbidding at the move, and I shivered.

"Take your shirt off," I ordered.

He jerked up his chin. "You first."

There was a moment when we both froze like that, unwilling to give up control to the other person. Then we collided. His mouth took mine, rough and hard and deep. His hands boosted underneath my ass, and I wrapped my legs around his waist.

Lips and teeth and tongue, slick and slippery and messy. I'd been waiting for this, I thought, since the moment I saw him in the elevator. Waiting for the strength of his body against mine, overpowering me in the best possible way.

He tasted minty and cool, and his tongue twined around mine as his fingers dug into my flesh until it hurt.

This wasn't sweet, and it wasn't slow as I tugged at his shirt.

I wanted my hands on him, now that I'd given myself permission for this. Nothing short of that would suffice until we were both gasping and spent and sweaty in the middle of that exceptionally large bed. He tossed me back onto it, and I bounced with a laugh.

But my laughter died at the look on his face.

This was a man pushed to the edge of his sanity. By me.

I'd done this to him, and it sent such a wet, hot rush of power through my body. Something overtook me at that realization, and I sat up on my knees as he ripped his shirt off and threw it onto the floor. My shirt went with it, and his eyes darkened even further as I laid back and started pushing my shorts down in slow, rolling movements of my hips.

"Stop," he growled.

My hands froze. One finger played idly with the elastic edge.

Noah shoved his shorts down, his boxer briefs with them, and I licked my lips at the sight of his glorious, glorious nakedness.

This was my best idea *ever*.

I didn't even realize I'd said it out loud until a wide, bright smile broke out over his face. That brief pause from the harsh, dangerous version of Noah, the one who looked ready to eat me whole, had a whole different effect on me. One that was just as potent.

"It's been a while for me," he admitted, sliding his hands up my legs as they fell open for him.

"Has it?" I gasped, tilting my chin up when he caught the edge of my shorts with tightly bound fingers and tightly bound strength. "F-for me too."

"That's why this first time will be fast and hard." He leaned over me and took my mouth again in a kiss so dirty, I started squirming for relief.

"Yes, please," I begged.

He smiled again. My shorts were whisked off, and he leaned back to stare at me unabashedly.

"Next time," he said in a rough, uneven voice. His hands gripped my hips and pressed me into the bed. "Next time, I'll take my time." He cupped one breast and rolled his thumb. "Here." His hand slid between my legs. "Here." He bit my bottom lip. "Everywhere."

"Noah," I groaned.

He prowled between my legs, and as I registered the feel of each slab of muscle on his chest and stomach pressing against my soft skin, my back arched so I could feel more, more, more.

There was a pause before he delivered on his promise of fast and hard, both adjectives equally as exciting to me, and at that moment, his eyes held mine.

This matters.

It was hard to remember our promise of two nights, of this protected space to exorcise whatever had been brewing between us when we shared a look, a moment, a breath so heavy and poignant. But then he shifted forward, forward, forward in a long, slow slide, and with a long, slow groan from deep within his massive chest, I forgot everything but him.

He didn't stop until he was tight against me, and his arms curled under my shoulders and tucked me firmly against his chest. I had to swallow a loud sob of relief at the way he was wound around me, in me, filling me.

For another moment, he held impossibly still, and it had me shift my hips up in a restless, anxious movement. He sucked in a breath through gritted teeth.

"Molly," he groaned. "I can't... I can't..."

I gripped his face and sucked at his lips. "If you stop right now, I'll murder you in your sleep."

Noah rolled his forehead on mine. "Once I move, I can't hold back. I don't want to hurt you."

I brushed my nose against his. "Give me everything," I whispered. "I can take it."

And he did.

With harsh pants of breath against my skin that felt like he was branding me with hot strikes, Noah pulled back and, true to his word, gave me everything he had.

It was all I could do to hold on as he moved with ruthless, unrelenting snaps of his hips, unleashing his strength in the bunching muscles that had me pinned to the bed. I clapped a hand over his mouth when he groaned loudly, and I had to bite down on my own lips when I felt the cresting, rolling wave of pleasure, the bright burst of ecstasy that split me wide open.

Behind my fingers, he shouted roughly and then slowed his movements. I tilted my pelvis up to draw each last pulse of pleasure and finally opened my mouth to kiss him deeply. He tangled his fingers in my hair and let the full weight of his body collapse onto mine. I wrapped my arms around his back and held on with deep, shuddering breaths.

When he tried to roll off me, I tightened my arms, and he chuckled. His skin smelled like masculine soap, and I wanted to get high off it. I practically already was. In this bed, in this room, I could easily pretend that nothing existed but me and Noah.

"You're not allowed to leave yet," I informed him haughtily.

Noah pulled back in surprise. "No?"

I shook my head. "That's part of the South Dakota agreement. If we only get two nights, I get maximum bed sharing."

His eyes traced my face, and the sated smile he wore did funny things to my insides. I'd never seen him look so at peace. So happy. "Just running to the bathroom, greedy girl."

Greedy. *Such an appropriate term*, I thought as I watched him stroll naked from the bed into the adjoining bathroom. He let out a satisfied groan, which had me burying my dumb smile in the pillow under my head. Yes, greedy was right. The dim light from the bathroom bounced off the angles and curved lines of his muscles as he walked back.

I wanted to hoard him. Clutch him to me and impatiently demand more of his lips and tongue and hands. If I could only collect a handful of these salacious memories of Noah Griffin, I'd need them to be good.

He must have been feeling the same way because for the next couple of hours, he was insatiable. More than likely the byproduct of withholding for as long as he had. If the rumors were true, Noah had years of unspent sexual tension that needed be unleashed somewhere, and oh sweet mercy, I was glad it was me who was benefiting. Again. And again. And again.

By the time I lost count of how many times he brought me over the peak, I was so exhausted that my eyes could hardly stay open, and still his hands didn't stop running over the tight tips of my breasts or the curve of my ass ... he really liked it there. The hollow of my belly button. Noah was storing up memories of his own, and it was past two before we fell into a deep sleep, his arms curled around me as I laid tucked against his side.

I woke briefly when he climbed out, and it was still dark outside.

"What time is it?" I mumbled as he kissed my forehead.

"Early. I just need to get downstairs before anyone else wakes up," he whispered. "Go back to sleep."

Like a good girl who'd been screwed into oblivion all night, I did as I was told.

When I woke, it was bright, and the sounds of the small farm echoed through my room. I stretched and couldn't stop the happy wince at all the places I felt evidence of my night with Noah.

Deliciously sore, as I'd read in almost every romance novel that I loved so much.

It was used so much because it was effing accurate.

I showered and left the room with my game face on.

There would be no sex-drugged looks in his direction.

No daydreaming of how tight his hands held my hips during the third—*or was it the second?*—round.

No staring at him and remembering what he looked like when he pressed my knees up and braced them on his chest.

And we did well.

Feeding the horses with his grandma was as exciting as I thought, and she laughed at me when I bounced on my toes at the thought of brushing them out for her. Occasionally, I felt eyes on me as we worked in the barn, but I never caught Noah looking in my direction.

When Rick suggested they walk around the property, I followed along. And even though I had the thought that my presence was completely superfluous to this entire process, nobody seemed to question it.

Noah didn't need anything from me, especially because his honest reaction to this whole adjustment was the point of the documentary in the first place. Rick and Marty didn't really need me either. They'd done this before and knew that anything negative caught on film would be caught in editing and removed, probably at Beatrice's request.

Why had she thought it necessary for me to be here?

It was strange to come to that realization now, of all places. The place where I'd felt freer than I had in a long time. Where Noah clearly did too. But it was the truth. I watched from behind Marty as they filmed Noah and his grandma fishing in a pond that had been hidden from view behind the barn. I couldn't help but be thankful that I was here, but the truth was that there was no reason for it. My sisters questioned it, but now I wondered if there wasn't another reason.

Rick came up to me and found a seat on the grass. "You're quiet today."

I smiled at him. "Just enjoying the day."

He nodded. His mouth opened like he was going to say something, but he shook his head and stopped.

"What?" I asked him.

"Just ... curious about something," he said carefully, watching Noah and his grandma laugh. We were sitting far enough away that we were out of earshot, and I liked it better that way. Give them privacy where they could take it. "Why do you think he's stayed away for so long?"

My eyebrows popped up at his question. This was the first time Rick had asked my opinion about something of this magnitude. But I supposed it was his job to delve into the hidden layers of his subjects. It was what made him good at his job.

"And you want to know what I think?"

He nodded. "I do. You're intuitive. You've got good instincts when it comes to dealing with someone like him, who was clearly hesitant about this. Now look at him. He barely notices when we're around anymore."

I laughed. "I don't know about *that*." It wasn't lost on me that I'd ignored his compliment, focusing instead on his observation about Noah. "But thank you," I said carefully. "I like my job. I always have."

"You're good at it." He nudged me with his shoulder. "That's why I'm curious what you see when you look at him."

My face went hot, and I was so incredibly thankful that Rick wasn't looking at me. I thought so, so many inappropriate things when I looked at Noah, none of which Rick needed to know about. I cleared my head of the more lurid ways I could answer that question and focused on the scene in front of us.

"I think," I started slowly, "that it's easier for someone like Noah to stay focused when he keeps blinders on to everything else besides football. Probably to his detriment. Time with his grandma this way, it probably feels like, I don't know, an intrusion on his process, if it comes at the wrong time. So he ignores it. I don't think it means he loves her less, but I think he's so good at compartmentalizing his life that he's separated himself from everything outside of football that matters." I sighed. "And that's sad."

Rick's gaze was heavy on me, but I didn't turn to meet it. I didn't want to know what he'd see in my eyes, in my face, at my answer.

"I think you're spot-on," he said after a minute.

I looked at him when I felt like my face was into a more controlled mask. "Yeah?"

"But it's more than sad," he continued. "It's heartbreaking. When you observe people for a living, like I do, like Marty does, you see where they're headed. Sometimes before they do. And someone like Noah will let his entire life go by unnoticed by the time he retires. He'll finish playing and have nothing left, except for some trophies that mean nothing. Records that hold no weight, except some arbitrary importance that a single, small group of people put on it. Records that can, and will, be broken by someone else someday."

My eyes welled with tears, and I blinked rapidly to push them back.

"And there's nothing I can say that would change that for him," Rick said sadly. "He has to figure that out for himself." He paused and glanced at me again. "I just pray he doesn't ..." He stopped and exhaled heavily. "Shit, I don't know."

"What?"

Rick pierced me with a serious look. "I pray he doesn't hurt someone amazing in the process."

My mouth fell open.

He knew.

"Rick," I whispered.

He held up a hand. "Just the rambles of a man who's seen a lot. Okay? That's all it is."

Even though my heart was thrashing in my chest, I nodded slowly.

His words flipped and turned and tumbled in my head for the rest of the day. I made it a point to stay behind Marty because I was so afraid of what he might catch on my face if that camera turned in my direction.

I was quiet through dinner, another delicious carb and meat heavy affair that was made with obvious love. Noah kept glancing in my direction, but I kept my eyes off him because I was afraid it would be written all over my face.

I could fall in love with you so easily.

And you would break my heart if you couldn't love me back in the way I deserve.

Because Rick was right.

It wasn't my job to fix Noah's priorities. It wasn't my job to show him that he could have it both ways. He could have a life filled with love and family and be the best at his job while he was fortunate enough to do it.

I pretended to read a book while the guys played a card game with Noah's grandma and everyone slowly marched off to bed.

Before Marty went upstairs, I said good night and kept my face even as I clicked the door shut behind me. One single tear slipped out as I washed my face, and I turned the faucet to ice cold to snap myself out of it.

About an hour later, as I stared mindlessly at the screen of my phone where I was huddled under the covers, I heard Noah approach the door. I held my breath, and when he knocked softly, I climbed out from under the blanket and opened it for him.

His eyes searched my face as he walked in. "Are you okay? You were so quiet today."

If one word escaped my lips about how I was feeling, I'd coat the walls with my messy emotional state. So I nodded, my hands reaching for the hem of his shirt to tug it up over his head. He complied but looked concerned as he tossed it to the ground.

"Molly," he said, sliding his hands around my waist. "It's clear something is wrong. Talk to me."

I took a deep breath. "We have one night, Noah. Do you want to spend it talking? Because I don't."

Indecision warred in the handsome, chiseled features of his face. "I do if there's something important on your mind."

With a self-control I didn't know I possessed, I slid my hands up my chest and pulled his face down to mine. A groan came from his lungs when I tugged on his lip with my teeth. Goose bumps broke out over my skin at the sound of it.

I pushed down everything except the way he felt under my wandering fingertips, every worry, every doubt, every instinct that told me that this one last time would only make it harder for me when we got back to Seattle.

But I wouldn't ignore the opportunity when it was given to me.

Making this choice felt important.

I leaned up on my tiptoes and kissed him, digging my hands into his lush, silky hair and tugging. He changed the angle of the kiss, and I felt the moment when his brain switched off and his desire took over.

For the rest of the night, that impulse reigned over us, and we allowed it with every touch and kiss and whispered plea into each other's skin.

When he wanted to see all of me, I straddled his hips and rose above him, hands braced on his chest, for a slow, sweet round that left my body gleaming with sweat from delayed satisfaction.

When I wanted him to unleash every ounce of his strength, he turned me over onto my stomach where the pillows muffled my sobs of gratification when it finally broke wide open.

And when we knew he should've been leaving the room, we

allowed ourselves one last time. Not a single word passed between us, but he touched me everywhere, tasted me everywhere, and I did the same. He moved so slowly and with so much purpose, letting the desire grow and grow and grow until I swallowed a scream when we finished at the same time. A tear rolled down my temple as I lay under him, trying desperately to catch my breath, and he caught it with his lips.

I watched silently as Noah pulled on his shorts and T-shirt, his face an unreadable mask.

The blinders were going back on.

So were mine.

He stood over the bed and looked down at me, and when I thought he'd turn to leave, I scrambled out of bed. He caught me, wrapping his arms tight around me and taking my mouth in a searching, searing kiss.

It came down slowly until he did nothing more than hold me while I breathed him in.

"I know this is the right thing to do," he said into the crown of my head.

My eyes fluttered shut as I snuggled my face into his chest. "I do too."

I didn't, though. I wasn't entirely sure I believed that. Right. Wrong. They were so subjective based on who you were asking, weren't they?

Maybe the statement that I could agree to was that this was the *smart* thing to do instead. The most likely to allow him the success he was still chasing after with both hands and give me the same result.

"But I'll think about this," he admitted in a rough voice. "I'll think about you, Molly, and I want you to know that."

I had to roll my lips together to keep from telling him that I was falling in love with him. Because he had no space for something like this in his life, and I had no room for that kind of complication in mine. So all I could do, knowing we were leaving the next day, back into a world where we'd pretend this hadn't happened, was give him another soft kiss and lie about what he meant to me.

"I'll think about you too, Noah."

He pulled away from my embrace, and in a few strides of his long legs, he was gone.

CHAPTER TWENTY-ONE

MOLLY

THE STRANGEST PART of returning to Seattle was the fact that no one seemed to notice that anything was different. When I got home, Isabel greeted me with a smile, wanting to know how the weekend went.

When Paige stopped over a couple of hours later because Emmett wanted to show us something, there were no curious, lingering looks at my face, and no one asked if something had happened.

And as protective as I felt over those two nights and what happened in that big bed, I was relieved.

For the first time since I could remember, something happened in my life that I didn't want to share with my family. My sisters were my best friends, and Paige as close as a mother to me, but I didn't want to confide or discuss or pick apart anything about my time in South Dakota.

Normally, we would.

But the rest of my Sunday back in Seattle was just ... normal.

I arrived at work, feeling rejuvenated after a good night of sleep, something I didn't have at all in South Dakota due to one

Noah Griffin. And the lack of sleep from that weekend was nothing that couldn't be hidden by a good concealer, which I applied liberally when getting ready that morning.

My office was quiet and tidy when I let myself in, and I'd barely gotten through the items waiting in my inbox before a message popped up from Beatrice on my phone.

Beatrice: Would love to hear how the weekend went. I'm free after lunch.

It wasn't so much a suggestion as a summons. And I got a pit in my stomach as I thought about facing her across the expanse of her desk. Beatrice had been so very, very far from my mind in that cabin in the mountains. Her request for no fraternization had as well, something I'd broken. A few times. But there was really no point in counting how many times, honestly.

Ignoring the ramifications of what would happen if she found out, I'd already begun to formulate the opinion that all this forced proximity with Noah didn't help either of us. Especially not now. I was a glorified errand girl, hanging around the filming crew the way I'd been doing. Maybe that was the sharp, unpleasant edge to Beatrice's promotion in the first place.

Putting lipstick on a pig, so to speak.

She acted like she was doing me a favor, but in reality, the job I'd done before was more challenging, kept me busier, and on the whole, could generate just as much revenue for Washington if I did that job well.

Glancing at the filming schedule tacked to the pinboard behind my desk, I knew that Marty and Rick weren't around today. Probably at their own offices going through everything they'd caught over the weekend. As I tapped the side of my pen on the desk, I thought about the past few weeks. I thought about

Marty. And Rick. The pen slowed; my heart rate sped up. And I thought about Noah.

Facing him.

Being around him.

Trying to pretend nothing had happened and watching him do the same.

It was a recipe for disaster, and I couldn't even care what it said about me that I didn't think I could shove it down and do my job. Nothing was sexy about us trying to sneak around now that we were back to reality in Seattle.

Even if we'd agreed to try, I saw nothing fun or exciting about trying to hide a relationship with him. We were both too pragmatic for that.

I pulled a pad of paper out of the top drawer of my desk and started scribbling things down. Flipping back and forth between that and my computer whenever something came up, I felt ready to meet with Beatrice by the time I'd scarfed some cold leftovers for lunch. Being away from Noah meant my head was clearer, and that was hard to admit.

Something about him scrambled my brain waves, and if I was honest with myself, that had always been true. My breaking-and-entering career kicked off at the ripe age of sixteen because of the Noah effect. And look where that had gotten all of us.

Now I stood to lose something even more precious if I wasn't careful. I stood to lose my heart. Two nights in South Dakota was one thing, but seeing him in front of me, day in and day out, was another.

I pushed back from my desk and shoved my feet back into my flats before making my way down the hallway to Beatrice's office.

Out of respect, I rapped my knuckles quietly against the door even though it was propped open, and I could see her typing away at her computer.

She turned in her chair and gave me a small smile. "Come in, Molly. Perfect timing."

"Yeah?"

Her face smoothed out into that placid, pleasant expression she favored even though I could sense her studying me carefully. Since I got home, no one had looked at me like that, and I fought not to fidget as I took a seat across from her. "I've been trying to get a hold of Rick, and he seems to be ... how do I phrase this ... ghosting me?"

My eyebrows bent down. "Really? That doesn't seem like him."

"It doesn't. Yet I've asked for more raw footage, updates on how it's going, and he's ignored every request for the past two weeks. Either he evades me with a bland update, or he outright avoids answering my questions." She steepled her fingers in front of her. "Do you have any idea why?"

"No," I answered honestly. "Filming has been going really smoothly. They got a lot of great stuff over the weekend, so I can't imagine why he wouldn't want to show you."

When she didn't reply right away, I got the distinct feeling she was weighing the sincerity of my answer. But no matter what conversations I might have had with Rick, I was being truthful with Beatrice about this. I couldn't fathom why he wouldn't want to show her any of the footage they'd recorded.

"Okay," she said. "I'm glad to hear you say that. It makes me feel better since I know you're present whenever they're filming."

"Good." I took a deep breath. "But that's something I wanted to talk to you about, actually."

She tilted her head, raising an eyebrow in question.

"I've been there every day since they started. Very little has been filmed without me being there."

"I know. That's part of your job."

"I'm questioning how necessary that is, though," I said evenly.

Her face didn't move. Not a single muscle. Yet I felt a stunned reaction from her like a wave pulsing through the room. "Why's that?"

I shifted in my seat before answering. "Rick isn't trying to undermine us. He's not trying to manufacture drama or instigate something false. He clearly cares about Noah and wants to capture the raw truth of what this is like for him. And Noah ..." My voice wavered on his name, just the slightest hitch, but I covered it up by clearing my throat. "Noah is so much more comfortable in front of the camera than he was when this started. They don't need me there, Beatrice. I feel like I'm wasting my time, and Washington's money, by hanging in the background to make sure everything is going smoothly. And I"—I blew out a slow breath—"I wonder if that's something you knew would happen when you gave me this opportunity. That I'd feel unnecessary. Like I could be doing more or make a bigger impact elsewhere."

Her eyes narrowed. "Do you think I'd trick you?"

I licked my lips. "Not trick, no. But you were very honest with me about why you were doing this. You felt like I hadn't earned my job, that my last name meant I didn't work as hard as someone else might were they in my position. And even though I know that's not true, not fully, you flat out told me to prove it to you. But continuing with this setup, I'll never be able to do that."

"Why's that?"

Because I'll fall in love with Noah if you keep shoving him under my nose and will inevitably make more horrible decisions when I know I can't stay away from him. I blinked the thought back.

"Because this role is a waste of my talent. I can do both things, but I don't need to be with them every day they film. I can meet with Rick and Marty once a week to make sure they have all the access they need within the organization, and if Noah isn't working with them as he should, then I can step in as necessary. I've already proven to be able to communicate with him effectively."

The words were coming out of my mouth when I was slammed with a vivid memory of how effective our communication was for those two nights.

Yes, just like that. You feel so good, Molly. So, so good.

My face felt warm, and I kept my gaze steady on my boss.

Beatrice leaned back in her chair and set her hands in her lap. "You're right," she said after a long moment of silent regard. I didn't say anything, but inside, I was deflating with heady relief. "A good employee will do what's required. A great employee will find ways they can benefit the company they work for beyond what's asked of them. And you admitting this is a sign that you're a great employee."

"Thank you," I answered meaningfully.

Already, I felt the burden lift off my shoulders, the one I'd been trying to figure out how to carry ever since Noah walked out of my bedroom in the early morning hours.

"Which is why I hate that my mind immediately tries to connect your request with the timing of Rick ignoring me."

My brain jerked to a halt as I processed her words.

"Wh-what do you mean?"

"I'm going to ask you this once, Molly. Did something inappropriate happen that Rick doesn't want me to know about? That you don't want me to know about, which is why you don't want to be present for the filming anymore? If someone tried something or has made you feel uncomfortable, then I want to know about it."

I shook my head, stunned at the turn of the conversation. "I promise you, I'm not asking because *anyone* is making me feel uncomfortable."

"So the contract hasn't been violated?"

My mouth opened. Closed. If I admitted what happened between me and Noah, everything I'd worked for, that he'd slowly started creating here, would be gone in an instant. "No, Beatrice."

Oh, shit. It was out of my mouth. My stomach curdled dangerously, but she seemed to believe me.

Her face was hard, but her eyes were kind as her shoulders relaxed. "I'm sorry that I have to ask this, and that this is the culture we live in, but I understand what it's like to be a young woman surrounded by powerful, influential men. The absolute last thing I will tolerate is someone taking advantage of your desire to gain my approval."

And that only made me feel worse.

Guilt was so much more insidious than you realized before the lie slipped out of your mouth. It promised that everything would be fine. She'd never find out, and everything was better this way.

But instead, I was faced with the realization that she wasn't pushing it because she didn't believe me. She wanted to make sure I was safe.

I held up a hand. "Beatrice, please, I promise you that I would never put up with the kind of treatment you're talking about. If anyone under this roof so much as looked at me in a way that was disrespectful, my brother would rip their head off."

By the downturn in her mouth, maybe that wasn't the best answer, given what her initial opinion of me was, but it was the truth.

"And I know this gains me no favors, but I won't deny it either. A lot of the veteran players have known me for ten years. They were rookies when Logan retired, and now he's their coach. They all love me like I'm part of their family. And Allie Sutton-Pierson is my sister-in-law's best friend. Trust me, not only do I have about as good of a work support system in this place that anyone could ever ask for, but I know how to put my kneecap between any guy's legs in a way that would have him singing soprano for a month."

Beatrice exhaled a restrained laugh and relaxed a bit as she let her smile fall. "I get it. And you're right, it's hard for me to get over the fact that you're so entrenched into the fabric of this place, but ..." She shook her head. "But I know now that you don't use it as a crutch. You're a hard worker, Molly. And I'm proud to be your boss."

My eyes burned, my throat swelling with emotion. "Thank you."

"Please don't cry," she said dryly.

I laughed. "Yes, ma'am."

"I may have handled you wrong from the get-go, Molly, and I can't promise that I won't make more mistakes."

"You didn't handle me wrong," I argued. "You had every right to be wary."

"No, it was unprofessional of me to start off on that foot, and even worse when I ambushed you about your past with Noah."

A rock sank heavy in my gut, slicing neatly through the pride and warm happiness I'd felt just moments earlier, my skin going cold and prickly as it did.

She kept going. "Obviously, certain situations warrant a strong warning, but this isn't one of them."

My lips stretched in a tight smile. "Obviously."

"If you're telling me that this request to shift your schedule isn't born from that, from some situation that you don't want anyone to know about, then I'll trust you. Because you've earned that."

I felt two inches tall.

This wasn't the way I wanted her to believe in me. Believe that I was worthy of her respect and trust.

"So," she continued, "if you'll accept my apology, then let's take this as a fresh start, shall we?"

I found myself nodding weakly. "Apology accepted," I said quietly.

Beatrice nodded back. "Good. Let me know if Rick has any problems with the change in your role, will you?"

"I will."

On autopilot, I walked back to my office and sank heavily in the chair. I sent an email carefully worded to outline the changes to Rick, and I cc'd Marty. And just before I sent it, I added Noah as well.

After I'd hit the button, I read it over again, trying to reconcile, yet again, the whole concept of smart versus right.

Sleeping with Noah wasn't smart. But it felt so right.

Separating myself from him now that we were back was smart. But it felt wrong.

Falling in love with him ... the jury was still out on whether it was smart or right.

Every cell in my body was wailing dangerously from the wrongness. That was how strong my desire was to seek him out somewhere in these black and red hallways.

My cell phone rang in my hand, Noah's name appearing like I'd summoned him. I exhaled shakily and then drew a fortifying breath before I picked up the call.

"This is Molly."

"What the hell is that email?"

I sat back in my chair. "Excuse me?"

"You heard me. What the hell is that email about?"

Quickly, I stood from my chair and went to close my office door. "You can read just fine, Noah. I don't need to explain it to you."

He made a sound of muted frustration. "I just don't ... I get that it'll be difficult to be around each other for a little bit now that we're home, but that will fade. It doesn't mean you need to hide."

"I'm not hiding," I said fiercely.

Liar, liar, pants on fire.

"Bullshit."

"This has been a really fun chat, Noah. Thanks for calling."

He sighed. "I'm sorry." He gentled his voice. The sound of it, oh, I had to press my hand to my chest from what it did to my insides. "I'm frustrated, okay? I didn't think you'd disappear after what happened. Practice today was shitty, and your brother cursed my ass out for not paying attention this close to preseason, and all I could do was keep watching the doors to see if you'd show up. And it's not your fault that I couldn't pay attention, but hell, Molly, I didn't expect to come out of the locker room to that email saying you won't be around at all."

I sank back in my chair as I processed what he was saying. And what he wasn't.

In the span of one day, I'd gotten everything I thought I wanted.

Beatrice's approval and Noah's notice.

And it felt all wrong.

I didn't want to make his life harder. I didn't want him to screw up at practice because of me. I didn't want him to be frustrated about it, upset that his attention was split in this way, because he'd never tried to balance his focus before. The only thing that would do was make him resent me.

"I should have told you separately, Noah. I'm sorry I sprang it on you like that." I raked a hand through my hair, pulling the band out and wrapping it around my wrist. "But this is the best option. The smartest choice." I closed my eyes and fought the burn of tears building at the bridge of my nose. "And I think you know that."

He was quiet on the other end of the phone. And even

though I ached, oh, I ached to see his face to help me decipher what he might be thinking, I knew that if he was here, if he was in my office, I'd reach for him.

"I do," he finally admitted quietly.

His agreement didn't feel good.

It felt like he shoved a rusty sword through my gut. Irrationally, I wanted him to argue. To tell me it was worth the frustration to be able to see me. But the pain served as a good reminder.

He'd always choose football.

And in turn, I had to choose myself.

"Now what?" he asked.

I leaned back in my chair and stared up at the ceiling. "Now we both do our jobs. If you're having a problem with Rick or Marty, send me an email, and I'll take care of it. And you kick ass on the field starting this weekend."

The rough sound of Noah letting out a harsh puff of air had a tear slipping down my cheek. I dashed it away with the palm of my hand.

"Okay, Molly," he said. "I can do that, if that's what you want."

"That's what I want," I said in a remarkably, miraculously steady voice. If he'd been able to see my face, he would've seen the lie immediately.

But he couldn't. So he didn't.

And we started the season like that. Him with his blinders on. And me, the liar with the broken heart.

CHAPTER TWENTY-TWO

NOAH

THERE WAS a moment at the start of every season when you're standing on the sidelines before the whistle blows and the football was kicked from the flimsy plastic stand. Before it went end over end in the air, and the crowd roared, phones glowing in the stands as they captured another game, another snap, another beginning to their favorite sixteen weeks of the year.

That moment was usually hope and anticipation. It was unruly energy that finally had an outlet after months of practice and preparation. It was what we trained for, suffered for, risked injury for.

And for the first time, I felt nothing at that moment.

For the weeks of preseason that led up to it, I felt nothing. I showed up and played a few snaps, then found the bench for the rest of the game while the rookies and the second string got time on the field.

I felt nothing when I sat at the table with the mics in my face and talked about whatever game we were going to play next.

I felt nothing when we won the first game of the regular season, and I ended it with three QB sacks.

No visceral satisfaction when we won the second game as well, this time with two sacks added to my tally.

No chest-thumping celebration when we pulled out a one-point win during the third, thanks to a forty-nine yard field goal straight through the uprights as the clock ran out.

Oh, I managed to fake it well enough. I pounded helmets and smacked the pads of my teammates who performed well. Nodded my thanks when they got in my face, and roared their appreciation when I took down the opposing quarterback and ripped the ball from his hands.

Only three people watched me with a bit more interest as the weeks passed. Logan, Rick, and Marty. I saw it in the way their gaze lingered on me after a big play. When I kept to myself in the locker room and during team meetings and workouts. When I went to bed even earlier than usual, which meant the camera crews had to get the hell out of my beautiful home with its beautiful view that I hardly took the time to notice.

Each day that passed, I found less and less satisfaction in the knowledge that while I was achieving everything I wanted on the field, it dissolved like ash in my mouth. Not simply unsatisfying, or impossible to sustain me, but it left a bitter aftertaste that I hadn't expected.

Instead of ripping the lid off why, I buried myself in work. My body was in better shape than it had ever been in my entire career. My performance in game five was one for the record books.

And I couldn't bring myself to care.

The cycle I'd found myself in, with apathy at the wheel, started manifesting in strange ways. The longer I felt nothing about this job that I'd worshiped like a deity my entire life, the more it irritated me.

If irritation was the only feeling I could manage, then I'd channel every ounce of it during the minutes I found myself on the field. And when the clock ran out on our fifth game of the season, just before our bye week, not only did we have another win under our belt but my teammates also buffeted me with violent congratulations.

Kareem laughed at me when he saw the confusion on my face.

"What are they freaking out about?" I asked.

"You seriously weren't keeping track?"

I shook my head as players milled around us on the field. I didn't even have to look to feel Marty zoom his effing camera in on my face.

"Man," he said, slapping a hand against my chest, "you just broke the single game sack record. Seven and a half sacks, Griffin."

For the first time all season, I felt a tiny kindling of excitement flicker behind my chest. "I had no idea."

He grinned. "Whatever you're doing, man, keep doing it." He tipped his head back and bellowed over the post-game noise, "Beast mode, y'all!"

His words had the same effect as tossing a bucket of ice water on that small flame. Did I want to keep doing what I was doing? Not like this.

I found my eyes wandering through the crowds of people allowed on the field after the game as I absently greeted the team we'd just beaten with nods and halfhearted handshakes and fist bumps.

A skinny young player from the other team approached with a nerve-filled smile. "Hey Griffin, amazing game, man."

I nodded. "Thanks. You too."

I had no clue who he was, but my answer inflated his chest all the same. "You're, uh, you're kind of my idol. Have been since you played at U Dub. I told my wife if I got the chance, I'd ..." He inhaled sharply. "I'd see if you'd be willing to swap jerseys."

As Marty moved around us to film, I propped my hands on my hips and really studied the kid for the first time.

He looked like a teenager, and he was talking to me about my college days and about his wife. And the conversation immediately had two incredibly strange, incredibly humbling effects on me.

The apathy tumbled headlong into emptiness. Everything about this game felt empty.

The win.

The record.

And the fact that I invested my entire life into seeking both of those things above anything else.

Without answering, I started tugging my jersey off, and his face broke into a relieved smile. It was all I could do to meet his grateful gaze.

He lost the game, he didn't break any records, hell, he probably didn't stand on that turf for a single second of the game, and here he stood, happier than I'd felt since ... since South Dakota.

The thought slipped into my head, slithering easily underneath the iron brackets I'd kept around my heart since the day I talked to her on the phone.

That should have been my warning, that I couldn't even think her name without feeling like everything around me would tumble down, unprotected and vulnerable to every vivid second with her. Every kiss. Every touch. Every moan I'd unleashed in her. Every quiet moment when all I did was hold her in my arms as she slept.

He said something, and I blinked back to the present in time to take his jersey as he handed it to me. It was pristine—no sweat, no dirt, no grass stains—unlike mine.

"Remind me of your name again," I said slowly, tucking the jersey carefully under my arm so that I didn't drop it.

"Michaelson," he said hurriedly. "Eric Michaelson."

I held out my hand. "It's an honor to have your jersey, Eric."

"The honor is all mine. I can't wait to tell my wife about this." The returning pump of my hand was so vigorous, so enthusiastic, that I found myself smiling for the first time in weeks.

"Did she come to the game today?"

He shook his head, still beaming. "No, she stayed home. We had our first baby a few weeks ago." In the next breath, he pulled out his phone and showed me a picture of a wrinkled, red-faced baby. "Her name is Molly."

A steel beam to my temple would have had less of an impact. It knocked the breath clean out of my lungs for a second. I patted him on the back and managed a polite smile. "She's beautiful. Congratulations to both of you."

He left, and I managed to get off the field and into the locker room uninhibited while Marty trailed me quietly.

Filming had been that way every week.

Quiet. Uneventful.

Boring as all hell, if I tried to imagine it from his perspective.

Before I showered, I spoke to a few people from the press in the locker room about the record, answers I gave by rote about the honor it was, the work I'd put in, and the solid play by our competitors. By the time Rick approached me when I was dressed and clean and packing my bag, I couldn't even remember a single word I'd said.

"Great game, as usual." His smile was subdued.

"Thanks." I shoved my cleats into my duffel. "Can I do something for you?"

"Do you have a few minutes to talk?"

I sighed. "What is it, Rick? I'd like to get home."

"Why? Need to work out more? Watch film? Stare blankly at the wall?" My jaw clenched, and I straightened to my full height. He smiled, completely unintimidated. "I have something I'd like to discuss with you before I bring it to Beatrice for her approval.

We have ..." He paused, clearing his throat slightly before continuing, "I have an idea for the documentary. A new angle I'd like to explore."

I studied him. "Will I have to be there when you meet with Beatrice?"

"I think you should be, yes. Just giving you the opportunity to talk about it beforehand."

"When are we doing this? Because I'd rather not sit through the same meeting twice, if we can get it out of the way."

Hearing myself talk, it was no wonder everyone had left me alone. I could practically see people tiptoe around the invisible forcefield I was projecting. But Rick, that asshole, was undaunted. *She* would've been too, if she hadn't created a forcefield of her own. It was a toss-up whose was more impressive, but I had a feeling I would lose if I went to head to head with her on that.

"If you're sure," he said, eyeing me carefully.

"The sooner we do this, the sooner I can go home."

He held up his hands. "You got it. If you're ready, let's head down to that empty office past the press room. She said she had time to chat with us when you were done with the media."

Since the Wolves headquarters were housed with the practice facilities outside of Seattle, I didn't have to worry about passing Molly's office on the way to see Beatrice. My mind only stumbled slightly as I thought her name, and I had the distinct displeasure of recognizing that my heart did the same thing.

The hallways were a blur of glossy red and black, the Wolves logo everywhere we turned. It was strange how even now, months after I'd arrived, I didn't immediately recognize it as my home team. The press room was still buzzing with activity, our QB taking his turn up at the table, and I kept my eyes on the empty office space where we were headed because I'd given enough sound bites about the game. I didn't want center stage.

My face creased into a frown as I realized it. The thought was there, clear as a bell and just as loud, and I couldn't figure out when that had changed.

But I couldn't pull on the thread any further, not until later, as Beatrice waved us into the room with the phone glued to her ear.

"That sounds great, thank you. Send me a draft of the press release before anything goes live, okay?" Her eyes darted back and forth between me and Rick. "Yeah, bye."

We took the seats across from her as she hung up. Marty took his position in the corner of the room, still filming. Always filming.

Beatrice smiled in my direction first. "Congratulations on your game, Noah."

I nodded. "Thanks."

"Just so you know, we have a press release going out about the record, and we may want to record a snippet we can put up on Instagram thanking the Washington fans for all their support so far this season. We're already editing some footage of Coach giving you the game ball in the locker room."

Again, I nodded.

Beatrice folded her hands and directed her attention to Rick. "I was happy to hear from you, Rick. As you know, I've been salivating for a taste of what you three have been working on, but you've been such a tease."

My attention sharpened, but I kept my face forward.

Rick pulled his laptop out and set it on the desk, angling it so both Beatrice and I could see the screen. "There's a reason for that, as you can imagine."

"I certainly hoped that was the case." Her face was pleasant, but the edge to her voice was clear. "Should Molly be present for this? She assures me that you maintain open lines of communication, and there haven't been any issues since the season started."

196

My stomach clenched tight, and I fought to breathe evenly. I hadn't been in the same room as her since she left the airplane upon arriving back in Seattle.

"Not just yet," Rick said. When he sat back, he took a deep breath and gave both Beatrice and me a protracted look. "I'd like to make a change in the direction we're taking with Noah's story."

Her eyes narrowed. Mine didn't. Probably because I couldn't bring myself to care much about the documentary anyway. The change he most likely wanted to make was firing my ass from sheer boring footage.

"What kind of change are we talking?"

"An entirely new narrative," Rick said. "And the season would focus solely on him."

Beatrice sucked in a quiet breath. "I'm interested."

I rolled my lips together but kept silent.

"Marty and I found ourselves editing footage every week, and it became apparent to us—pretty much from the very beginning—that the reason we came to film Noah was the not the story that we should be telling." He gave me an inscrutable look. "Noah's nickname is The Machine. Over his young career in the league, he quickly established himself as something more than human. His stats are beyond impressive. His discipline is well-known, and he's respected by teammates and opponents alike for the way he methodically dismantles the competition with his body and his brain."

"All of which we knew," Beatrice supplied.

"We did," Rick agreed. "But nobody knows the very human side of him. He's created his career to mask it. No one questions what's underneath The Machine because the façade is so impressive. And from day one, Marty and I noticed something. Something that had both of us glued to the screens as we went through the hours and hours of footage from your day-to-day life, Noah."

I lifted my chin, mind racing but face implacable. "And what's that?"

His face softened, and there was an apologetic glint to his eye that made me want to clap a hand over his mouth even before the words came out. "We watched her dismantle The Machine with hardly any effort. We watched you fall in love with her. And her with you."

The bottom dropped out, and everything I'd been so carefully juggling in the air crashed down with his simple statements. I hardly registered the way Beatrice sat back in her chair.

I was shaking my head immediately, my heart thrashing wildly, my stomach an icy, iron block of denial. I felt like someone had opened a hidden trapdoor, the one I'd worried about on the very first day of this entire project, and now my feet dangled helplessly over an endless black pit. It was all I could do not to plummet inside of it. "You don't know what the fuck you're talking about."

"Molly? We're talking about Molly?" Beatrice asked quietly.

Rick nodded. Then he turned his attention back to me. "Noah, don't bullshit me right now. It is my job to see the stories where they unfold in people's lives. You can't tell me it's not true. We watched the way she was with you, and the way you were with her. Every single day, that woman singlehandedly brought out the human side of you. It wasn't me, and it wasn't Marty, even though we're damn good at working with the people we film. And it was a beautiful thing to watch. It was real and heartbreaking and compelling."

Bracing my elbows on my legs, I gripped the sides of my head. Over the roaring sound of my pulse, I registered the sound of Beatrice asking him what he caught on film. I lifted my head.

"Did you film us without our consent?" I asked in a low, dangerous tone. "Did you get footage of her without her knowledge?"

Rick started to speak, and I stood, whipping around to Marty. "Turn that camera off." He didn't move quite as quickly as I wanted. "Turn it off or I will break it with my bare hands," I yelled.

Marty clicked a button and dropped the camera. His face was drawn and pale. "I never filmed anything when you didn't know I was there. I swear to you, Noah. I'd never do that to either of you."

My chest heaved with jagged, uneven breaths as I struggled to rein in my temper.

"Did you sleep with my employee?" Beatrice demanded.

I glared at her. "Remind me why that's any of your business."

Her face went glacial, but she was the least of my problems. "Rick," I said, "you better start talking now."

"Beatrice," he said quietly, "can I have five minutes with Noah, please? I should have insisted I speak with him privately first, and that's on me."

"I'm not sure I should be kept out of the loop anymore," she snapped. "This is unacceptable."

He pinned her with a deadly look. "What's unacceptable about it? That Washington stands to make more money if he gets his own season? That we found a story that's real and true and is the kind of television we dream of making? It's not up to you to decide whether it's unacceptable or not. I'm telling you about this as a courtesy, but the decision will be made by Noah and Molly." He pointed a finger at me. "And you will hear me out before you do so."

I couldn't spare any of my rioting attention to Beatrice, but the fact that she stood and walked briskly from the office was answer enough. Silence descended when she slammed the door shut behind her. Closing my eyes, I tried to remember what it had felt like just an hour earlier.

Apathy sounded like heaven.

Not caring sounded like the best kind of escape I could have imagined.

And in that, I recognized it for what it had been: protection. I insulated myself in numbness because without it, I would have had to admit what Rick was telling me now. That Molly slid through an unseen chink in my armor and planted herself there, right next to my heart. A hole in my rib cage I hadn't known about before she showed up in that elevator. That space inside me belonged to her now.

I wanted to scream.

I wanted to rip down the walls.

I wanted to find her.

"You hate me right now," Rick said calmly. "And I don't blame you."

Slowly, I lifted my head and stared at him. The side of my jaw twitched, and I knew I couldn't let a single word escape my mouth until the rage lessened. But all I could think about was her. How she'd feel when she heard about this.

"If I find out that you got a single second of footage of Molly without her consent, or a single moment we thought was private ... if there's a fraction of a frame on that film that makes her look like she's being disrespected, I will make your life hell on earth," I vowed.

In the seconds after I spoke, it took me a moment to realize that he started smiling.

"What?" I snapped.

"And you still don't see it," he mused.

I shoved my hands into my hair and tugged on the strands. "Quit talking in circles, Rick."

He leaned toward me. "Think about what you just said to me. It wasn't about how *you* look, if you come off bad, or if it tarnishes your reputation. You'd tear my life apart if I did something to *her*."

My hands dropped numbly into my lap.

"She stepped back because she cared more about you being focused going into this season. She stepped back because it hurt her too much to be around you. And you let her. I'm not saying that you care less about her, but holy hell, Noah, for such a smart man, you are a fucking idiot when it comes to what you feel."

I swallowed roughly.

He turned his laptop and punched a few buttons. "There, I'm sending you our rough concept trailer. I'd intended to show it to you today before you and Beatrice lost your ever-loving, control-freak minds," he mumbled. After he snapped the laptop shut, he faced me again.

"H-how did you know?" My voice sounded like someone took a rusty, chewed-up chainsaw to my throat.

"Please," Marty said. "The day she stopped filming with us, you flipped the switch into Terminator mode. It was like watching a cyborg pretend to be a human."

I gave him an unamused look.

He tapped his camera. "Can't argue with me on this, buddy. I have it on film."

Rick held up a hand. "On film or not, whether you agree or not, I like you and I like Molly. I think you guys are great together." He leaned in. "But if you can't pull your head out of your ass long enough to realize what you found in her, then you don't deserve her."

Chewing on his words was slow and uncomfortable because the grain of truth was so big that it was unavoidable. I stared at him for a minute before speaking.

"I thought you weren't supposed to force action."

He laughed. "You know, my wife was filming a nature documentary a couple of years ago, and a flock of penguins got stuck in a ravine. The crew had to watch, completely helpless, as dozens of birds tried and tried and tried to get out to no avail.

And if they did nothing, that entire flock would've died. So they broke their rule about intervening and carved stairs in the ice and snow, and the penguins marched right out of that ravine as soon as they had the chance."

I shook my head. "Not sure that's a flattering comparison if you're me."

He slapped me on the back. "They were smart enough to climb those stairs, Griffin. All I'm asking you to do is open your eyes. Once you do, your life will never be the same."

CHAPTER TWENTY-THREE

MOLLY

MY OFFICE WAS quiet as I typed out a reply to an email that had been sitting in my inbox for all of two minutes. The plus side to absolutely no social life for the past eight weeks was that I was on top of my game at work.

Sure, the dark circles under my eyes were as dark as the movies I'd been bingeing, and I'd accidentally bawled my eyes out watching a holiday romance movie on Netflix when I was too lazy to get up and find the remote, but at work, I was slaying.

Turns out having your heart bruised up was excellent for your professional life.

I was a quick email replier, and Noah was breaking sack records left and right.

Okay, fine, my accomplishment didn't sound as impressive as his, but I'd take my victories where I could get them.

I typed harder, ignoring the impulse to pull out my phone and watch the footage of him getting the game ball in the locker room from the day before. He'd looked ... bored.

In the seven times I watched it the night before, tucked under my covers so Isabel couldn't hear me and hide my phone, I studied his face. He was smiling, but behind his eyes, I saw no spark. Absolutely nothing. And it tore uneven holes in my heart.

Someone knocked on my office door, and I called over my shoulder, "Come in."

"I hope I'm not interrupting," my boss said quietly.

Something in her tone had me pausing before I swiveled my chair to face her.

"Not at all," I said, watching her warily as she walked into my office and closed the door quietly behind her. "How was your weekend?"

She didn't sit, simply curled her fingers around the back of the chair facing me on the opposite side of my desk.

"Enlightening," she answered cryptically.

"What happened?"

"I need you to answer a question for me, and answer it honestly, Molly."

Her formality, reminiscent of when she first started, had me sitting up straight. "What is it?"

"How long have you been in a sexual relationship with Noah Griffin?"

My skin prickled hot, then ice, ice cold, sweeping between both extremes in a rush from the top of my head to my toes. "I'm not in one," I said instantly. "I haven't spoken to him in weeks."

Eight weeks and three days and like, six-ish hours. Not that I was counting with every miserable beat of my heart.

Beatrice exhaled slowly. "Then I'll clarify. Have you ever been in a sexual relationship with him?"

The breath halted painfully in my lungs as I opened my mouth, but no words came out. At her question, all the memories I'd locked tight into a black box in my mind came tumbling out, one after another, after another. The pieces of my time with him that I missed so desperately. And it showed on my face, I knew that like I knew my own name.

"Dammit, Molly," she said under her breath. "You lied to me. You *lied* to me."

I stood slowly, hand clutched to my chest. "Beatrice, I'm so sorry."

"I wish you hadn't done that." She shook her head, gripping the back of the chair even more tightly. "I can't make an exception for you, Molly. I had a rule, and you violated it."

The reality of what she was saying had my skin rushing hot again, blood pooling under the surface in a way that had my face blazing with embarrassment. "Beatrice, please."

She held up a hand. "I had specifically laid out the rules in that job agreement that we discussed and that you signed. One was my no fraternization with the crew or any subject of the documentary. And two was the discussion we had about honesty. About trust." She paused, and her eyes went suspiciously bright. "Do you know how furious I was when I thought someone had taken advantage of you? I looked you in the eye, and I took you at your word when you told me nothing had happened. I trusted you."

My voice cracked when I interrupted, a messy, inconvenient truth falling from my lips. "I fell in love with him, Beatrice. It wasn't some meaningless fling."

It was the first time I'd admitted it out loud, and my heart squeezed painfully.

"And in the process, you broke the trust I had in you," she threw back. "Now, I look back on you requesting the change in your role, and I question it. I question your ability to set your emotional state aside and do your job. I question your ability to think through your choices before you make them."

Dashing a tear away from my cheek, I cursed how easily I

seemed to cry when it came to anything surrounding that giant brute of a man. "I've been doing my job," I told her. "And I've been doing it well. You know I have."

"Was it about Noah? Your request?"

Slowly, I nodded.

Beatrice dropped her head and sighed heavily. "Thank you for being honest, Molly." Then she lifted her gaze back to me, and I felt very much like someone about to face a one-woman firing squad.

Ready.

Aim.

And her finger squeezed.

Fire.

"You have until noon to clean out your desk. Your employment with the Washington Wolves has been terminated. Someone from HR will be here shortly to take care of the paperwork."

I sank back into my seat and dropped my head into my hands, tears falling freely now as she walked quickly out of my office. For my whole life, this place had been a hub, a central figure for my family. Even before my dad died, before my mom walked away. I couldn't remember a time when I hadn't run through the halls like I owned them. And now, I'd be walked out with a box in my hands. The fact that she'd left me alone at all should've made me feel slightly better because even though I'd lied, even though I'd broken her rules, she trusted me enough to give me some privacy.

At a moment like this, a girl would normally call her mom. My hands shook as I picked my phone up from my desk and thumbed down my favorite contacts. The phone rang once before Logan's wife, Paige, picked up.

"What's up, buttercup?"

At the sound of her voice, I broke down, blubbering and crying and failing to get even a few intelligible words out.

"Molly, Molly, calm down," she instructed. "I'm driving, and hang on, I'm pulling over, but I need you to tell me if you're hurt. Are you okay?"

"Beatrice just fired me," I got out.

"*What?*" Paige yelled. "Oooh, I will burn that bitch's house down."

A watery laugh escaped me. "I messed up, Paige."

"Oh honey, you couldn't have messed up that bad. You're so good at your job," she said. "Hang on, let me text your brother."

"No, Paige, don't interrupt his practice." I inhaled, slowly getting control over my tears. "I'll come over after I leave here. I have until noon to clear out my things."

She was quiet and, knowing my sister-in-law, quiet was dangerous.

"Paige," I said again.

"Hmm?"

"What are you doing?"

"Nothing. Just ... imagining you having to box up your desk and how that makes me want to rip her hair out."

I laughed again. "I hope Emmett isn't in the car with you. You're way too bloodthirsty to be in mom-mode right now."

"Hi, Mol," he piped up in the background. "Mommy looks scary right now. She's got angry eyes."

"I'll bet." I rubbed my forehead. "I need to start going through my things. And, ugh, someone from HR will be here soon."

"Bullshit, this is complete and utter bullshit," she muttered. "What happened? What's her reasoning for firing you?"

"Can we talk about it when I come over?" I asked wearily.

"Yeah, sweetie, we can." She was quiet for a second. "I love you. It'll be okay."

"Love you too, Paige."

The call disconnected, and I snatched a tissue from the box behind my computer monitor, noisily blowing my nose. It took me a few minutes of doing my best zombie impression before I started opening drawers and staring blankly at what needed to stay and what I should take with me when I heard two things at once.

The stomp of a man's feet.

The click of heels coming from the opposite direction.

"Paige," I whispered. "What did you do?"

Logan arrived at my door just before Allie Sutton-Pierson did.

"What happened?" they asked in tandem.

Logan ripped his hat off and rushed over to me, wrapping me in a hug that had me fighting not to go blubbering again. "I'm so sorry, Mol. This is bullshit."

I was wiping my face when Allie closed the door to my office.

Allie was just past forty, and as she stood, arms crossed, worried expression stamped on her stunning face, she looked barely over thirty-five. "She wasn't in her office when I walked down, but I will have words with her as soon as I see her."

"It's okay, Allie," I said. "You don't have to do that."

As the owner of one of the most financially successful football franchises of the past decade, Allie wasn't accustomed to people telling her what she could and couldn't do. "I know I don't have to," she said calmly. Underneath that calm was steel. "But you, your sisters, Emmett, you are part of my family. And I do not like people messing with my family."

Logan rubbed a hand on my back. "Let her help, Molly. You don't deserve this happening to you."

I gave him a sad smile. "You don't even know what I did."

"Because it doesn't matter," he replied instantly.

I rolled my eyes. "Yes, it does. What if I punched her?"

"Did you?" Allie asked.

"No."

"Did you sexually harass her?"

"Of course not."

Logan shook his head. "I knew I didn't like her. Not from that very first meeting."

"Come on, you guys, people get fired all the time. It sucks, but I'll be okay."

Allie propped her hands on her hips, which were wrapped in a sleek black skirt. "People who are phenomenal at their job do not get fired all the time."

Logan chimed in. "Exactly. And you are good at your job."

The two of them started building off each other, tossing ideas back and forth. Words like harassment. Unlawful termination. Performance Improvement Plan. Firing Beatrice. I closed my eyes and tried to tune them out, but finally, I held my hands up, and yelled, "Stop, please!"

They went quiet.

"I screwed up, okay?" I looked at both of them. "I-I slept with Noah on a filming weekend, then lied to her about it when she asked if I'd violated her contract, which included a no-fraternization policy."

Logan's face flushed red, his jaw clenched tight, and he stared at the floor like it held the world's secrets.

Allie deflated like a snipped balloon. "Oh," she said weakly.

"I've stayed away from him since then," I continued, tears building in the back of my throat, "but it doesn't matter. She knows. I-I thought that I'd thought it through all the way. That I knew what I was getting into. That's always been my problem, right?" I wiped my face, daring Logan to argue with the look on my face. "How many times have you had to step in over the years when I didn't think something through? When I did something because I felt like it or because it was fun or silly or ... felt right at the time."

"Molly," he said on an exhale. "You're young. Making mistakes is a part of life."

"I know. But so is stuff like this, Logan." I shook my head. "I don't regret my time with Noah, but I knew it was a risk when I did it. If this is the fallout of the weekend I got with him, then I'll take it."

Allie sighed. "It still feels wrong, Molly. There's no rule in the Wolves handbook that prohibits a relationship with a player and another employee."

"No, but Beatrice's contract is different. It's separate from that." I swallowed. "It was a stipulation that Beatrice specifically added to my job description, which hinges on the relationship with Amazon."

Logan glanced at Allie. "So she's right?"

Allie shrugged. "I'm not involved enough when it comes to those types of situations, but"—she nodded—"I think she's right. And not only that, as long as Beatrice isn't firing her for any discriminatory reasons, Washington is an *at will* employment state. She can fire her at any time without providing a reason."

"That's dumb," he said sullenly.

"You sound like Emmett," I told him with a reluctant smile.

My brother wrapped his arm around me. "I'll take that as a compliment, kiddo."

Allie watched us with a sad smile. "Do you want help with your desk?"

I shook my head. "I'd rather do this alone, if that's okay with you guys."

"Of course." She met me in the middle of my office and gave me a tight squeeze. "You're a rock star, Molly. If there's anything I can do moving forward, let me know, okay? We're always looking for help at the Team Sutton Foundation."

Another job I'd get without blinking because of my last name. I smiled at her all the same. "Thank you, Allie. I will."

Logan took longer to convince, but after three more hugs and five more offers to stand outside my office while I cleaned up to make sure whoever came from HR was nice to me, I all but shoved him out of the room that wouldn't be my office anymore.

He was just beyond the corner when I called his name. His head popped back through the open door. "Yeah?"

"Not a word to Noah."

Logan opened his mouth to argue.

"No." I pointed a finger at him. "It happened weeks ago. I am an adult, and so is he. You don't get to interfere this time."

He narrowed his eyes. "Define interfere."

After a second, I ticked off the most obvious answers on my fingers. "No yelling, no telling him what happened, no threatening, no embarrassing him or me in front of the guys, because Logan Ward, if you march back in that practice and get in his face about this, I am the one who is embarrassed. Do you understand me?"

Paige had these scary eyes that she used on my brother when she went from *I'm serious* to *I will end you if you cross me.* I'd seen them often over the past ten years, and I gave it my best attempt. It must have worked because he grimaced. "Fine."

"I mean it."

He held up his hands. "I promise! Geez. You're as bad as Paige," he mumbled before he left.

I was grinning as he went back to practice. And given the current situation, that was pretty impressive. Everything after that went as smoothly as possible.

I signed some papers. Filled two file boxes. And the security guard who walked me out started tearing up because I'd known him since I was five.

"Ain't right," he said under his breath.

I wrapped my arm around his thin waist and gave him a squeeze. "I'll be okay, Rod, I promise."

He hugged me back, wiping at his face with the sleeves of his shirt after he took my security badge from me. Before I walked out the door into the parking lot, my eyes watered up again as I stared at the red and black logo of the wolf tossing its head back in a howl.

I let out a slow breath and left the building.

Everything held a surreal quality as I walked numbly to my car. Like when you have a cold and your head feels disconnected from your body. Or everyone around you is moving at a different speed. There were boxes in my hands, but I hardly felt them, like someone else's arms were holding them up.

My car was right where I left it, and I set the boxes on the hood so I could dig my keys out of my purse. With the trunk opened, and the boxes set carefully inside, I couldn't get over the strange sense of detachment I felt.

Later, I'd probably cry again at the loss of a job I loved.

I'd probably cry at the knowledge that I wouldn't see Noah anymore. Then I snorted. Please, I hadn't seen him in eight weeks unless it was on a TV screen.

That was when I heard him. "Molly?"

The sound of Noah's voice sent chills racing down the length of my spine, one after another, tumbling on top of each other to see which could go faster. They were powerful enough, those racing, chasing chills, that I shivered. Just once.

For the past eight weeks, I'd fought against every impulse to show up at his door some night. To catch a glimpse of him after a game or when he was sweaty after practice. But I'd been right to stay away. Because I knew, I knew so deep in the darkest, most vulnerable part of my heart that *I* couldn't go to *him*. Not this time.

With my hands still braced on the lid of my trunk, I took a deep breath, dropping my arms slowly as I turned to see Noah, watching me with a careful expression on his face.

If his voice gave me chills, then his face melted me to my core.

"Hi, Noah," I said, keeping my own expression just as neutral.

His jaw clenched. And I held my breath to see what he'd say next.

CHAPTER TWENTY-FOUR

NOAH

She looked terrible.

And beautiful.

Her nose was red, and her eyes rimmed like she had a cold or had been crying. There was no messy bun today, the kind I was used to, the one that she'd no doubt done and redone a dozen times, and her hair was down in messy waves.

It was shorter, just below her shoulders.

Molly's eyes surveyed me in much the way that I was her, and it occurred to me, after a few beats of awkward silence, that it was my turn to talk.

"How are you?"

If I'd ever wanted to find the situation in life that I sucked at the most, it was this, right here. I couldn't have sounded more painfully polite. More disinterested. But inexplicably, her eyes softened at my robotic tone.

"It was kind of a rough day," she answered quietly. "Or not nearly as good as yours was yesterday, at any rate."

I grimaced. "Yeah." My eyes searched her face. "What happened? Are you okay?"

When she smiled sadly, I knew she wasn't going to answer me. "Congratulations on breaking the record." She shook her head. "You've looked great out there."

My eyes held hers, and she blushed.

"Or played great," she stammered. "Not looked great. Not that I can see your face under the helmet."

"I knew what you meant." I gentled my tone. "And thank you."

Molly glanced away, staring hard at the facility behind me. I had to close my eyes for a second and try to formulate a plan. Walking out to my car, I hadn't expected to see her or have this awkward facsimile of a conversation with the one person I never struggled to talk to. Rick and Marty's words about her rang through my head, louder and louder until I wanted to smack my temple and dislodge them. Empty my ears like they were water I'd allowed in while swimming.

"Are you still liking the house?"

I nodded. Good plan, Griffin. Stand awkwardly until she felt forced to speak because you couldn't get out of your own head.

"Yeah, umm, I'm still slow at buying furniture and stuff. I don't do much besides sleep and eat there."

That made her look sad. For me.

"Did you get your telescope at least?"

"Yeah." I rubbed the back of my neck. "It's still in the box they shipped it in."

This was getting better and better.

She gave me a tiny smile. "I found a constellation the other day."

"Yeah? Which one?"

"The Big Dipper."

I smiled widely, and it felt like that simple motion cracked a concrete mask off my face.

How far had my blinders extended? I'd been so focused on

work—eating it, breathing it, sleeping it—gladly allowing it to drown out every other thing in my head so that I didn't have to dissect what was remaining. And in one uncomfortable conversation, she sliced them off with the neat clips of a blade.

No wonder I never dipped my toes into the ocean of dating and women. I sucked at this. I'd managed one stupid question, the kind you'd ask a stranger.

But this was Molly. The same woman who made me laugh, when laughing was the last thing I wanted to do. Who made me smile, and surprised me when I thought I was beyond surprising. The same woman who singlehandedly obliterated my legendary control because I couldn't imagine not kissing her or tasting her. The only thing I could do was be honest.

But she spoke first. "I should go."

"Wait." I strode forward, stopping just shy of touching her. "Why is this so hard?" I asked.

Molly slumped against her car and gave me a miserable look. "Come on, Noah. You know why."

"No, I don't," I said. I ran my hands into my hair, a helpless gesture when what I wanted to do was tug her into my arms and feel my soul settle again. "Help me understand why it's so hard to see you, why we can't talk like normal."

"What's our normal?" she asked quietly, shaking her head as she did. "We hated each other until we didn't. We slept together, then stopped talking. And here we are."

I raised an eyebrow. "That's a massive simplification of what happened between us."

"I know it is."

"Nor was it my idea to stop talking," I reminded her gently.

That made her eyes flash dangerously. "Can you blame me for backing away? Would it have been easier to try to pretend that weekend didn't happen? Film, work, be around each other every single day and just ... pretend." Her voice sounded thick. "That sounded like hell to me."

"No, it wouldn't have been easier. I hate pretending. I don't ... I don't think I could have." I took a step closer. "But this hasn't been easy either, has it?"

She dropped her head into her hands and exhaled shakily. I got the distinct impression that the only thing allowing her to keep hold on her emotions was if she physically blocked out my presence like that. I took a step back.

"What do you want me to say, Noah?" she asked, voice muffled behind her hands. "I had a shitty day, and I'm tired, and I don't know what you want me to say right now."

"I want you to be honest with me." Curling my hands around her wrists, I gently pulled her hands away from her face. "I know you said that we never had a normal ... but ... I don't know what to make of that. You were my friend, Molly. I talked to you more than I talked to anyone. I miss you," I told her fiercely. "It was easy to ignore how much when you weren't around, but I do. And I hate how weird things are right now. Don't you?"

I couldn't believe what had just tumbled out of my mouth.

Unpracticed.

Unrehearsed.

Hell, I'd barely registered how I felt, but standing in front of her, it was like someone took a wood-chipper to whatever I'd been using to block out everything I'd suppressed for the past eight weeks.

It was impossible to believe that only a day earlier, I was able to stand back and monitor just how little I felt about my life. Like someone who'd lost the ability to feel pain. You could set your hand on a stove and not register the sensation of blistering skin. And now, watching her expressive face work through what I'd blurted out, I felt everything.

Every pinch of her lips and every shift of her eyes. When they filled with bright tears, I wanted to do anything, *anything* humanly possible to make it stop. Just the threat of tears on her part, and I felt them like a blowtorch to my gut. But if withstanding the heat, if pressing into it further was what she needed from me, I'd step closer and hold the flames against me for as long as she needed.

Oh, hell.

Rick was right, that asshole.

I'd ... I'd fallen in love with her, and it happened without me realizing it.

"Noah," she started, completely oblivious that my heart had just splattered to the ground at her feet. "Of course I do. But ..." She trailed off, eyes snapping beyond my shoulder. "Shit. I need to go. I cannot be on camera right now. Not after my day today."

I glanced back and saw Marty sprinting toward us like he was about to catch me mounting Molly on the hood of her car. I pinned him with a look and held up my hand, but he just kept barreling toward us. Thank goodness he was so out of shape. He stopped about forty yards away and braced a hand on his knee to breathe for a second.

"Molly," I begged. "Don't go."

"Please don't make me do this right now. Not on camera." Her eyes were huge and pleading. I nodded and stepped back.

I knew at that instant that I'd do anything she asked of me. Anything, even if it meant letting her drive away.

"Have a good rest of the season, Noah," she said, just before she slammed her door shut.

"What?" I went to grab the door handle and ask her why the hell that sounded like a goodbye, but I stepped back when I heard Marty's pounding footsteps and obnoxiously loud breathing behind me. "You rotten asshole," I told him.

"You let her leave?"

I whirled. "Yeah. She didn't want to be on camera, you dick. You think I'd force her?"

Marty sighed, watching Molly's car leave the parking lot once the security guard lifted the gate. "No."

I gave him a dry look. "Your timing leaves a lot to be desired."

"Molly got fired," he blurted out.

"What?" I yelled.

"That's why I was running out here. I overheard her brother say something about it when I was packing up my gear after practice. You looked like shit today, by the way."

"Why did she get fired?"

"Why do you think?" He shook his head. "She lied to her boss about what happened in South Dakota. I guess Beatrice had added a no-fraternization stipulation in Molly's contract for this project that covered the cast and crew." He pointed at his chest. "And she ain't sleeping with the crew."

I ran my hands over my face. "Shit, shit, shit. She said she'd had a rough day." My hands curled into fists. "Shit," I yelled. "I really want to punch something."

Marty gave me a warning look. "Don't even think about it."

With fumbling hands, I pulled out my cell phone and tried to call her. It went right to voicemail.

"Her phone is off," I muttered.

"Probably a work cell. I bet she had to leave it."

"Do you know how pissed I am at you and Rick?"

"Us?"

"Yeah." I glared at him. "My life was perfectly fine before you two showed up. And now I have an old man informing me that I fell in love without knowing it, and another old man who can't run for shit interrupting the first chance I've had to talk to her. I hate you guys."

Marty grinned. "We love you too."

"I can't believe she got fired." My chest pinched tight. And then tighter again. Love was awful. Even imagining what she must be feeling made me want to hurl an unsuspecting vehicle across the parking lot.

I knew how she felt because I went through it. I loved playing at Miami. One stupid choice on one stupid night, and a career I'd been building for years was upended.

Upended, but not ruined.

I liked Washington.

The team was strong.

The coaching was top-notch, even if one of those coaches was probably currently plotting my demise knowing that I slept with his sister.

The culture was accepting and warm. Stable. That was harder to find than you'd expect.

But there was no way I could have known that when I was shipped here just before the season started. And no way for Molly to know right now, caught in the muck and mire of feeling dumped by a place that was so important to her.

"She's a smart girl," Marty said, interrupting my thoughts. "This is a tough knock, but I'd put my money on her any day." He nudged my shoulder. "I mean, if she can go head to head with you without backing down ..."

I smiled. She had, too. Thinking about all those moments now, I was such a fool that I hadn't seen how quickly she got under my skin. But she was there now, and I didn't want her gone.

"I need your help, Marty," I said, still staring at the road where her car had disappeared.

"Anything."

"Before you promise that, it may require you to be chained to that computer for a day or two."

He eyed me. "What do you need?"

I slung my arm around his shoulder, and we walked back

toward the building "The way I see it, you and Rick owe me, right? For ambushing me in front of Beatrice. But I guess I owe you too, for bringing it up in the first place. I can be a little ..."

"Blind?" he helpfully supplied. "Clueless?"

"Hyper focused," I amended, "when I'm in football mode. So that little trailer he sent me? I'm going to need more from you."

"I was afraid you'd say that." He sighed. "If she doesn't have a phone, how are you going to get in touch with her?"

I glanced back at the Wolves facility. "I know a guy."

"Just ... let me film it when you ask him, okay?"

I laughed. "Shall we get it over with now?"

Marty's face blanched as he looked at the building with me. "Now?"

"Why do you look so nervous?"

His eyes never wavered. "Because I'm worried I'm about to catch your death on film. And Rick will never forgive me."

I let out a deep breath. "Logan won't kill me."

Marty glanced over at me.

"Okay," I hedged. "It won't be pleasant. That's why I'd rather rip off the Band-Aid now."

He swept a hand forward. "Lead the way."

I KNOCKED on Logan's door. Marty shifted behind me, probably making sure he had the optimal angle to catch whatever happened next.

"Come in," Logan said.

My exhale was slow and steady before I pushed the door open. His head was bent over his computer, face hidden by the brim of his black hat.

"Do you have a minute, Coach?"

Logan's frame froze imperceptibly at the sound of my voice. As he lifted his head, I braced for what I'd see on his face.

It wasn't pretty.

He crossed his arms over his chest and leaned back in his chair. Logan's expression was forbidding, carved from granite for as little as he gave away.

Right. Another member of the Ward family who would wait me out and force me to talk today.

"I'm assuming you know what happened," I started.

His jaw clenched.

"And I'm also assuming you aren't very happy with me right now."

His nostrils flared. I'd take that as agreement.

"But even if that's true," I said, holding his terrifying gaze as steadily as possible, "I have no way of getting in touch with her, and I'm hoping you'll help me with that."

His eyes narrowed dangerously, and behind me, Marty shifted uncomfortably.

"Her?" he spoke slowly. "By *her*, you mean my little sister? The one you slept with after I told you to stay away from her?"

"Yes." I lifted my chin a fraction. "That's who I'm talking about."

The line of his mouth flattened.

"Logan," I told him, hands raised by my sides, "I can find another way to reach her if you won't help me."

He tilted his head. "Do you think that's the best angle to take when you're trying to convince me this is a good idea?"

"I'm being honest because I respect you enough not to lie to you."

One eyebrow rose on his forehead, slowly, incredulously. I felt my face flush hot, because disbelief radiated off him in strong pulses.

"Your sister is important to me. It ... it took me a while to realize just how much." I swallowed roughly. "And I could stand here all day trying to convince you of that, but no offense, I won't admit anything to you that I haven't said to her first."

His face went slack with understanding.

I fell in love with Molly, and now he knew it.

Slowly, Logan unfolded his arms, his gaze searching my face for ... something. Proof. I wasn't sure. Then he ran a weary hand down his face and nodded. "I'll help you. Just tell me what you need."

I glanced back at Marty, who was grinning behind the camera. "Right now, I just need a little time to pull something together."

CHAPTER TWENTY-FIVE

MOLLY

WHEN I LEFT, I knew I could've gone home to my apartment with Isabel. But the only thing that waited for me there was the temptation of day drinking and the inevitable crying into my pillow.

So I kept true to my word and drove straight from the Wolves facility to Paige and Logan's house about thirty minutes away. The neighborhood had tall, mature trees and shrubs, and the houses were set back off the road. They were big but not obnoxious. And selfishly, especially at moments like this, when I felt my most vulnerable, I wanted to return to the place that felt like home.

And nothing felt more like home to me than here.

I parked my car behind Paige's and ascended the concrete steps to the solid oak door, opening and closing it quickly since it had started to rain on my drive.

"Back here," Paige called from the kitchen. I smelled garlic and carbs, and instantly applauded my decision to come here.

Emmett skidded around the corner, knocking into me with an

oof. His skinny arms wrapped around me in a hug, and I leaned down to kiss the top of his head.

"Hey, bud. No school today?"

"Nope. Mom said you needed the tightest hug ever."

My throat pinched. "I do. Thank you."

He set his chin on my stomach and looked up at me with huge eyes. "Can you help me with my math homework? You're good at it, and Mom said she doesn't do that bullshit."

"Traitor," Paige yelled over the sound of my laughter. "And that's a buck in the swear jar, you little potty mouth."

"It's not swearing if I'm repeating something you said."

"Ooh, get her with logic," I whispered. "I approve."

He grinned. "Is that a yes?"

I rubbed his back. "I'll tell you what, you give me thirty minutes of girl time—no interruptions—and then I'll help you."

"Deal!" He ran off, feet pounding up the stairs toward his room.

Paige leaned her shoulder against the wall by the kitchen and gave me a small smile. Her red hair was braided over her shoulder, and as usual, she looked so beautiful, it was hard to stare for too long. That was the problem with having a former supermodel for your surrogate mom. "How's my girl?"

I shrugged. "I don't know."

She held open her arms, and I walked into them without further encouragement. Paige sighed, running her hands down my hair. "Tell me what you need from me because sometimes I take my violent, angry support too far, and I'm told by parties that shall not be named that it's not always the most helpful thing I can do."

I smiled, burying my face in her shoulder. "Logan said that?"

"He's such a killjoy." She leaned back and cupped the side of my face. "You look sadder than I thought you would after talking to you. I mean, I know you're sad. You loved your job. But your heart." She swept a thumb over my cheekbone, and it came away wet from the tear that escaped. "It hurts, doesn't it?"

The canny observation—one that could only be made by someone who really, truly knew me—had me sinking into her arms again. I sniffed noisily. "I saw Noah in the parking lot, a-and," I sobbed, "he said he missed me, and I miss him too, but what does *that* mean, right? He's such an idiot. He hasn't said one word to me in weeks. Weeks! And then he's asking me why it's so hard to see me, and why it's so hard to talk to me. Ugh. Why do I have to answer those things for him, you know?" I hiccuped as Paige turned us, her armed wrapped tight around my shoulder so she could steer me toward the couch in the living room. "It's not like I'm sitting around waiting for Noah Griffin to explain things to me now that we've had sex. Like, figure it out on your own, you moron."

"Ohhhhkay, my husband left out a few things when he texted me," Paige said under her breath. Once I was tucked into the corner of the couch, I tugged my favorite pillow into my lap and toed off my Chucks.

Once the plush weight was clutched to my chest, I watched her over the silky edge. "Logan didn't tell you about the whole *I slept with Noah and that's what got me fired* thing?"

Her eyebrows lifted so slowly, so high on her forehead that I worried for a moment that they'd get stuck. "No, no, he did not."

"Erm, yeah. That was, well, that was why I said maybe we shouldn't resort to pyrotechnics against Beatrice. I kinda earned my spot in the ranks of the unemployed."

Paige let out a slow breath, her thoughts stamped loudly over her face. Concern was first and foremost, and the thing I saw most clearly. Very deliberately, she spun on the couch, crossed her legs, folded her hands primly between them, and faced me fully. "What shall we tackle first? The job or the sex?"

When she put it that way, maybe I'd been a little close-lipped with my family since I got back from my weekend away. I frowned. It wasn't like me to keep stuff from them, not big things like this, but I'd been in survival mode, convincing myself that I was fine with what happened in South Dakota stayed in South Dakota.

I'd worked overtime to keep a lid on the part of myself that missed him, missed talking with him, laughing with him, and teasing him until he allowed a crack in his reserve. It had been easier not to talk about him at all than to face the reality that it had only been one weekend, despite what it had meant to me.

Paige shifted restlessly when I didn't answer immediately.

"Please, give me guidance, because my mind is about to explode if I don't get clarification"—her voice rose in pitch and volume—"on the fact that you slept with the boy who used to live next door, and I didn't know about it, and it cost you your job. I don't know what to say about any of it, Molly, and you not telling me is freaking me out," she cried.

I smiled, leaning forward to grab one of her hands. "Deep breaths, okay?"

It was similar enough to what she had told me earlier when I called from my office that we both laughed. "Sorry," she said. "It's just ... you're throwin' a lot at me, kiddo. What do we deal with first?"

My swallow was rough, hard to get down, but it was Paige, so I had to be honest. "This may not be the empowered female answer where I say that nothing matters except my career and he's just a guy, and I don't need a guy to feel complete or happy or to love myself."

"There is a time and place for all of those things," she interjected. "But there's no one size fits all for what makes people happy, okay? If there was, we'd have a black and white checklist to follow."

I nodded.

227

"We will talk about Beatrice, and your job, and what you'll do next," she promised. "But if Noah—whatever happened with him —is the thing weighing on you the most right now, then let's start there."

The words came easily, like I needed her permission to unload them into the safe space that our couch represented. All four of us girls had cried there through middle school, high school, and college. If Logan ever got rid of that couch, there would be a mutiny within the Ward family. The cushions sank a little where I was sitting because it was everyone's favorite spot, but that couch was the next best thing to being in a therapist's office.

Paige listened without interruption as I told her everything. She smiled about the yoga, sighed when I got to our first kiss, blushed like only a mom would when I got to South Dakota, and her eyes got suspiciously glassy when I told her about my decision to pull back from him, how I lied to Beatrice, and up to what had happened that afternoon in the parking lot.

My throat was dry when we were finally caught up, but so were my eyes because there was some strange power in the telling of what led to my current predicament. I wasn't angry with Beatrice. I was frustrated with myself. I wasn't mad at Noah for being clueless because the man's longest relationship was with an inanimate object covered in brown leather with white laces and that was just sad AF, in all honesty. I asked for space, and he'd given it to me. It wasn't fair to hold it against him when all he'd done was respect my wishes.

I felt heavy from all those things combined. Weighed down with the various components of what lost me my job but had me falling in love with a man who had the emotional availability of a rock.

"Damn, girl," Paige said when I finished. She was slumped against the cushions of the couch.

"I know." I held my breath as I watched her process everything. Trust me, I knew it was a lot. I'd had weeks, and I still found myself a little confused. "Was I stupid for pulling back?"

"Oh geez, Mol, it's not that simple." She blew out a quick puff of air. "I don't think you were stupid, no. But I happen to think you and your sisters are four of the six greatest human beings to walk this earth, so I'm prone to believe whatever you decide is correct and will thereby defend it to the death."

"Yeah, right." I snorted. "Where was that logic when we were in high school?"

She smiled. "I know, I know. Easier for me to say now that it's not my responsibility to decide how to weigh the consequences of your actions. Now, my child, that burden is yours. Yours to live with, and yours to work through."

"I'm so glad I came to you because this is making me feel much better."

Paige laughed. "Listen, what I will say is this, being in a relationship with an athlete is no piece of cake. But I don't need to tell you that because it's been a part of your life longer than it's been a part of mine. I get it, he's driven, and he's talented, and he's at the top of his game. He's never put anything ahead of football and that makes him a scary bet. That wasn't the case for me and your brother." She smiled. "He had you guys, and nothing, not even football, was more important than the four of you."

"I sense a but ..."

"But," she said slowly, "it's not up to you to make that decision for him when he had an incomplete picture, Molly. And that's what you did. He respected you enough not to push you on it, and that was before he had any clue that you could lose your job for what you did. What would he have done if he'd known you were falling for him? What would have happened if you talked to Beatrice and told her it was a serious relationship? There's no way of knowing, not now. Maybe he would've panicked, but maybe not. Maybe Beatrice would've fired you earlier, but maybe not." She shrugged.

It was like trying to untangle of knot of multi-colored yarn in my lap, one the size of my head. I couldn't tell where it started, where it ended, or just how long I'd been looping and looping and looping in the wrong direction. It was hard to say whether the first wrong turn had been as far back as the elevator when I saw Noah for the first time. Or thinking I could be friends with him, kiss him, sleep with him without involving my heart. That I could prove something to Beatrice that she'd never fully believe in the first place.

All those things equaled one massive coiled, complicated mess.

"What's going on in that head of yours?" she asked. "Just ... blurt it out. First thing you wish you could understand."

"Noah in the parking lot." I blinked at how quickly the words came out. "I was surprised at how awkward he was. His confusion that the awkwardness was there between us at all."

Emmett came around the corner, and Paige held up her hand. "Ten more minutes, kid. Back away."

"But—"

"Ten minutes, unless you want my help with the math instead of Molly's."

He disappeared in a flash of mahogany-colored hair, and I laughed.

"Honestly," Paige said, "that's a piece of cake. Men are incredibly clueless sometimes. And if you take a man like that, who lives by the x's and o's of a playbook, who is in complete control of just about every piece of his life except his opponent, they get really good at reading the competition. You took that away from him by removing yourself from the equation. Not only that, but you are also a woman, and from the sounds of it, Noah has had little-to-no experience with that area for the past few years. His choice, but still. You rocked his world, Molly." She grinned, and I hid my face behind the pillow with a groan. "And then you disappeared. The fact that he's still puzzling out how he feels about that means he's got it just as bad as you do."

I slumped back, keeping a tight grip on that pillow. "Why does it sound so easy when you explain it?"

"Because I'm old and smart and happily married to an incredibly stubborn man. It's the trifecta of good relationship advice."

Curling into my side, I grinned at her. "You're humble too. Don't forget that."

"It's a terrible burden to bear," Paige announced gravely. She clapped her hands. "Okay. So now that we understand the man, what do we do about it?"

Unfortunately, I knew the answer to this. "We don't rush into anything."

Her face fell. "We don't?"

I shook my head. "I've gone headfirst into so many situations without paying attention to anything other than my feelings. Noah is a perfect example. Twice now, when it comes to him, I've let my feelings override common sense. I agree with you, I think Noah does care for me, and I think we could have something amazing." I swallowed. "But it's not my responsibility to make him understand that. Or to prove to him that I'm worth a spot in his life. I know that I'm worth it. I know he's worth more than what he does on the field. But I think"—I breathed unsteadily—"I need him to climb through my window this time. Do something that feels risky and crazy for *me*. I deserve that."

Paige surged forward on the couch and flung her arms around me. I was engulfed by almost six feet of gorgeous, overwhelming, maternal-influence love.

"You deserve that times a million," she gushed.

I patted her back with a laugh.

"Can we eat carbs now?" I asked.

Paige disentangled herself from me and held out a hand to help me up. "Yes. Let's go brainstorm your other issue over garlic bread."

I grinned. "Oh, I already have an idea for that. I won't be unemployed for long."

CHAPTER TWENTY-SIX

NOAH

"This is not what I had in mind when you asked for my help, Griffin," Marty said. His head was resting on his arms, his whole body slumped in exhaustion. Or maybe it was irritation, I couldn't really tell. Didn't really care either because once the plan starting formulating in my head, I dialed in like a ravenous dog onto a medium rare chunk of prime rib.

I crossed my arms and pointed at the massive screen I had mounted above the fireplace of my family room. "Back it up about forty seconds and look." I swept an arm out. "We need to cut right there." I rolled my eyes when Marty groaned. "If you watch carefully, you can see what I'm talking about *right there*."

"If you make me watch this clip one more time," he growled.

I glanced over my shoulder. "You'll what? Glare at me to death?" My hands snapped together in a sharp clap, and Marty jumped. "Do I need to mark it up on the diagram again?"

"No," Rick and Marty answered.

The diagram had been an immense source of joy for me over the past forty-eight hours. It laid on my dining room table, spiral bound with laminated pages so I could mark on it with dry erase markers. My own playbook because I could understand that structure for how to move forward.

Offensive Campaign: M Ward

The title needed work, but what was found inside the pages was nothing short of genius. I'd never fancied myself a filmmaker, but over the past two days, the three of us had honed, hacked, edited, tweaked, and cut my relationship with Molly down to a short film that was fucking Oscar-worthy, if you asked me.

Rick and Marty just didn't appreciate my approach at directing, which looked a bit more like my attempt to channel my inner Bill Belichick. I was ruthless, making them loop the same thirty-second scene over and over and over until we caught just the right cut of the moment that Molly tipped me over when we were doing yoga.

The only reason they hadn't tied me up and stuffed a gag in my mouth was because I'd agreed to let them film the entire thing once she was here. A camera guy from their office came over after Marty and I had our parking lot brainstorm, then cleared everything with Rick.

The parking lot brainstorm was full of excitement and optimism and hope.

Now, they were actively plotting my demise with every request I made to play back another chunk of the footage.

"Okay," I said, "let's move back to South Dakota. I think we can give that more impact."

"No," Rick mumbled.

My eyebrows lifted. "Sorry?"

"No, no, no." He stood from the couch and pressed two fists into his back as he stretched with a groan. "You are the Hitler of romantic gestures, and if she doesn't love this exactly as it is, then holy shit, Griffin, we can't help you."

Suppressing my irritation that they weren't taking this as seriously as I was, I crossed my arms over my chest and faced him with spread legs. "It has to be perfect, Rick."

My tersely spoken words hung in the air as they stared at me. Didn't they understand?

This was my chance. This was the way I could make her see.

Seeing Molly like that—when I was unprepared to speak to her, unprepared for the gut check of being around her, and seeing the way every emotion played out over her face—it flipped on every light that had been dark in her absence.

Maybe I hadn't seen it right away, that every second we spent together, every second she spent gently coaxing me out from behind the wall I'd built, had been us falling in love. But I saw it now.

I couldn't help but see it, in the hours and hours of film I had at my fingertips.

Watching the film was preparation.

Watching the film helped me understand myself and my opponent, and currently, the thing opposing me was the clock. Washington had a bye week, so the time for a big romantic gesture couldn't have been better.

But the time ticked down all the same. Bright, shifting numbers that got closer and closer to some imaginary buzzer going off.

And I was fighting against myself.

Showing Molly that I was capable of allowing room in my life for something other than football—not just something, *her*—would need to be big.

Those were pages fifteen through eighteen of the playbook, which included sketches of string lights across my back deck, a movie projector, and a giant screen stretched through the branches of the trees in my backyard. And some vague idea of moving my mattress onto the grass and topping it with pillows and blankets so we could watch our movie under the stars. My telescope was out there somewhere too, since I'd mapped out precisely what would be visible in the night sky.

This was the way to do it. Everything lined up correctly, the best defense against my own cluelessness. My own ambition blinded me to all the other things that could matter just as much as my career did. If I could pull this off correctly, if I could do this right ...

My thoughts started stuttering in that same place every time. The *if*.

Rick must have sensed the change in direction in my head because I couldn't entertain the idea that maybe I'd read Molly wrong in all of this.

He laid a gentle hand on my shoulder. "Noah, it's perfect."

I shook my head. "I can make it better. I just need a little more time."

Marty and Rick shared a look.

"Molly won't need perfect," Marty said quietly. "You know that girl. Even when you were a giant horse's ass, she felt something for you. Because she knew the real you was underneath there somewhere."

Rick nodded. "All you need to do is show her that she wasn't wrong about you. That what she saw, what she put her trust in, even for that one weekend, was worth it."

"Worth her job?" I asked dryly.

"Worth taking a risk," he corrected. "She took a risk because you were worth it to her. This"—he gestured to our little command center—"is you taking a risk too. Because you could get through everything you have planned, and she still might not say yes."

Panic was an icy claw that dug straight into my chest, gripped my spine tight, and threatened to tug. "Please never be a coach because that is the worst pep talk I've ever heard."

And I thought that figuring out how to get her to the house would be the hard part. I'd convinced myself up until the current moment that convincing *Logan* to help me was the hard part. But the hard part was letting go of the edge, one finger at a time, until I could fall back freely into whatever happened next.

In my ears, I could hear the hard pulse of my heart because I knew Rick was right.

Before I could talk myself out of it, I yanked out my phone and sent a text to her brother.

Me: Here's my address. Tell her whatever you need to get her here, but I'll be ready at 8pm tonight.
Logan: Understood.

I let out a slow breath.

Rick smiled. "All set?"

"I have eight hours to get everything set up."

"Plenty of time," he assured me. Then he eyed my face with concern. "You're going to shower, right? Because you look a little ..."

"Homeless," Marty answered. "He looks homeless."

"Will you both shut up? Yes, I'm going to shower. But I have more important things to worry about right now."

Marty's eyes widened. "More than how terrible you look? I highly doubt it."

Rick smothered a smile. "What do you need?"

"Do I have a projection screen?"

He nodded. "Our guy can be here in two hours with everything you need. He'll get all the A/V set up for you. All you'll need to do is hit play."

"Is the mattress idea stupid?"

Marty laid his head down on his folded arms again. "I know now. I know why you didn't get laid for years because you have to question whether a mattress is a good idea."

My exhale was slow and steady. "Fine. Keep the mattress. I just didn't want to be, you know, presumptuous."

"And you're doing the constellation thing, right?" Marty lifted his head. "Stars are some romantic shit, Noah. You can stand behind her, all that touching, show her where to look and everything."

I rubbed my temples. "Yes, Marty, we should be able to see Pegasus pretty clearly. But I thought, I don't know, shouldn't I tie it in? Make some connection to our love story?"

"That's on you, buddy. I'm just here to run the camera."

"Yeah," I said dryly, "make sure you zoom in properly if she breaks my heart."

"She won't," Rick said. "What's the story of Pegasus?"

I grimaced. "It, uhh, sprang from Medusa's severed head. That's how he was born."

Rick swallowed like his mouth was full of sand. "Maybe ... don't use that." He patted me awkwardly on the back. "Why don't we watch the tape from the beginning one last time, all right?"

Marty groaned. "I can't. I can't do it. He's made us watch it eight thousand times in the past two days, Rick. I see them almost kiss one more time, I'm going to lose my mind."

I glared at him. "And whose fault is it that you got it on film?"

"Like I knew what you guys were doing when I came back upstairs! I didn't even realize I caught anything until I got back to the office."

Rick held up his hands. "Okay. Marty, go take a breather. Noah, you and I can take it from the top. But I promise," he said, "it's perfect. She'll love it."

"This better work," I muttered. He started the video we'd

made again, and just like I had every single time we watched it, there was an unsettling sense of rightness in every second. The fact that I missed it, from the very first day, seemed impossible now.

We watched quietly, and I found myself smiling when we got to the snippets from the day we did yoga. Marty fought tooth and nail for the scene where I blatantly checked out her ass, and he was right, it was funny. A chink in the armor, a break in my control, almost as though she'd scripted it herself from the very beginning.

There was a brusque knock on the door, and I sighed, punching the pause button on the remote.

"Want me to get it?" Rick asked.

"No. It's probably a neighbor or something. I keep managing to avoid the greeting committee."

I yanked open the door.

And there she was.

"Wha-" I stammered. "Molly?"

Her brother stood behind her, a cunning grin plastered across his face.

She glared over her shoulder at him. "He just ... showed up here and wouldn't tell me why."

When she faced me again, her cheeks were flushed bright pink, her eyes bright with nerves.

The fact that my house was a mess, nothing was ready, no lights were strung, and no soft music was playing under a sunset-dim sky or that I looked like a crazy homeless person didn't matter. There were a thousand details that could have made it the most perfect night in the world, but suddenly, they were completely inconsequential.

The excess boiled away, reducing the moment down to the bare truth, the unbreakable bones of what I needed to know, what I needed to trust in.

She was here. And I loved her.

"Will you come in?" I asked.

Molly blinked. "You knew I was coming?"

I gave Logan a loaded look. "You were supposed to be delivered a little bit later," I said meaningfully, "but yes. Logan agreed to help me."

Her lips curled in a smile. "Then I'm sorry I'm early."

"I'm not," I answered.

The smile widened, and it blew through me like a veritable wrecking ball. That was always what Molly had been to me. A weapon of mass destruction, testing every limit I'd ever given myself. And I didn't want it any other way.

Standing back so she could enter the house, I glared at Logan. "What was that for?" I hissed.

He leaned up to smack me on the shoulder. Hard. "That was for sleeping with my sister, asshole." Then he grinned. "Welcome to the family."

As he ambled back to his truck, he whistled, and I couldn't help but shake my head at how this entire thing had played out. Ten years in the making, an inevitable conclusion that was impossible for me to avoid.

I shut the door and tried to regroup because well ... I'd just been blitzed. Outmaneuvered. And I never saw it coming.

Rick was grinning as he greeted Molly. "He's been an absolute terror to put up with since you left."

"Is that your way of saying you missed me?" she asked. Marty stormed up the stairs when he heard her voice and wrapped her in a massive, rib-cracking hug that had her laughing. "I guess that answers my question."

"Don't leave us alone with him," Marty begged.

Molly tucked a piece of hair behind her ear and gave me a shy glance that had my heart thudding—big, big, bigger—until it felt stretched over my entire body. "I'll see what I can do," she said.

I smiled.

It was so right having her here. This was what made it feel like my home. Her.

Her gaze tracked over the space, and even with how messy it was, she looked happy. Then the smile froze, her eyes widening as she caught sight of the TV screen. "That's us," she said numbly.

Rick and Marty shared a look. Rick gave me a thumbs-up and disappeared downstairs. Marty picked up his small camera and moved back into the kitchen, so he could be out of the way and still catch what needed to be caught. It was our compromise.

Just far enough out of earshot that if she and I spoke quietly, they'd struggle to hear us. The other cameraman flicked off his machine and followed Rick downstairs. He nodded encouragingly too. Maybe I ought to learn his name before it was all over.

"It is us," I said, coming up behind her. "It's ... hell, this is not how I wanted to do any of this."

She reached down to the coffee table and carefully picked up the remote. Before she hit the play button, she let out a shaky breath.

But my brave girl, not knowing what she'd see, or what I'd intended, she lifted her chin and started it over.

I'd seen the film enough, the blossoming of our love condensed into eight minutes, so I could unabashedly watch her.

One minute in, she was smiling at the scene where she knocked me on my ass by telling me I could be better.

Two, she had a hand covering her mouth as she breathed out a laugh at the sight of me storming out of the tiny house.

Three, and I caught the sheen of happy tears during our yoga session.

At four minutes, the realization that Marty caught our almost first kiss. She pressed a shaky hand to her mouth.

241

It was impossible to be so far away from her, so I approached quietly from behind, letting out a slow breath before my palms coasted up the sides of her upper arms. I cupped her shoulders, warm and firm, and her soft hair tickled my fingers. She leaned back against me, giving me her full weight, and I exhaled my relief, wrapping my arms around the front of her chest as she watched the footage from South Dakota.

This was subtle to anyone else watching, but to Molly and me, it was bright and obvious, a spotlight on everything we'd been denying. The camera caught me constantly watching her off the screen. Everything I couldn't understand was right there in my eyes.

I tightened my arms, and her hands came up to grip my forearms. With her tucked against my chest, I could set my chin easily on the top of her head. She dropped her mouth and laid a soft kiss on the tender skin of my wrist.

"I was such an idiot," I whispered.

She kissed me again, just above my thumb. "Only a little."

The laugh was out before I could stop it.

"Shhh, I'm still watching," she chided gently.

I closed my eyes and breathed her in. How had I ever thought I could live a full life, a satisfying life, if I didn't have this in it?

What a fool I'd been.

She sniffed when she watched the blank, robotic version of me after she pulled away. It was the part I hated most—what I would have accepted, what I did accept, as a normal, healthy life.

Then she laughed when she saw the end. The part Marty caught in his failed attempt at a sprint in the parking lot. The screen went black, and Molly turned slowly in my arms.

"You did this? For me?"

My hand cupped her face, and my eyes feasted on the small details that I'd missed so much. The jut of her chin, the delicate nose, the weight of her body against mine. "I had a little help," I admitted with a smile. "And there was going to be a much better delivery."

"Yeah?"

"A screen in the backyard. Lights. A big bed on the grass where we could watch it."

Her eyebrow lifted, but she was running her hands over my chest, so I figured I wasn't in too much trouble.

"And the stars," I continued. "I found Pegasus and had every intention of trying to make it romantic, but ... it's not. He came from a severed head, so it's probably best that it didn't work out anyway."

The laughter started low in her throat, bubbling out the longer I rambled. Finally, she took pity on me and laid a hand over my mouth. "Stop."

I kissed her fingers. "Okay."

"Why'd you make that?" she asked quietly. "The movie."

"Because there needs to be a record somewhere," I told her. "There should be proof, undeniable proof, of the very best thing I've ever achieved in my life." I wrapped my arms around her back and lifted her up in my arms so I could whisper where no one but us would hear. "Falling in love with you is the greatest thing I've ever done, Molly Ward."

Her arms were so tight around my neck that I felt the way her body trembled. Within the circle of my arms, she let out a sob of relief. "I love you too," she whispered back.

In the next moment, her mouth was on mine, hard and sweet and deep. The fierce fullness of the kiss pulled a groan from my chest, and she wrapped her legs around my waist so she could hold tighter and move more firmly against me.

I wanted her.

I loved her.

She loved me.

And, I thought as I froze, we were being filmed. I pulled back, and she followed with a whimper.

"Camera," I said against her lips.

Molly went still, another bright smile spreading over her face. "Oh, yeah."

"But as soon as we chase them out of here ..." I promised with a growl.

She hopped out of my arms and called for Rick to come upstairs.

I glanced over at Marty, who was wiping tears from his face unabashedly.

Rick skipped lightly up the steps. "You called?"

"Yes," she said. "You and I have to talk tomorrow morning. But right now, you need to leave."

His face creased in confusion. "Tomorrow morning?"

Molly nodded, herding them gently toward the door. "Yes. I have a job proposal to go over with you. I think you should hire me."

My eyebrows popped up in surprise. So did his.

"He says yes!" Marty interjected as he hastily started wrapping up cords.

Rick gave him a look. "Tomorrow," he promised. "But can't we, I don't know, film a little happy cuddling?"

"No," Molly and I answered.

"We have other things to discuss," Rick said. "A lot has happened this week. You don't even know about our new idea!"

"Out. Or I will start stripping," she warned. "And that will make my future employment awkward. And you'd violate the nudity clause if you film me in any state of undress."

My head tilted back on a booming laugh, and Rick gave me an exasperated look.

In another two seconds, she had them out the door, and the

deadbolts flipped decisively. I set my hands on my hips as she turned, her back flush against the door's surface.

"Now," she said, "let's recap."

"Okay." I stepped closer to her.

"I'm your girlfriend."

"Yes." My hands found her hips.

"You're my boyfriend."

"Mmmhmm." My lips found the soft curve of her neck.

"W-we're finally alone. With no cameras. Or microphones. Or family members under the same roof." Her fingers pushed under the soft cotton of my shirt, and I hissed when she trailed them along the edge of my shorts.

"That's correct." I bit down on the delicate line of her collarbone, soothing it with my tongue when she moaned.

"You love me," she said quietly.

I pulled back and held her gaze steadily. "I do."

"And I love you," she finished.

My voice was rough when I was finally able to speak. "Yeah."

"That's good. I like all of that."

I smiled. "How should we celebrate? Every big win needs a big celebration."

"Like ..." She dropped her voice like a sports announcer. "You just won the Super Bowl, what will you do next?"

"We're not going to Disneyland, sweetheart," I promised. But the fact that she could bring me to the edge of laughter in a moment so laden with sexual tension, so rife with want and desperation to *take, take, take*, was how I knew that Molly was the exact right person for me.

She inhaled with a satisfied smile pulling up the edges of her lips. "Take me to your big bed, in your big room, because we are about to break it in, Noah Griffin."

I swept her in my arms, relishing in the happy shriek that left her mouth. "You're the boss."

We stayed there all day and all night, only stopping briefly for food. A shower. And endless conversations. The playbook was probably still lying open in a useless heap on the dining room table. But that was the point.

I couldn't have scripted this, couldn't have planned it, couldn't have controlled it.

Because sometimes, the best things in life come straight from your blind side.

EPILOGUE

MOLLY

"Oh sweetheart, did you see this one?" Grandma Griffin tossed the *Us Weekly* into my lap as she passed the couch. "You're way too pretty for my grandson."

Noah groaned as I flipped to the article she'd dog-eared. "Another article?"

I elbowed him. "People love us. We're cute."

It was a quick mention. Never in a million years would I have anticipated having a corner of a magazine page dedicated to me and my hot boyfriend and our red-carpet style.

Amazon had gone all out for the *All or Nothing* season featuring Noah, and to my never-ending surprise, me. Instead of red, we'd done a black carpet, so that my red dress would stand out. And it had.

It was a picture I'd seen a lot. Instagram users seemed to like that particular one. Noah had his tux-clad arm wrapped tight around my waist, head bent toward me, and his nose pressed against my temple.

I was smiling widely, my shoulders angled toward him, and a hand placed against his chest. The Grecian-style dress that I'd chosen was a vivid scarlet that draped over one shoulder and was cinched tight around my waist with a gold belt. What the camera couldn't see because the length of the dress swept the floor were the spiky gold heels that had only lasted as long as getting our picture taken.

By the time we were in the theater for the screening of the first episode, I'd slipped into some nude flats.

It was our first night as a couple in the spotlight, and social media exploded with the release of the full season of episodes documenting our love story. Since Rick hired me before I even finished pitching myself, I was involved in crafting the finished product of our story from beginning to end. And it was damn good television, if I said so myself.

The last episode was my favorite, the one we'd shot during their final playoff game, which they lost 28-21. It encapsulated everything about Noah and me that I loved so much. Before the cameras moved to follow us through the game, it caught some sweet, quiet moments when he helped me unpack my things. I loved Isabel, but living with Noah was *way* more fun.

When the quiet moments were done, and we saw him play his heart out for four quarters, only to have the opposing defense stop us five yards shy of the end zone as the clock ran out. The devastation and disappointment on his face still made me cry, as it had that day. It was still hard for me to watch even though we were a few months removed from it by now. But the viewers loved it.

They loved how real we were with each other. They loved that the footage of me at the end of the game was just as emotional, that my sorrow for him was so obvious as I sat in the stands with the other disappointed Washington fans. It was what made the closing scene so poignant.

Me climbing over the barrier and into his waiting arms. Him, sweaty and disheveled and dirty, lifting me into a tight embrace on the chaotic post-game field. And he smiled.

Not a sad smile.

Noah Griffin smiled like he'd just won.

His grandma, our host for the week, told me she'd watched every episode three times. She kept every article that mentioned us and made sure to show me each and every one.

"You ready, son?" Noah's dad asked from the kitchen.

Noah nodded, dropping a soft kiss on my lips as he stood from the couch. "We'll be back for dinner."

"Okay." I grabbed the front of his shirt and tugged him back down for another kiss. "Have fun fixing fences."

He rolled his eyes. His grandma and I laughed.

Noah left the cabin first, and I smiled as I caught the embarrassed blush on his dad's face when he left the kitchen. It had taken a bit for him to get used to having me around and seeing the easy affection that Noah and I shared.

As I spent more time with his dad, it was so clear to see how Noah fell into the patterns that he had. Slowly but surely, his dad was relaxing around me. My goal was one week every summer that Noah, his dad, and I came to South Dakota together. Eventually, I'd break him into the Tuesday family dinners. He just didn't know it yet.

And that was why Grandma Griffin proclaimed that I was her new favorite person in the entire world.

She rubbed my shoulder as she passed behind the couch. "Need anything while I'm up, sweetheart?"

I smiled up at her. "I'm good, thanks. I have some work to do for Rick while they're out there unless you need my help with anything."

"No, no, one set of hands is all I need to do some weeding."

"I'll come out when I'm done," I told her. "It won't take me too long."

She set her wide-brimmed hat on her head and paused before she walked out front. "Actually," she said, tugging her gardening gloves on, "I know how you can help."

I glanced over. "Yeah?"

She lifted her eyebrows. "A great-grandchild would be *lovely*."

As she walked outside, I was still laughing because she found so many ways to remind Noah and me that she needed a baby to spoil.

The door swung back open, and my smile softened when Noah strode back into the cabin.

"Forget something?" I asked.

He snatched his water bottle from the counter. "It's hotter than hell out there."

"I'll take another kiss while you're here."

He was already sweaty, one of my very favorite looks on the man I loved so much. When he came around the couch to cage me in with his arms and take my mouth in a deep, searing kiss, I felt that desperate urge rush through me, just like it always did.

Honestly, it was a miracle I *wasn't* pregnant with how often he took me to bed.

Noah had proven that frequent sex did not hurt his performance on the field in any way. Mr. Defensive Player of the Year had proven it well, too.

I licked my lips when he pulled back. "And your dad would notice if you didn't come back outside right away, right?"

Noah hummed. "Yes."

I trailed my finger along the edge of his jaw. "Okay. I can wait until tonight."

His eyes searched my face and landed unerringly on my mouth. "Can you?"

My heart started pounding wildly, and my toes curled up. "Yes?"

"I can't," he stated.

My lips spread in a slow smile. "No?"

As usual, my big man was quick to make his decision. "Nope."

And he scooped me up, both hands under my ass. My legs wound around his waist as he straightened, turning us toward our bedroom.

I loved the bed in that cabin. It was my second favorite bed in the world.

"Noah?" I said breathlessly as he sucked along the edge of my throat.

He growled something unintelligible into my skin.

I gripped the sides of his face so I knew he was paying attention to me.

"Wha?" he said. He already had that dazed look in his eye that he got when my clothes started disappearing.

"Make sure to lock the door," I said. "I don't want any interruptions for what I'm about to do to you."

He grinned. His hands tightened on my body as he walked us into the bedroom, his foot delivering a swift kick to the door.

No matter how our love story started, as long as it brought us right here, it was perfect.

CLAIRE

Searching the internet for glimpses of your mother brought

about strange emotional reactions. Unless you'd experienced those reactions, it was hard to put them into words. Occasionally, we'd get a postcard from her with an updated address, or a caption-less picture would show up on the usually quiet Facebook account she still had access to. Those tiny snippets were the only way my sisters and I knew where Brooke was currently spending her days.

My heart and my head warred mightily when I studied the last few pictures she'd posted. I wasn't furious at the thought of her; it was hard to be when we had such a happy life in her absence. But I didn't feel nothing either. Sometimes I wanted to punch her. Sometimes I wanted to hug her. Most of all, I wanted to sit across from Brooke Ashley Huntington-Ward and pick apart her brain. That was the most desperate feeling of all of them, fighting for first place in my head. I wanted to understand why, and it drove me abso-friggin-lutely batshit crazy that I might never have that understanding.

As I scrolled through, counting five pictures posted in the last three years, my twin sister's phone lit up on the desk next to me where it was charging. My eyes cut to the screen, a force of habit because it was often a group text from one of our other sisters or Paige.

It wasn't from any of them, though. What appeared was a text from Finn, my twin sister Lia's best friend, and like I'd trained my body to do it, my heart sped up at the sight of his stupid name.

Finn: Lia, PLEASE, I'll owe you a million favors if you help me out.

"I'll help you," I mumbled miserably. It didn't even matter what he needed help with. I'd do it. I'd do it without a million favors. If I closed my eyes, I could picture every detail of his face.

The way his smile was a little lopsided. The width of his shoulders that seemed to expand every year. The shy exterior that hid a personality that was so, so funny and dry and sarcastic. But I didn't close my eyes because picturing my twin sister's best friend was another thing that made my head and heart war mightily. And every single time, my head won.

Leave him alone.

It would be too weird.

He doesn't even look at you that way.

Those were all the things I told myself when my crush on Finn flared out of control. And it had helped for years.

"Text from Finn," I yelled.

"What does he want?" Lia called from our kitchen, right around the corner from my bedroom.

I swallowed heavily as I read the text again. "Help. He'll owe you a million favors."

Lia groaned. "He could offer two million, and I still wouldn't be able to do it."

"What does he need your help with?"

"Some fancy-pants dinner and award ceremony. He needs a plus one, and since he refuses to find himself a date, his mom practically demanded that I go with. I think she actually put my name on the guest list because she assumed I wouldn't say no."

My heart clenched with unwelcome jealousy. "It's just dinner. Why not go?"

"I can't. I have something that night, and moving it isn't an option. He just thinks I'm being stubborn."

I rolled my eyes. Lia was physically incapable of admitting when she was being stubborn, which was about ninety-two percent of her existence.

The sound of her footsteps approached my doorway, quick and loud. "Wait," she said.

I spun my chair to face her. "What?"

A devious smile spread over her face.

"No," I said instantly. Twin telepathy, y'all. It was a real thing.

"Oh, yes." She rubbed her hands together. "We haven't done a twin swap in years, Claire. Come on, won't it be fun?"

While my head tried desperately to wrap around the idea of pretending to be my sister for the first time since high school, it was a faint whisper compared to what my heart was doing.

That particular organ buried in my chest was roaring and thrashing, screaming at me to *do this one thing* that would grant me my greatest unfulfilled wish.

Time with Finn.

"He'll know," I argued weakly.

Lia blew a raspberry through her lips. "Nah, he won't. You know how to be me, Claire. It's one dinner. Then I'm off the hook, and his mom gets off his back."

One dinner with Finn. One night to soak up his attention instead of playing the third wheel to the clearly non-romantic friendship between him and my sister. They'd never even hinted that they wanted to cross that line, which was the only reason I was even considering this insanity. Because for one night, I wanted to know what it felt like to have his eyes on me. To wear a pretty dress and spend the evening by his side.

"One dinner," I said again.

She bounced excitedly in the doorway. "You'll do it? Seriously?"

I took a deep breath and held it, muting every argument that sprang into my head. "I'll do it."

FAKED (Ward Family series book 2) is coming Summer 2020! Pre-order your copy HERE!

Need more broody Logan, fiery Paige, and the ward sisters? Grab your copy of The Marriage Effect HERE.

See where the Washington Wolves began in The Bombshell Effect. Grab your copy HERE.

ACKNOWLEDGMENTS

This fall was a complete and utter BLUR of writing and travel, and I'm so incredibly thankful that my little tribe of people (friends and family) understood what that meant for me.

It was long stretches of writing, blinders on, and ignoring texts for days. It was to-do lists with no wiggle room and pretty much no socializing for three months. On nights and weekends, it was spending time with my family, and putting my phone away.

Being a writer is strange. It's a job that most people don't really understand, and that's okay. Where I'm SO FORTU-NATE is that the people in my life who don't understand it still love me and respect me when I have to ignore them.

So, here's that list:

To my husband. WE OFFICIALLY SURVIVED our first stretch of both of us working from home. YAY! Thank you for respecting every crazy boundary I put on my own 'office space', both mental and physical. You didn't so much as blink when I looked you in the eye and said, "If you need ANYTHING FROM ME, it can wait until after I get the boys from school. So, please, for the love, do not interrupt me for the next seven hours unless you are bleeding." I love you.

To my kids, because I think you're really awesome and funny and smart and kind.

To Fiona Cole and Kathryn Andrews, for every opinion on this book, whether I wanted to hear it or not. You make my books better, and I love you both.

To Najla Qamber Designs and Regina Wamba for a STUNNING COVER that I'm obsessed with.

To Jenny Sims for the editing.

To Michelle Abascal Monroy for her help keeping me sane during my last release, and my amazing ARC team and reader group!

To Enticing Journey for their promo help.

TO AMY DAWS for the light flare idea on the cover. She wanted me to dedicate this book to her because of how amazing it turned out, but I felt like if I caved to her demands, her ego would spin out of control.

Stay up to date on Karla's upcoming releases!

Subscribe to her newsletter

ABOUT THE AUTHOR

Karla Sorensen has been an avid reader her entire life, preferring stories with a happily-ever-after over just about any other kind. And considering she has an entire line item in her budget for books, she realized it might just be cheaper to write her own stories. She still keeps her toes in the world of health care marketing, where she made her living pre-babies. Now she stays home, writing and mommy-ing full time (this translates to almost every day being a 'pajama day' at the Sorensen household...don't judge). She lives in West Michigan with her husband, two exceptionally adorable sons, and big, shaggy rescue dog.

Photo credit: Perrywinkle Photography

Find Karla online:
karlasorensen.com
karla@karlasorensen.com
Facebook
Facebook Reader Group

Made in the USA
Columbia, SC
14 January 2021

30918138R00159